I0714702

CONCERTED CHAOS

THE CORBITT CALAMITIES BOOK 1

SARA LAFONTAIN

26
TREES
PRESS

26 TREES PRESS

Cover Design: Leigh McDonald

Editor: Marisa Coltabaugh

Concerted Chaos/ Sara LaFontain - 1st ed.

ISBN 978-1-958025-01-7

To Rowan the Great
(the person, not the tree)

ONE

There's a stranger in my shrubbery.

That's unusual.

Not his presence, per se. People do creep around in the bushes often; that's why we have so many security cameras. And that's why we have several large prickly pears and one side of the property is lined with jumping cholla. I almost always recognize the trespassers though, and either chase them away or invite them in for coffee, depending on what they're after and how willing my brother is to give it to them.

This one's a stranger. Could be a stalker. Could be a super fan. But given the size of the lens on this guy's camera, I'm guessing paparazzo. And I'm guessing he's new since I didn't get a text first. Most of them are polite, partly because they know if they stay on my good side, I might call in tips.

It's been five hours since the security system alerted me to his presence, and he's still there, shifting around uncomfortably behind the oleander. That's a foolish risk—he picked a place where we have sprinklers. I could turn them on and roust him that way, possibly damaging his camera equipment in the process.

But I think instead we should have a little chat. I'll clear him out in person.

As soon as I open the door, I catch sight of movement—he's spotted me. Sunlight glints off his massive lens. Wait, what? He's taking *my* picture? Oh, this guy is definitely an amateur. He's shooting the wrong person.

I was planning to send him away with his dignity intact, but if he's going to take photos of me, I'm going to pose. Let someone else tell him his mistake—like whoever hired him. That's not going to go well.

I redirect my path and instead of a casual conversation through the fence—a conversation peppered with words like *police* and *restraining order*—I head toward the Porsche I parked in the middle of the driveway last night. Surely I left something in there I need to retrieve. His lens follows me.

That's right, camera jockey, watch me unlock this car door. Check out how sexily I get . . . nothing. I keep my car clean; there's nothing to grab. Oh well, he's not going to care about what is or is not in my hands. Am I tossing my hair provocatively? Putting my finest *asset* on display? Yes, I am. And this guy is loving it. He's not even trying to hide now. He's standing, openly grinning as he keeps snapping away. I throw a few more poses.

"Get everything you need?" I call out, and he has the audacity to wink.

"What's your name?" he asks, confirming my belief that he has no idea what he's doing and is about to make some gossip column editor very unhappy. My response is a blown kiss. I feel his eyes on me as I sashay my way back to the house. *Enjoy watching me walk away.*

It only takes half an hour for my phone to ring. The display shows the office of *Hot News Now*, one of the sleazy gossip sites. Ha! That's exactly the type of scumbag I expected.

"Cassidy Blaine-Corbitt, how dare you!" the head editor's voice shouts in my ear.

"Good morning to you, too, Eduardo. How dare I what?" I ask in my most innocent tone.

"Why are you wasting my photographer's time?" He's angry and aggrieved, but he shouldn't be; he only pays for the pictures he wants. He's not out any money on Oleander Man.

"I assure you, I have no idea what you're talking about. I was merely minding my own business, on my own property . . ."

"You knew I couldn't use any of those pictures!" He's slightly out of breath, so he must be pacing circles in his tiny office as he shouts into the speaker phone. Serves him right.

"That's what you get for sending some rookie who doesn't know what he's doing. Next time send someone with a basic knowledge of his quarry."

"Actually the problem is my tip line. Someone said they saw Powell Corbitt leaving a bar, drunk, with a hot brunette. How was I supposed to know they meant you?"

"Don't say 'you' so derisively. I am a hot brunette, thank you very much. You know my brother's not a cheater. And even if he were stupid enough to cheat on Zahna, he certainly wouldn't do it where nosy bystanders could see him. If there were anything worth reporting, it would have been leaked to you and you'd have had the opportunity to acquire some tasteful candids. I don't appreciate you sending some stranger to sneak around in our bushes."

That's a complete lie. Not about my brother; he's not a cheater, ever. But calling Eduardo with a tip? Lie! I do leak tips on a regular basis, usually at the insistence of my brother's publicist. Unfortunately for Eduardo and his website, he got himself bumped to the bottom of my list of gossipmongers deserving access to free information when he drunkenly groped my ass at an industry event two months ago. I don't forgive easily, and I never forget.

"Stop dying your hair. You're messing with my people," Eduardo snaps. This attitude is getting him bumped even further down. I'm going to leak to the Home Shopping Network before I call him again.

"I'm a natural brunette, always have been. And I'm not going to run it past you anytime I want to add or remove highlights. My face hasn't changed. Hire better vultures." I hang up before he can say anything else.

"Who was that?" Powell's muffled voice comes from under a blanket. He is curled up in an armchair, covered almost entirely. Some of his famed golden hair peeks through a tiny opening, and even that looks wretched. My brother is not much of a drinker, so his binge last night is hurting him badly. He hasn't moved since I dropped him in that living room chair when we got home last night. I'm strong, but not strong enough to carry a full-grown adult man all the way to his bedroom, especially when he's whining and protesting. Alcohol makes Powell regress to toddlerhood. I probably should have offered him a binky when I got him a blankie.

"Eduardo. He sent a new guy and got about a thousand shots of me," I say, hoping to make him laugh. No luck. A strange groaning sound emits from his blanket cocoon. "You're going to have to come out soon, you know."

"I live inside here now."

This situation requires gentleness and coddling, two things I'm not usually good at. "Powell," I say cajolingly. "I'll make you coffee."

"This is the worst," he complains, still muffled by his coverings.

"The hangover?" I can imagine. When I received a middle of the night phone call from Powell's favorite bar, I knew he was in trouble. He's lucky they helped him to a back room and called me. I snuck him out to the car, hoping no flashbulbs would go off. Apparently, based on the lurker in the oleander, someone did see, but not well enough to identify that it was merely his little sister taking him home.

"All of it. I'm getting dumped. I hate it."

Notice he said he's *getting* dumped? Like it's not a completed action? That's because celebrity relationships take more work to end. If I ever had a boyfriend, I could easily tell him it was over and walk away. Powell can't do the same. The publicists have to discuss the situation and select the optimum time. Then they have to craft a heartfelt joint statement with cheesy phrases about growing apart and still having the utmost respect for each other. This must be followed by a carefully managed public image campaign, determining what emotion the breakup should have evoked and then playing it up in the media. Should he be heartbroken? Relieved? Moving on immediately? Should he go out partying with his friends, or should he stay out of the spotlight as he wallows? It's complicated.

"Have you called Miriam yet?" His publicist is fantastic. If he hasn't called her, I should. She's an expert at public breakups, breakdowns, and any other possible celebrity breakages.

"I texted her last night. She wondered if we could hold off for a few months, until after the Last Barons reunion concert. But since Zahna is sleeping with a Czech race car driver, I'd rather not wait."

"She always did like fast cars." That's the one thing he and the up-and-coming model had in common. They could talk cars all day long. There was nothing else of substance in her pretty little head though. And I'm not saying that because I'm dismissive of supermodels. My closest non-relative friend is Brixley. Yes, *the* Brixley: the internationally famous, globally worshiped beauty with an IQ in the stratosphere. There are plenty of highly intelligent individuals in the modeling biz. Just not Zahna.

"I'm going to have to find someone else now. Cass, I just want to get married and make a bunch of babies. Why can't I meet a nice normal girl who wants that too?"

He finally pulls back the blanket to reveal his face. And I refrain from pointing out that his face is why he can't find a nice normal girl. His face that appears on album covers and billboards. His recognizable face, attached to his objectively attractive body (yes, he's my brother, but I'm mature enough to admit that others drool over him), and his impressive musical career. Not to mention all his money. Powell can't meet a normal girl because he's not a normal guy. But this is not the time to remind him.

"I'm sure you'll produce dozens of gorgeous babies someday," I assure him, certain that our parents will be extremely disappointed in him if he doesn't provide them with at least a couple of grandchildren. "But let's not focus on that right now. You're scheduled to be getting on a plane in less than an hour."

It's a minor lie intended to convey urgency. He has three hours, in reality, but he also possesses a rich and famous person's understanding of time—he believes it's flexible and bends around him. Fine if he were traveling on a private jet, but he's booked on a commercial flight. He's going to be flying out to Los Angeles to participate in location scouting. The once beloved boyband Last Barons of Sound are getting back together to release a brand new video—something fans have spent the last nine years begging for—just before the long-awaited reunion concert. My brother is going to be spending the afternoon on a helicopter, searching the outskirts of LA for a wild and desolate—yet easily reached—filming spot. My only job this morning, aside from clearing paparazzi off the property, is to get him out the door and to Sky Harbor airport.

"Don't make me go. I'm hungover and miserable," he says with a pathetic expression marring his handsome face. "Deedee, I don't wanna."

I take sympathy on him. How could I not? He pulled out my childhood nickname, and I can't resist that.

"Fine, I'll make some calls. Does someone from the band have to go?"

"That was the agreement. We never book a video location without one of us approving the site. Remember the disaster when we were slated to film at a zoo and Xander had a meltdown?"

"He always has meltdowns. Who's in Los Angeles at the moment?" I could probably check social media and find out myself. Mason isn't; his baby is due any day now, so he's holed up in his Mumbai villa impatiently waiting. Devon is always around, but his fear of flying is legendary.

"Besides Devon? Xander and Jace both should be. But Xander is worthless."

Truer words have never been spoken.

So I call Jace. Jace Monroe, awarded the coveted World's Sexiest Man title two years in a row, the hottest member of the former Last Barons, and current superstar from the duo JaDed (with his best friend Devon, Mr. Cries-on-planes-even-private-ones). Beyond being a sex symbol, he's also my friend, and he's generally willing to jump in and do favors, even last-minute ones like filling in for my hungover brother.

"Caaaaassidy," Jace drawls when he answers. He has this way of stretching names out in his ridiculously sexy voice. Everything about him is sexy, except sometimes his personality. With a couple of rare exceptions—like my brother—most entertainers who shoot to stardom as teenagers end up as adults with a hefty degree of jerkiness and assholery. "I was just thinking about you."

"You were?" While I have no interest in Jace as anything other than a friend, still, his attention is like the sun. When you stand in his spotlight, you are delighted, and grateful, and oh so warm, and then he looks elsewhere. The light fades, and you are left cold and alone.

"I was. I was thinking to myself, hmmmm, only a dozen people have my personal number, and which one of them is monstrous enough to call me this early in the morning? Of course your beautiful face immediately popped to mind."

"Haha. This is important. How would you like to go on a helicopter ride?" I say it with as much enthusiasm as I can muster, as if that will trick him into thinking it's an exciting adventure rather than work. Yes, I'm trying to manipulate him like I would a child, but if it works on Powell, it should work on Jace, too.

"Maybe. First fill me in on the hot gossip. Rumor has it your brother was out hooking up last night. Trouble with his girlfriend?"

How on earth did he hear that, especially if I just woke him up?

"False, and I'll let Powell share when he feels up to it. Meanwhile, are you in LA? He needs someone to cover him for the video location scouting today."

"Mmmmmmmmmm," Jace hums as he ponders his willingness to assist. "Cassssssidy, my sweet, I'll do it. But you owe me one."

"*I* owe you? Take it up with Powell."

"No, *you* owe me. You're going to be my date for the concert."

"Absolutely not. I'll be working." I'll be busy working backstage as Powell's assistant, making sure everything is running smoothly and allergen-free. It's the role I prefer anyway. Being on crew is way more fun than sitting in the audience. It'll be like old times.

"Just show up at the after-parties on my arm. That's all I ask." His tone demonstrates his absolute confidence that I'm going to say yes.

I've been his date to many award shows and events. Spending time with him is usually entertaining; he's got a keen eye and a sharp wit, and it's kind of fun as long as his barbed commentary isn't directed at me. But I hate getting my photo taken and appearing in the tabloids as fans wonder why he's settling for somebody like me, rather than the movie star, supermodel, or glamorous heiress that he deserves. I get why he does it though:

sometimes celebrities like low pressure dates, ones with zero expectations or obligations. Plus I do look fabulous in a gown.

"Agreed," I concede. "You go in the helicopter; I'll buy a fancy dress." *And make Powell pay for it.*

"It's a date. Love you, Cass."

"Love you too, Jace. I'll text you the details."

While Powell goes off to try and shower the smell of stale alcohol sweat away, I make a food run. Big greasy burgers, while hard to find so early in the morning, are Powell's favorite cure. Fortunately, there's a nearby diner where they make delicious ones, and they're very mindful of his deadly peanut allergy. His exorbitant tips guarantee that the food is always safe and we are well taken care of.

"Morning, Cassidy," Mama Nina, the owner, greets me. "By yourself today?"

"I'm getting a to-go order," I reply. "Powell was out drinking last night."

She frowns in concern. "That's unlike him. Is he alright?"

I shrug, not willing to share exact details. "Sometimes he needs to let off a little steam. He's suffering for it though."

She laughs then, a deep belly laugh that lifts my spirits too. "No problem. It's been a while, but I remember exactly what that man needs. You take a seat while I get those burgers cooked up, and I'll send over some coffee while you wait."

See? That's the benefit of going where your brother tends to leave 120% gratuities. He's always been a spread-the-wealth kind of guy, and the overly helpful staff are fully aware of the benefits of catering to him, and, by extension, me. I tip well too, based on a combination of gratitude for excellent service, a tribute to the years my mother spent waiting tables, and the lack of limits on Powell's credit card.

As I sit and sip my coffee, a person suddenly drops into the seat across from me. This isn't a crowded coffee shop, and my table isn't the only one with an available seat. A diner is certainly not the kind of place people should plop down at a stranger's table uninvited.

"So your name is Cassidy Corbitt?" The man says. He looks vaguely familiar, but I can't quite place him. Messy dark hair, a couple of days' worth of stubble, unruly thick eyebrows. Where have I seen those lately?

"It's Blaine-Corbitt, actually. And you are?"

"Tanner. Tanner Smythe. With a y."

I don't say anything, merely raise my own neatly groomed eyebrows and wait. I've got nothing to offer complete strangers who believe they have the right to harass me in public. When this happens, it's usually someone who wants something from my brother—a charity donation, a public appearance, perhaps a date.

"This morning?" he finally reminds me.

Oh, him. The face behind the lens. The snoop with the wrong scoop. "You were trespassing on my property. You're lucky Sir Scrappy and Lady Yip didn't find you."

"Who are they, your security team?"

"No, just the coyotes that live somewhere on the mountainside. They've been known to attack."

"You're bluffing," he says, but I can tell he is thinking back to any strange noises he may have heard. Typical city boy. Afraid of a little desert wildlife.

"We also have javelina," I tell him, and, when he looks confused, I explain. "Wild pig-like creatures. They're mostly blind, really stinky, and they will attack. Mr. Garbagebreath and his pack trapped a guy on top of his car once. We waited forty-five minutes before calling animal control. Figured he deserved it. You don't want to rile up our desert friends."

I smile smugly and watch his reaction. Yep, he is definitely not from around here. I can tell he is itching to pull out his phone and look up *javelina*. I'm betting he spells it wrong.

"Thanks, I'll keep that in mind for the future." He shakes off his momentary concern and seems entirely unrepentant for his trespasses. That's not a surprise with his type. "I like how you name the animals."

"Did you get the shot you needed? I hope it was worth the wait." I smirk a little. Sometimes I amuse myself.

"Got some lovely pictures of the wrong woman," he says. "You knew I couldn't use those."

I shrug. "Some strange creep lurking behind my fence, how am I supposed to know you aren't looking for me? I could have a stalker."

"You're lucky my editor recognized you. He could have run those pictures and outed you as your stepbrother's secret lover. That scandal wouldn't play well."

"Last time that happened, the lawsuit bought me a gym," I reply, making full and complete eye contact. You have to treat paparazzi like the threat that they are. They skulk about, always hoping to catch you at your weakest. You have to make it clear that you see them and aren't afraid. It works; he blinks first.

"Wait, really? Like an actual gym?"

"Yep. When I was seventeen, some fool at one of the tabloids ran a whole story about Powell taking my virginity. They went fully in on the incest angle, claiming some anonymous source. Not only was it not true, but it also would have been a crime since he was twenty-one and I was under the age of consent. We sued for defamation, got a huge settlement, and the tabloid ended up folding. We Corbitts don't back down from litigation."

I always talk about it so flippantly, but that lawsuit marked one of the worst periods in my young life. I was still a virgin at the time and having to reveal details about my young body in a deposition was utterly humiliating. And even after we won the case there were whispers. Still are. I suppose it doesn't help that Powell and I are super close, and he takes me to awards shows—as a guest, not a date—whenever he's single. We've both heard people gossiping, and we do our best to ignore it. He may not technically be my blood relative, but he is emotionally and legally my brother. I can't think of him any other way.

Tanner is watching me rather intently. His eyes, I can't help but notice, are an intriguing green, the kind of color that only exists on Sci-Fi aliens or on exaggeratedly attractive love interests in romance novels. He's probably wearing colored contacts, but I'm not going to comment on them. Zahna would have asked where he bought them, and she'd have shown up to her next runway show with emerald irises.

"That must have been rather upsetting for you," he says, and he sounds like he means it. He's the only person I've ever encountered who didn't immediately jump on how fortunate I was to have those false rumors bring me a ginormous windfall. Lawsuit lottery, more than one jealous acquaintance called it.

"It was, but it all worked out in the end, didn't it?" I give him my fake cheerful smile, one I've perfected over the years. I've learned from the best in the business.

He tilts his head to the side and bites his lower lip. He looks like he wants to say something else, which sends off warning bells in my head. He must be an aspiring journalist. I hate them the most—the ones who slum it as paparazzi until they can break a big story. They steal our stories to use as the subjects of their unauthorized documentaries. They're far more invasive than the usual camera jockeys.

"I guess so. You seem to have your whole life together."

I can't tell if he means that as a dig, so I assume he does.

"Oh, you do too, Mr. Smythe-with-a-y. A career of prowling in someone else's bushes. How fun. But you're new, aren't you? They don't send their best out to Arizona when LA is packed with opportunities."

"I am new, in fact." He does not rise to the bait. "But it's working out for me so far. It's mostly athletes out here, and they're much more interesting than some floppy haired ex-boyband singer."

Ouch. That is a rather dismissive description of Powell's career. He's done quite well for himself as a solo artist. Maybe he's dropped down to filling arenas rather than stadiums, but he's also achieved critical acclaim, maintains a large fan base, and more importantly, earns a significant steady income from his music.

"To be fair, you haven't even caught a glimpse of the award-winning triple platinum musician you tried to stalk." I will always talk my brother up to other people, especially the ones who act like they aren't impressed with his considerable musical accomplishments.

"True. Here, take my card. Maybe you can shoot me a heads up if anything interesting is going to happen." He gives me a cheeky grin and slides his business card across the table. I pick it up. *Tanner Smythe Photography*, with an area code I don't recognize. Not that I'm likely to call anyway.

"I doubt I'll need this anytime soon. Now, if you'll excuse me, I believe my order is ready." Mama Nina is carrying the bag over to me with a polite customer service smile on her face, but her eyes are filled with fury. As I leave, I hear her angrily lecturing Tanner about the importance of privacy and not harassing her diners. I suspect he'll learn his lesson. Probably won't be seeing him again.

TWO

Powell looks much healthier and more alert after scarfing down two cheeseburgers and a pile of fries. If I tried to eat a heavy meal like that with a hangover, I guarantee I'd see it again soon after in a much more disgusting state. For him, that kind of food is revitalizing.

"You're lucky you aren't on a diet yet," I remind him, as he wipes the last of the grease from his lips and tosses his napkin on his plate.

"I've got a couple of months left."

The big concert is less than four months away, so soon he has to go into a full-on must-look-good-for-the-masses body improvement regimen. Diet, exercise, mandated sleeping periods, the works. I usually suffer alongside him, not just because that's how our kitchen is stocked, but because I want to look good in the periphery. Especially if Jace is making me go as his date. I need to look my best from all angles because if I don't, the gossip blogs run with it. That's why I prefer staying out of sight backstage. It's better for my self-esteem if I don't have to read critiques of my hair and clothing and speculation as to my relationships.

"True." We move from our patio table, where he consumed his grease-feast and I drank a healthy smoothie, to the poolside. This is where we come to forget the world. When we're relaxing on our loungers, or swimming in the cool water, or soaking in the hot tub, nothing else matters. Not Zahna, not scummy photographers, not the impending media storm of Powell's latest relationship implosion. None of it.

The rest of the morning and most of the afternoon passes peacefully. It's one of those perfect late-February days where the temperature hovers around eighty degrees. We alternate between lounging and swimming until we're thirsty enough to need a refresher other than water. Unfortunately, our outdoor wet bar hasn't been restocked lately. That's Powell's fault—our alcohol supply seems to dry up whenever he invites his local musician buddies over for a jam session. He's a generous host.

"But it's tequila o'clock," Powell complains when the only thing I can pull out is a half-drunk bottle of sickly-sweet Midori.

"Are you kidding me? Isn't that what made you so miserable in the first place?" If he's requesting tequila, he must be fully recovered from last night's binge. Anything I make him will be very weak though—I'm not dealing with a repeat.

"Shots at a bar are different than sharing a refreshing cocktail with my little sister. Besides, I'm trying to mend my broken heart."

"Then write a sad song."

"I'll do that later. Please? There's more inside." Powell waves toward the house. "Check the Corbitt Cantina."

"I'm not calling it that." The remodel of the basement bar was finished a month ago, and he's been trying to come up with a name for it. So far I've vetoed everything. Powell's Palace? Veto. Cheers to Life? Veto. Bar-Baron-a? Mega-veto.

"The Baron's Last Stand?"

"Powell, seriously, no. What's wrong with you?"

"The Rowdy Rathskeller?"

"You can't make up words."

"It's German for basement bar. It's perfect. Brixley suggested it."

"No, Powell, we're not outsourcing the naming rights." A flash of selfish inspiration hits me. "How about the Downstairs Drinkery?"

"Hey, that might actually work." Powell nods thoughtfully at my suggestion. He doesn't see my ulterior motive. My nickname is Deedee, so I'm going to special order a neon bar sign that says DD. I'm staking my claim. "Okay, get it from the Downstairs Drinkery."

"You're the one who wants it. You go get it."

But he doesn't move from his seat. I wait, arms crossed. Nope, he's still reclining like a hungover diva. "Take care of me, baby sis. I'm newly heartbroken."

"Your legs aren't broken." He still doesn't get up, and now he's giving me puppy dog eyes. I give up. "Fine, I'll go fetch some margarita fixings. Stay here and wallow in your misery."

His thousand-watt grin belies his supposed misery.

When I open the glass doors to enter the house I am greeted by a cacophony of phones. Oh no. This does not bode well for the remainder of our day.

Our kitchen charging station has all four phones plugged in—we each have one personal, one business. And they are all going insane. Beeps and chirps and ringing come from three of them, and Powell's personal phone has vibrated itself off the counter and is doing a little rattlesnake dance as it dangles from its cable. Crap. Word of Powell's breakup is out. Respite officially over. I'm going to need to call Miriam and tell her to get a handle on this, though I'm sure she's already trying.

After returning Powell's vibrating phone to a safe place on the countertop, I check my personal phone. Hundreds of texts that I don't have the time or inclination to skim, and my mom's number is showing up as it rings in my hand. She's probably mad that she read it online instead of hearing it directly.

"Hi, Mom," I answer, deciding to ignore everything else and go ahead and make the drinks. I won't tell Powell the news is out yet. He can find out later. He deserves one last peaceful afternoon.

"Cassidy!" Her unexpected scream is so loud I have to hold the phone away from my ear. My mother is not prone to screaming, and she doesn't even like Zahna that much. "I'm so relieved you finally answered! Did you . . . did you hear about Powell?"

"Yeah, of course I did," I tell her. She should have known that I'd be the first to find out. "Mom, you know this is something I can handle."

"Can you? Because I can't!" She starts sobbing. "Oh, Cassidy, when you didn't answer your phone I was so afraid you were with him."

"When, last night? I was." Of course I'd be the one caring for him after the break up. Technically, it's my job. My brother pays me as his assistant, though I don't work regular hours or anything like that. I make sure Powell leads an easy life, and a nice chunk of money appears in my bank account every two weeks. It's a fair exchange. But I'd have been the one he called no matter what, even if I wasn't salaried. I'm more than his sister, I'm his best friend.

"It's just . . . Powell . . ." She cries even louder. She's not usually like this, but she has been complaining about the start of menopause lately; maybe this over reaction is a side effect. Perhaps I should ask my stepdad to —gently—suggest that she schedule a consultation with her doctor.

"Mom, he's with me right now," I say, already heading out the door to the pool deck. Powell is going to hate me for passing this off, but I'll let him deal with explaining why he and Zahna ended things. There are limits to what I'm willing to take care of for him. Once mom hears about the affair with the race car driver, she'll understand.

"Of course he is, he will always be with you. Always. Don't ever forget your brother. I just . . . Hank is so devastated. We never thought we'd have to bury one of our children."

I freeze mid-step. "Bury?"

"Well, not literally." She chokes on the words.

This is such an overreaction. I know they want grandkids someday and Powell is their best shot, but there's no need to be so dramatic. I'm about to tell her that when she continues.

"They haven't . . . I don't know how many details you've been given, but there's not going to be enough left to bury. . ." I can't make out the rest of what she says through all the crying.

"What's going on?" Powell peers over his sunglasses at me, probably wondering why I'm not bringing him a cocktail and am currently in violation of our no electronics rule.

"Mom's hysterical. Something about burying you."

He sighs. "It was a break-up, not a death sentence. Tell her there are other fish in the sea, other stars in the sky, as one door closes another one opens. Take your pick."

I roll my eyes at his ridiculous platitudes. "Mom, Powell says there are other notes in the song." I wink at him. That was a good one. He should have thought of it himself, given his musical inclinations. "It was a breakup, and not even a bad one. I didn't even know you liked Zahna. You said she was shallow, remember?" I have to raise my voice to be heard over her wailing.

"Cassidy, I don't know anything about a breakup. I'm talking about the helicopter crash."

The what now? I'm pretty sure my heart stopped beating.

"Helicopter crash?" I repeat for Powell's benefit and quickly switch to speaker phone.

"Sweetie, I thought that's what we were talking about. It's been all over the news. The police called us. Powell was doing location scouting outside of LA, and they crashed. The chopper exploded. I'm so sorry . . ." she breaks off into sobs again.

"Ginny!" Powell shouts. His eyes are huge and round and starting to shine with tears—we've both come to the same horrifying conclusion. His voice can't penetrate her hearing, so he brings out the big guns. "Mom! MOM!"

Powell doesn't normally call her "mom." His preferred names for her are Ginny, or Gin, or, when annoyed, Hey-Lady-Stop-Embarrassing-Me. He was seventeen when our parents got married, far too old and too cool to need a maternal figure, though he requested an adult adoption later, to make our family official and complete. The rarity is what makes it the magic syllable, the one thing that can get through to her. She stops immediately.

"Mom, I'm alive. I wasn't on that helicopter."

"Powell? Powell!" Then she blows out our eardrums with a high pitched, "Hank! Powell's alive! He's on the phone right now!"

I toss him my phone so he can reassure his father, and sprint back into the house, grabbing the other three. My work cell is full of messages, condolences, requests for a statement, for an interview. Powell's phones aren't receiving calls; they're going crazy with social media notifications. I open up a browser to check the news and the biggest headline reads *Superstar Powell Corbitt, Three Others, Killed in Tragic Helicopter Explosion.*

"I'll call Miriam," Powell is saying when I return. "She'll fix this." I love the level of confidence he has in his publicist, but this may require more than just her.

"No, I'll call her," Hank says. He used to manage Powell's career and still knows all his people. "She thinks you're dead. It's probably best she doesn't hear your voice from beyond the grave. I'll get Jace's publicist on the line, too. We're leaving now, see you in five." They should have thought to come over to comfort me earlier. We live in the same neighborhood; a quick drive or a short walk could have saved them a couple of hours of misery. Though I suppose they assumed I was in California.

When we hang up the phone, my brother and I stare at each other in wordless silence. It hasn't quite sunk in yet. Can Jace really be dead? I just spoke with him a few hours ago. I . . . I asked him to get on that helicopter. Did I send my friend off to his death? This is so surreal.

Powell reaches out and pinches my forearm.

"Ow!" I jerk away.

"Sorry, I was just checking to see if this was a dream."

"You're supposed to pinch yourself!" I smack his arm and he winces.

"Ow! Okay, I guess it isn't. Cass, this is . . . this is real." Now instead of trying to hurt me, he hugs me instead. I can feel his shoulders shaking as he's trying not to completely break down. If he's going to emotionally crash, that means I can't. He might be the older sibling, but I've always been the strong one. I'm going to need to handle this for both of us.

"Go get dressed," I tell him, switching into damage control mode. "If we're about to announce you lived and Jace died, you shouldn't be in a swimsuit. Put on something somber, and I'll get a photographer." While Hank is gathering publicists, I need to make some calls of my own.

On my way to change into clothing more sedate and appropriate than a bikini, I grab my purse and dig through it for Tanner's card.

Fortunately, he answers the phone.

"Tanner, it's Cassidy. From this morning?"

"Cassidy, I saw the news. I'm so sorry for your loss." Well, that is a sweet reaction. He sounds genuinely sympathetic.

"Are you still in the area?" I ask, trying to keep my voice as steady as possible. Jace, my friend—who I sent in Powell's stead—was blown up. I can't let the horror of that overwhelm me. Not yet. There's time to mourn later, but for now I need to do my job and focus on the task at hand. When he affirms his nearby location, I let out a breath of relief. Good. "If you want a picture that's going to boost your career, come to my house right now. Call your agent on the way and tell her to be ready with an offer."

"Cassidy, you're in mourning. I don't think this is the appropriate time for something like that." A pap with a conscience? That's new and unexpected.

"Seriously. Tanner, I have someone else I can offer it to instead, but I'm giving you a chance. Can you please come over? Quickly?"

"I'm on my way."

Next, I call the security guard at the gate house to inform him that Tanner—and only Tanner—is allowed to be buzzed through. The guard, a lovely former Navy SEAL named Omaha—yes, like the city—was relieved to hear my voice. He has also been trying to get in touch with us. Reporters from local stations have already been by, and per protocol, he told them nobody was home, but he wanted to warn us that the vultures were circling. Omaha is the king of conspiracy theories, so his belief that smartphones are secretly government tracking devices means he wasn't aware of what was going on and why the media were there, but he wasn't going to offer them up any carrion.

But after that phone call comes the worst one. This is going to hurt. Jace's closest friend and musical partner still doesn't know about his tragic and untimely demise. I take a deep breath to prepare myself and dial Devon's number.

"Cass, I heard about Powell. Jace and Brix and I are so sorry," he says as soon as he picks up the phone. Wild hope flairs in my chest.

"You've talked to Jace?" I can't breathe. Is it possible? Maybe this whole thing is a misunderstanding. Maybe there wasn't a helicopter explosion at all. The witnesses were confused, or it was swamp gas or solar flares, like all those fake UFO sightings.

"No, he's not answering his phone. But I know he's just as devastated as I am. Powell was a brother to us." Devon's voice is hoarse as though he's been crying. His words strip away that brief moment of hope.

"Devon, Powell is . . . alive." It shouldn't be so hard to say, but it is. My brother is alive. And I'm about to change Devon's life forever and he doesn't see it coming.

"He's alive?" Devon whoops with joy. "He's alive! Cass, that's amazing! Was this a hoax? Or . . . oh, tell me this wasn't a publicity stunt. That's so ridiculous. Powell needs to fire whoever came up with that dumb idea."

"No, it wasn't a stunt. Devon, Powell wasn't the one who went up in the helicopter. I'm so sorry."

I can almost sense how Devon's mind is working. He's flitting through all the possibilities of how there could be these horrible news stories but a living Powell. And I can feel the moment he understands what I desperately don't want to say.

"Who was it? Who was in that helicopter?" He'd be familiar with Powell's words from earlier: *One of us always has to participate in location scouting.*

"Devon, I'm so sorry, I am, but—"

"Who was it Cass?" he interrupts me. His voice has risen to a vocal register I didn't know he could reach.

"It was Jace. He went in Powell's place."

The sound that echoes in my ear is a scream that will haunt me for the rest of my life.

When I am able to end my call with Devon, I'm emotionally drained. I want time to mourn too. I want a quiet moment to contemplate how terrible it is that the world is still spinning and Jace is no longer on it.

But I can't do any of that because the doorbell rings. It's Tanner, who evidently either doesn't believe in speed limits or was already harassing someone nearby.

I open the front door and Tanner stares at me wordlessly for a second, before repeating his earlier condolences and enveloping me in a tight hug. Now, truth be told, I am awfully devastated, and I do like a good hug. Okay, I *love* a good hug by a strong man who oddly smells like he's spent the day in a bakery. But I can't let myself enjoy it—it's too much of a distraction from what needs to be done. When he releases me, I step back.

"Why'd you do that?" I ask, somewhat affronted at the unexpected invasion of my personal space. Also curious about the cinnamon smell, but mostly affronted.

"You looked like you needed a hug," he says, and then raises his camera and takes a picture. Of me, because he's an asshole. That is so not why I called him.

"Why are you taking *my* picture?"

"Isn't that why you called me? To document your mourning?"

I'm not sure I like his attitude. He swung so quickly from being comforting to being snarky. Or maybe he really does think I'm the type of person who wants to publicize my own grief. If so, he's greatly misjudged me.

"Don't make me regret inviting you. Come with me, I'll show you why you're here." I lead him into the living room.

"Holy crap," he gasps out, rather unprofessionally, when he sees who's sitting there. So much for him not being impressed by floppy haired ex-boyband singers.

"Yeah, he wasn't the one on the helicopter. Want the shot?"

THREE

I haven't seen any of Tanner's work before, so I was taking it on faith that he was a decent photographer. Faith and the massive lens I saw this morning. Pricey equipment can create usable images no matter who is clicking the shutter, right?

As it turns out, Tanner has a great eye for lighting and detail. He takes a gorgeous and evocative photograph of Powell, slouched over on the couch, blankly staring at a news report about the helicopter crash on his tablet. Within minutes, Tanner sets his laptop up and gets the image sent off to his agent. It doesn't take long before he lets out a rather loud yelp.

"Everything okay?" I ask, going into the kitchen where he is working. I'm glad to have an excuse to leave the living room, actually. My mom and Hank are really overdoing it with the emotions. They are clustered around Powell, making it clear how relieved they are that he is alive. They can't stop touching him and leaning on him. I had to shoo them away so Tanner could get his picture, and they got right back to it the second the photography session ended. Mom keeps running her hands through his hair—and he keeps trying to smooth it back down. Hank has his arm draped over Powell's shoulders and won't stop squeezing his son tightly. Ordinarily my brother would protest such a display of parental affection, but this is not an ordinary day.

"I'm getting out of debt with this offer." Tanner stares at the screen, mouth agape. He shakes his head and scrutinizes his computer again, blinking as though that might change what he's seeing. "Wow. I've never . . ." He shakes his head again. Is he going into shock? If he is, it's unwarranted. The figure his agent sent him is far too low.

"Good, your agent sold it to Eduardo. Let me make a call." I've already had ten missed calls from him, so I know Eduardo will pick up right away. He does.

"Cassidy! Is it true?" He's breathless with excitement. Fantastic. That means he'll be greedy.

"My sources tell me you just got a picture of Powell alive when the rest of the media is reporting his death. That's going to bring you a lot of attention. Your site will go viral."

"And?" Eduardo knows I have more news for him.

"You only have half the story. I bet you're wondering who was really on that helicopter." I swallow against the sudden lump in my throat. *Stay strong*, I remind myself, *for Jace's sake.*

"Who?" He's practically salivating, which means it's time for the bargaining.

"First you owe your man Tanner an additional 20k for the photo. I'll take double his payment for the info."

"I'm not paying you. It'll be out soon enough."

That's the wrong tactic to take with me, especially now, now when I'm struggling to control my emotions. Devon begged me to release it immediately and all I can focus on is getting through this phone call without breaking down myself.

"Sure will. I'm calling *Celebutante* next. You might have Powell's picture, but they'll have the real story."

"You catty witch!"

"You sure know how to sweet talk. My price is going up 10k every fifteen seconds. But in one minute, I'm offering it elsewhere."

"Fine, deal. Who was it?" He is putty in my hands now. I knew the mention of his competitor would break him. I pull out my other phone and open my banking app.

"I want to see the money appear in my account first."

"How do I know it's accurate?" Fair question. While in the past some of the tips I've provided may have been more Powell-serving than truthful, when it comes to a topic as serious as this, he should trust me. But how can I be absolutely certain Jace was on the helicopter and isn't hanging out somewhere without cell service? Well, for one thing, there was the selfie he texted Powell saying 'you're missing out,' sent from the doomed flight. That one is too tragic and personal for my brother to share with the world.

"If I'm wrong, I'll refund you my and Tanner's money. But I'm not wrong." There is a ding and a payment received notification flashes on my phone. "Good boy. It was Jace Monroe. He went in Powell's place, but they didn't change the name on the passenger manifest."

"Jace Monroe?" Both Eduardo and Tanner repeat at the same time.

"Yes. Jace is dead. The official announcement goes out in an hour. His team is putting it together. But you've got the scoop."

"I love you Cassidy!" Eduardo hangs up abruptly, no doubt about to start madly typing and uploading and whatever else he does to keep the gossip flowing.

I set my phone down and sink weakly into a kitchen chair. That call used up all my strength. Here I am, profiting from the death of one of my dear friends, though not by choice. Devon ordered me to break that story, and I couldn't say no. Tanner watches me, eyes wide in what I hope is awe and not horror.

"That was pretty freaking mercenary."

"Eduardo is a blood-sucking ghoul seeking to mine my pain for profit. He doesn't care about me; he only cares about the hits on his website. So yeah, I'm going to charge him for it." Not to mention making him pay was revenge on him for the December ass grabbing incident. I might have given him the story for free if he wasn't such a sleazebag.

"Are you okay?" Tanner asks. I don't know if it is meant to be a rhetorical question, or if he's referring to my mental health. I may have come across as an insensitive monster in my conversation with Eduardo, but it was the only way I could calm the storm of emotions inside me.

"Of course not. Someone I care about just died horrifically, and if my brother hadn't been so hungover this morning it would have been him. And I'm the one who . . ." I trail off as the guilt slams into me again. This is my fault. I called Jace and asked him to go in Powell's place. I handed him his death sentence. I'm never going to forgive myself. I should have had them reschedule for a different day, with a different company. A company that makes non-exploding helicopters.

The instant Eduardo's story goes live all the phones in the house start beeping, vibrating, and ringing. Even Tanner's, though his is likely his agent congratulating him on the increased money. And then the doorbell rings too.

"Already?" How did they get past Omaha? We're going to need to have a talk about his list.

"Cass!" Powell yells from the living room. "Was that the door?" Yes, Powell, excellent job, even in grief, you can recognize the sound of a doorbell.

"I'll get rid of them," I shout back. Really, I should ask Hank to do it. But I won't, because he hasn't left his son's side since he got here. He needs recovery time after spending hours thinking his baby boy had been killed. I hope the doorbell was a signal to him though, one that reminded him to bring some on-site security out here. There are only so many things I can do myself.

"I'll come with you," Tanner offers, jumping to his feet to follow me. He must think he owes me since I got his photo price bumped up. I still don't know why I did that, other than my annoyance at Eduardo.

I use my phone to call up the video feed from the security camera and discover, to my dismay, that it's not a reporter. The latest arrival is someone much more annoying.

"Xander, what are you doing here?" I ask my least favorite Last Baron as I reluctantly open the front door. I guess he managed to drag himself away from his busy lifestyle, partying with a bunch of D-list actresses.

"As soon as I heard about Powell, I jumped on my private jet and flew out here so I could comfort you," he proclaims magnanimously as he envelops me in an unwelcome embrace. Notice how he makes sure to point out he has a private jet? That reveals everything anyone needs to know about Xander's personality. Also, he's exaggerating. I know for a fact he only owns a share in it. It's not his personal private property.

Xander is the fourth person to hug me in the past twenty minutes. Hank was first, and his hug was supportive, as they always are. The first time he hugged me I was twelve years old and I knew in that moment I wanted him for my stepfather. Mom's would have been supportive, but she was crying and it quickly turned into a me comforting her hug rather than the other way around. Then came Tanner, with his warm cinnamon-scented embrace that was unexpected, yet strangely welcome.

But Xander . . . ugh. No physical contact from Xander is ever welcome, but his hugs are the absolute worst. Not only does he wear far too much cologne—so much so that it clings to everyone unfortunate enough to come in contact with him—but also, I always suspect he's subtly trying to use his chest to feel my boobs. Plus, he does this thing where he puts one hand on the back of my head to hold me against him. That's a power move, and I don't appreciate it.

I struggle to escape from this unwelcome cologne-transferring assault, but Xander is pinning my arms at my sides. If he were an attacker, there are plenty of self-defense moves I could use. The problem is I can't do them on the misguided and slightly creepy former bandmate of my brother's, because breaking his nose or kneeing his crotch would lead to worse problems.

"Get off me," I say, but he can't hear me over the sound of his own attempt at soothing.

"I'm so sorry, Cass, but don't worry, I'm here, I'll take care of you," he keeps repeating, which is absurd. Not only can I take care of myself, but he's the last person I would go to for assistance anyway.

"Alright, that's enough." A hand on my shoulder and another on Xander's pulls us apart as Tanner forces his way in between us. He keeps his body positioned in front of me so Xander can't molest me again.

"Who the hell are you?" demands Xander, sounding almost jealous.

"He's my bodyguard," I reply, and Tanner rolls with it.

"Sure. Yeah, that works. I'm her bodyguard. Keep your hands off her." He crosses his arms over his chest and tries to look intimidating.

"My shirt costs more than your car. Don't touch it again," Xander warns, brushing invisible Tanner cooties from his shoulder. I have no idea what kind of car Tanner drives, but it's entirely possible that Xander is correct. A pretentious asshole, clearly, but correct. "Cassidy, I'm here for you. Can we go somewhere to talk?"

As much as I loathe him, I do also slightly pity him. Sure, it was annoying that he hugged me. And yes, he was acting like a snobby jerk the way he talked about the cost of his shirt. But he was one of Powell's bandmates and, not only does he still think Powell is dead, he is about to find out that rather than Powell, with whom he's always had a somewhat contentious relationship, it was his close friend Jace who died instead.

"Let's go to the living room. There's someone you need to see," I say. Perhaps I'm being petty, but I lead him in with no warning.

He stops abruptly in the doorway, "What the . . . he survived? You're supposed to be . . . how . . . what? Powell . . . you . . ." Xander stutters and seems to be swaying on his feet. The shock of seeing my brother alive must really be getting to him. I almost feel guilty for the way I did the big reveal. But then I get a whiff of Xander's scent clinging to my shirt and the guilt evaporates.

Powell shakes off our parents to come over and greet Xander. They exchange one of those bro-hugs where their bodies barely touch and they both step back quickly. The contact wasn't nearly as intense as what Xander imposed on me, but I can tell from the way Powell's nose wrinkles and he wipes ineffectively at his own shirt afterward that he is also wearing some of Xander's cologne.

"I asked Jace to go in my place," Powell tells him. "I'm so sorry; I never expected this to happen."

"*Jace* was on the helicopter?" All the color drains from Xander's face as he processes the news.

"If Jace couldn't go, I was going to call you," Powell says, which is in no way comforting, but Xander doesn't respond. His knees give out and he collapses on the floor, head in hands. I nudge Tanner.

"This might make a good photo," I point out.

"Already on it," he says. Maybe I should have looked before I elbowed him in the ribs—I messed up his shot.

In times of tragedy, it's human nature to want to come together, reaffirm connections, and process the loss. That's why our house is starting to fill with people. Powell's local musician friends are all here, both to reassure themselves that he still exists on this earthly plane and to mourn the loss of one of their idols. Jace used to jam with them on his frequent visits.

Since we have so many visitors, I find myself stepping in and performing hostess duties, a welcome distraction from my pain. I order food from my favorite nearby Mexican restaurant. Mom and Tanner help me set out the trays of enchiladas and tamales. It's a little weird that he's still hanging around; he's already earned his photo money and no more celebrities are likely to show up. I'm not going to kick him out though. He's a lot more helpful than most of our guests. As the only one here who was not personally affected by the tragedy, he provides a calm and steady presence.

But I can't maintain my own calm and steady façade much longer. When it gets to be too much, I retreat to my room, over-whelmed and needing a break. Jace is dead. It still doesn't seem real. He was my first crush. In fact, as a pre-teen, I was such a huge Jace Monroe fan that my mom worked overtime to buy tickets to a Last Barons of Sound concert as a surprise for my twelfth birthday. She met Hank at that concert and changed the trajectory of both of our lives. If I'd been desperately worshipful of a member of a different boyband, who knows where I would be today?

Jace was my first kiss, too. It happened at the Y2K Round the World concert, a 24-hour live broadcast welcoming the year 2000 sequentially in each time zone. The Last Barons were performing in Chicago. The show was rough—the boys were all unhappy that they lost out on the coveted New York City spot, there were issues with lighting and sound, and their back-stage food requests were not adequately met. Just before mid-night, a producer grabbed me and four other young women and shoved us onstage. I was told to stand directly behind Jace, and I obeyed, though I had no idea what was going on. At the stroke of midnight, they spun around to kiss us. It was unexpected, but so very exciting. My crush, kissing me on live television.

Admittedly, the kiss was prim, a soft gentle pressing of his lips on mine, and nothing like the full-on with tongue make-out sessions happening on either side of us. I staggered off stage all dreamy eyed, to find my mom and Hank in an angry argument with a producer, the one who had accidentally grabbed the wrong 'brown-haired girl standing over there.' They were furious, with Hank repeatedly shouting "She is fifteen years old! *Fifteen!*" I was afraid my stepdad was going to punch the poor guy.

But I didn't care about the backstage argument, I was literally floating. That moment onstage has always been burned into my memory, Jace's eyes widening in surprise and his little half-smile before he cupped my face in his hands and leaned in for that precious tender moment. First, it served as fuel for many teenage fantasies and later, after his heartbreaking rejection of me, I would recall it with bitter-edged wistfulness. My crush terminated rather painfully but we eventually became close friends, and on that level, I truly cared about him.

How can he be gone? I just saw him two weeks ago when he flew out here to celebrate my birthday. I talked to him this morning. I can't believe that was our last phone call, the last time I'll ever speak with him. And I can't help but direct a smidgen of anger and resentment toward both myself and Powell. My brother was the one who said Xander was worthless and suggested we call Jace. I should have ignored him and called Xander anyway. While Xander might not be a fan of Powell, he's always willing to step up and do favors for me. He definitely would have filled in for him in an attempt to earn brownie points.

Of course, those thoughts make me feel like a horrifically bad person. Who am I to wish I had the power to trade deaths? Obviously, had I known the chopper would crash, I wouldn't have sent anyone up in it. And yes, Xander is an irritation, but that doesn't mean he deserves to die. But Jace . . . Jace deserved to live forever. Or at least longer than thirty-three years.

I open my laptop and start bringing up news articles. All the coverage of Powell's death has been replaced. Tanner's photo of my brother is everywhere, accompanying bios of Jace, memorials to Jace, and of course, news "analysis" about the crash. It mostly consists of reporters interviewing random experts who have neither investigated nor seen the crash site speculating about the cause. I don't want to read about that. I'd rather remember my friend as he was in the last photo he sent Powell, smiling and happy. I don't want to wonder how long he lived. Did he burn to death, or die of massive head trauma? Did the helicopter explode, as some witnesses seemed to suggest, killing him instantly, or did it crash to earth, giving him seconds to realize his own mortality before the end?

I put my head down on my desk. Sometimes I wish I could cry, really cry, just weep all the pain away. But I physically can't. I used up every sob in my body when I threw myself into the grave at my father's funeral, pounding on the casket and screaming and begging him to wake up. That was the last time I was actually capable of crying. Still, though, despite my inability to outwardly show the trauma I'm feeling, I need a moment to myself to do some private mourning before I drag myself back to playing the part of the gracious hostess who keeps everything under control.

I never heard my bedroom door open, but there are suddenly hands massaging my shoulders and a voice far too close to my ear whispering, "There, there, let it out. I'm here for you." There's no need to guess who it is, his pungency gives him away.

"Xander, stop," I say as I shrug his unwelcome hands off me.

"I understand. Jace was your first love." He sits down, uninvited, on my bed. Great. Now on top of everything else, I'm going to have to change my sheets tonight.

"First crush, not first love," I correct. Technically, I've never had a first love. It's not like I'm completely inexperienced or anything, I'm just not one for relationships. Fantasy fueled crushes, sure. Occasional flings, yes. But falling in *love*? Not for me.

"I'm surprised your boyfriend isn't here to console you," he says, glaring in the general direction of the rest of the house.

"Boyfriend?" If this is a sleazy joke about Powell, I am going to punch him in his snide mouth.

"The man with the camera. I didn't think you liked paps." Apparently, he finally identified Tanner's unfortunate career choice. Bodyguard, indeed.

"He's not my boyfriend. I've known him for less than a day," I respond.

"Let me guess. You picked him up at a bar last night, and he hasn't left yet. No wonder you didn't answer your phone all afternoon." Jealousy is not an attractive look on Xander, nor is it merited for a myriad of reasons. And not that it's any of his business, but I have never picked up a guy in a bar and brought him home. Never. That's not to say I've never had one-night stands. But not with someone I don't already know well enough to be sure they aren't using me to gain access to my brother. I made that mistake a couple of times when I was younger, but I learned my lesson and I'll never do it again. I don't like being used.

"He's a photographer, nothing more. He's doing a job. And I didn't answer because Powell and I were having a relaxing, technology-free day. If we had realized what happened, we would have dealt with it much earlier." By my calculations, Powell was dead to the world for about four hours. Tribute sites sprang up everywhere. I read his obituary.

"I don't trust him," Xander says. "He's after something. Here, come sit with me." He pats the bed next to him, a gesture that I'm sure has worked on hundreds of women. He is, after all, a former member of the Last Barons of Sound, legendary boyband. But I don't move. I'm not falling for that.

"You don't have to trust him. I don't either." That may be the one thing Xander and I will ever agree on. "But we needed someone, and he was in the right place at the right time."

"Unlike Jace," Xander mutters, and then falls over backward on my mattress. Gross. Xander is laying on my bed. And he is crying. I can't tell if he's making a ploy for sympathy or if his wailing is genuine. "Jace was my best friend," Xander sobs.

Maybe that is true. But he wasn't Jace's best friend. Jace believed in loyalty and was very tolerant of Xander, as were the rest of the Last Barons. But I'm not sure any of them liked Xander much. Sometimes people are part of our lives by choice, and sometimes by historical ties and record label contracts.

Despite my disgust and distrust of him, I'm certain Xander's pain is real, even if the tears probably aren't. But I don't want to be the one who helps him through it. I'm doing enough of that for Powell. I can't take on someone else's emotional load too. It's time to get Xander out of here and away from me.

"Have you talked to Devon yet?" I ask. Xander stops crying almost instantaneously, proving that he was exaggerating his distress to garner sympathy.

"No, but I should. When I heard Powell was dead, you were my immediate priority. I'd do anything for you, Cass." He reaches for me, but I manage to evade his grasp. He likely spent the entire flight on his private jet gloating about Powell and fantasizing about exactly how to comfort me, and I can only imagine it involved sex. His desires have always been transparent. I can't help but think he only wants me because I always turn him down. He's not used to rejection.

"You should go outside and call him." I'm not being mean; I'm positive Devon switched his phone to silent, so it won't be an annoyance. I would have told him to check in with Mason, but Mason's wife is literally giving birth right now, and his assistant is fielding his calls. I don't want his poor assistant getting yelled at by Xander.

"Let's call him together," Xander suggests, pulling out his phone. Yuck, no. I'm not putting my face close enough to his to share a call. I'm rather disgusted with the way he's acting tonight. I realize death sometimes brings out life-affirming horniness in survivors but he doesn't need to be so transparently desperate.

"No. Please get out of my room." I open the door that he had the nerve to shut and lock behind himself and gesture through it, urging him to leave. He doesn't move. "Seriously, I want some privacy now. Get out." With Xander you have to be firm. But he still ignores me. I can't leave while he's in here—I don't trust him not to go through my underwear drawer.

I finally give up and text Powell, telling him I need help, but it's Tanner who appears. He looks at us both, assesses the situation, and promptly demonstrates his remarkable skills at reading a room.

"I've been looking for you," he says, but not to me. "I want to take some photos for the press. Would you mind coming out and sitting with Powell?"

Xander jumps up so fast he creates a breeze of cologne. "Let me stop in the bathroom to fix my hair." He sweeps past Tanner and down the hall, thankfully not trying to use my attached bathroom. I don't have enough disinfectant for that.

Tanner grins and an adorable dimple appears in his left cheek. "I knew that would work."

"You're good at this." That's the only flattery he's going to get from me.

"You live here?" he responds as his eyes scan my room.

"This is my room, yes."

"Really? It looks like a spa."

He probably didn't intend that as a compliment, but I'm going to take it as such. My room is my refuge from all the pressures of the outside world, so I keep the space as Zen and spa-like as possible. With the exception of a pot of green bamboo in the corner, everything is white or light wood, and I have just the right amount of candles and a sound machine.

"It's supposed to. This is where I come to relax."

"Rather impersonal, isn't it? Except for that." Oh no, now he's walking in, invading my space, though in a less obtrusive way than Xander had. He goes over to the shelf near my bed. Other than a salt lamp and candles, it only houses two things: a framed photograph and a stuffed chickadee. The chickadee was my childhood comfort toy, the one thing I retain. My dad's wedding ring is on a chain around its neck. I'm twenty-eight now, but when I'm sad or feeling low, I still sleep with the ratty old thing. It will likely join me in my bed tonight. Once I've replaced the contaminated sheets, of course.

"Who's this?" He picks up the photo to examine it.

"My father."

"He looks different," Tanner says. "But I like the portraiture. Good lighting."

"Different from what?" When would Tanner have seen images of my father before? Was he stalking me online? After our run-in at the diner this morning, did he decide to do his research?

"The way he looks now. Did he have . . . oh, wait, I'm sorry. That's your stepdad out there, isn't it?"

"My father died when I was six." I don't need to get into this with him. Haven't there been enough talks about death today?

"That explains the hairstyle. His, not yours. In the picture. Because it's old. I'm sorry, I'm putting my foot in my mouth."

He flushes red and shoves his hands into his pockets, looking everywhere but at me. Am I making him nervous?

"Don't worry about it. In twenty years, we'll look back at our current hairstyles and laugh too."

"I'm ready now." Xander's voice and his freshened cologne waft down the hallway. Doesn't he understand that cameras don't capture smells? No need to poison everybody with the fumes.

"Speaking of hairstyles," Tanner mutters under his breath. Xander used the time to re-gel his already overly crisp hair. He's too vain to hire someone to advise him, because he holds the misguided belief that he's some kind of style icon. Some people have the eye for that sort of thing, Xander does not. Xander also doesn't have manners; he snaps his fingers and walks off, fully expecting Tanner to follow. Which, yes, he does, but not because of the snapping.

"Hey, Tanner," I call after him, and he turns to look back at me. "Thank you. For everything." Showing up unquestioningly, helping with the guests, getting foul-smelling parasites out of my room.

A smile flits across his face and he nods. "No problem."

FOUR

Jace's funeral has been scheduled rather quickly. It's only been a week since his death, and yet here we are, arriving in Los Angeles for a couple of days of press in the lead up to the main event. I cringe when I think about it. I'm not one of those people who believe funerals should be solemn affairs. I prefer the ones where we trade funny stories and celebrate the life of the deceased, rather than sit in mournful yet tasteful silence.

There's already a media circus at the airport. Fortunately, we're experts at evading them. Also, it helps that they *somehow* expect Powell to arrive on a flight from Phoenix. My brother and I drove down to Tucson and flew out of their much smaller airport, taking us to a different gate. Our parents are the Corbitts who came from Sky Harbor, and they are accidentally ambushed instead. Mom doesn't mind, she's been through this before. She likes to wave to the reporters and jokingly tell them to make sure they get her best side.

Powell owns a two-bedroom luxury condo in downtown LA, but he offered to let mom and Hank stay there. We go to Devon and Brixley's Los Feliz mansion instead. When we arrive, Devon greets Powell with a hug, but not one of those awkward barely touching hugs. No, this is a sad, desperate "our loved one has died and we have only each other to cling to" type hug that lasts minutes and ends with both of them wiping away tears. I am glad there are no photographers here. The moment is too poignant to cheapen by selling it to tabloids.

I follow them into the large living room, where Brixley is draped across a chair in the effortlessly beautiful way that models lounge around, in a pose that would break anyone else but makes her look glamorous and unapproachable. A very jet-lagged Mason is sprawled on one of the couches, but he springs to his feet to embrace me. His wife and newborn didn't make the journey, but in the first few seconds after greeting him, I am shown perhaps one thousand pictures of an adorable black-haired little baby with a wrinkled old man face. This is a privilege—the family hasn't released any photos to the media yet. Gossip blogs in India are offering bounties for the images, not because of Mason, but because his wife is a huge Bollywood star. Though he has a fanbase over there, too.

Mason moves on to show his baby off to Powell, and I am about to join Brixley when suddenly arms wrap around me from behind and I am enveloped in an overly pungent odor.

"I'm so glad you're finally here, Cassidy," Xander says, far too close to my ear. I don't understand why he's always so awkward and handsy with me but can behave with other people just fine. He's got good looks, wealth, and fame, so he should be perfectly capable of finding someone else to attach himself to, someone who can tolerate him. Someone who doesn't break out in figurative hives when he touches them.

"Stop!" I pry him off and go over to take the chair next to Brixley. I am unable to imitate her relaxed pose, but I try.

"Xander being a creep again? He has such a crush on you," she murmurs in a voice so low I can hardly hear her.

"No he doesn't," I say, but a chill runs down my spine. I don't want to think about Xander and his frustrated desires. I want to focus on losing myself in the moment and missing Jace.

"Always has. Remember his countdown to your eighteenth birthday? Don't worry, we all agree you're too good for him." She gives me a sad smile. "I wish Jace were here."

"Me too." Much like Powell, Jace always knew how to put Xander in his place.

"What kind of monstrosity is *that*?" Powell's shocked voice interrupts every conversation in the room. I turn to see him staring with an expression of wide-eyed horror.

"Good, Powell finally discovered the new piano," Brixley tells me in her quiet voice. "Devon's had it for weeks, and he's been so eager to post it on SwiftaPic, but he wanted to witness Powell's reaction in person first."

The piano in question has clear acrylic legs and an acrylic top, while the body of the piano—also acrylic—is bright red. My brother is examining it, both skeptical and appalled. He's a purist and a traditionalist. He still plays his mother's piano that she inherited from her own parents.

"Devon, it's ... *plastic*. Why ... what ... no ..." Powell sits down on the bench and winces as he tentatively pokes a few keys.

"Stop acting like a baby. The sound is great, check this out." Devon plays a few chords, and I recognize the beginning of *Only You*, one of JaDed's smash hits.

"Huh." Powell takes over playing, head tilted to the side, face screwed up in concentration. While he is making his assessment, the others disappear into Devon's instrument room. When they emerge, Devon is lugging his double bass, and both Mason and Xander are carrying borrowed guitars.

"That," Brixley indicates the guitar in Xander's hands, "is Devon's most expensive one. No surprise Xander claimed it."

Nope, no surprise at all. We watch as the boys set up and begin tuning. While they were all brought together by the record company on the basis of their singing and dancing abilities—as well as, let's be honest, their physical attractiveness—they also have numerous other musical talents. Powell is a piano prodigy, who plinked out songs before he could walk. He also plays every note on his solo albums, though obviously he tours with a backup band. Devon is a string genius. If something has vibrating strings and a soundboard, he can play it, even if it's an instrument he's never seen before. Both Mason and Xander play the guitar, and in addition, Mason has been—according to his social media profiles—learning to play a whole slew of traditional Indian instruments. He likes to post videos of himself serenading his gorgeous wife.

My heart aches as the remaining Last Barons start jamming. This used to be fun. Back in the old days, on tours, they would pull out their instruments when they were riding a post-show high, and everybody would dance to the improvised tunes. In the later years, they wrote many of their own songs. The lyrics always started out horrifyingly raunchy, but eventually evolved into romantic words that were catchy and palatable for the masses.

Now though, it's painful and melancholy. Powell is playing in minor key, and nobody is smiling. Jace isn't here to liven things up, Devon isn't demonstrating bizarre dance moves, Mason and Xander aren't competing to see who can play fastest or who can come up with the most obscene choruses. All the joy is missing.

I'm relieved when Devon's housekeeper interrupts. Apparently, there are investigators here who want to talk to Powell and me.

"Don't say anything without an attorney," Xander warns us both.

"You aren't under arrest," one of the investigators says. There are two of them, an older man with a scraggly ponytail, and a strikingly attractive younger one. They stand in the doorway somewhat awkwardly, possibly starstruck—though their eyes are fastened on Brixley, not the famous boyband.

"We're not the police. We're with the National Transportation Safety Board," the younger one explains, managing to tear his gaze away from the supermodel. "We couldn't arrest you even if we wanted to."

"Cass?" Powell asks me. I know what he's wondering. These are the kinds of decisions he relies on me to make.

"We don't need attorneys," I respond. "I'm sure they're only trying to build a timeline." No need to delay the inevitable. Besides, just the fact that Xander recommended we have a lawyer present makes me not want to call one. Yes, I'm petty. And I assume Xander is always wrong.

The younger investigator gives us a reassuring nod. "That's right. We just want to talk about what happened before the flight. This isn't a criminal investigation."

"You still need a lawyer," Xander mutters under his breath, but as usual, we ignore him.

While Powell is taken elsewhere by Agent Scraggly, I let the hot one, who introduces himself as Ethan, lead me into the kitchen for my interview. I think it's odd that they're separating us, but I suppose that's standard practice in most investigations.

My investigator sits down next to me at the kitchen table and looks deep into my eyes. "Before we start, I want to say that I'm sorry for your loss. I understand you and Mr. Monroe were close friends." There's real sympathy shining from his face, which I appreciate. I would have expected someone more . . . I don't know, detached? Someone who regularly investigates aviation disasters should be more cynical and dispassionate. More like . . . well, more like me.

"I've known him . . . I knew him for sixteen years," I say, grateful for the kindness in his approach to the questioning. "He was a good man."

"That's what everyone keeps telling me." Ethan's face transforms into a more serious expression. Oh no. This is going to be the part where we have to talk about the explosion. His lips start to form a question, and I hold up a hand to stop him.

"Wait. Before we get into this, I want to make it clear that although I'm willing to answer your questions, I'd rather not learn any specific details."

He nods in understanding. "Of course. We don't need to get into that anyway. I want to start with the morning before the crash. Can you talk me through why your brother didn't go?"

"He was hungover," I admit, and now I'm worried that my statement might make him sound like an alcoholic. That kind of speculation can ruin his image. Powell is a clean cut, usually sober guy. He just doesn't deal with getting cheated on very well. Nobody does.

"Can you give more information than that?"

"What are you going to use this for?" I'd love to be honest, but privacy matters.

"It's for my report," he says, which does not enlighten me.

"But is it confidential?" I'm sure it isn't, he already asked for permission to record. I just want to know *when* it will be made public. And how much of it. I hate when only edited versions of things are released. The media can twist our words so easily.

"The report will be released when the investigation is completed," Ethan tells me, again not giving me the information I seek. He leans forward intently. "You look like you have something you want to say."

"It's nothing important, just somewhat personal." The fact is, Powell and Zahna still haven't made their breakup public, because other things took precedence. Their *conscious uncoupling* is going to be obvious when she doesn't fly back from Europe for the funeral, but they haven't formally announced it yet.

"It usually takes at least six months, and I doubt many people who aren't aviation enthusiasts read these things. They're very technical."

The gossip mongers won't care that it's a technical write-up. They can all use ctrl+F to search Powell's name. But six months from now, the breakup will be old and valueless news anyway.

"Okay. I'll tell you in confidence, but don't sell this to any of the gossip magazines yet."

He looks insulted by that, so I continue, though still circumspectly. "Powell had an argument with his girlfriend Zahna the night before. He responded by drinking way too much, and the next morning he was sick. He's not a big drinker; he doesn't do that sort of thing. So he was hungover and didn't want to fly out to LA and get on a helicopter. We called Jace and asked him to go instead." Still not quite the full story, but enough of it that it should match whatever Powell is telling the other guy.

"What time?"

I unlock my phone to check the log and give him the particulars of that last call.

"And did anyone else know about this? Why wasn't his name changed on the passenger manifest?"

"That's beyond me. I have nothing to do with those arrangements. Although . . . neither of us thought to call the charter company to update them that Powell wasn't coming. Pretty much as soon as Jace agreed to go, Powell went to take a shower and I went out to buy him breakfast. We sat out by the pool for hours, without our phones, so he could take the day off."

"So you didn't tell anyone at all that Jace was going in his place?" Ethan is watching my face carefully. He appears really vested in my answer.

"Who would I tell? Why does this even matter?" Sure, he needs as much info as possible, but this seems a bit excessive. I would expect the investigator to be far more interested in the helicopter equipment than the passenger list.

"You said you didn't want details, but I'll tell you this much: we believe the crash wasn't an accident."

"You think Jace was targeted?" I ask, but even as the words come out of my mouth, I know how wrong they are.

"Not Jace," he says, and I stare wordlessly in shock as the meaning washes over me. Someone tried to kill my brother?

♪ ♪ ♪ ♪ ♪

I snag Powell as soon as he's done being questioned and drag him into the nearest bathroom for privacy. His naturally golden tanned skin has gone pale and he's shaky.

"Did they tell you about the bomb?" he asks.

"Bomb?" Maybe I should have been more open to hearing specifics.

"They're still combing through the wreckage, but that's what they expect to find."

"Ethan said you may have been the target." My stomach is tying itself into a knot.

"Yeah, I probably was. Cassidy, I might have murdered Jace. And those poor videographers."

"No! Don't ever say that! Some homicidal maniac murdered them."

"But Cass, if I had called someone and told them I wasn't coming, maybe the crash wouldn't have happened. Maybe the killer wouldn't have blown the helicopter up if he knew I wasn't onboard."

"Powell . . ."

"This is all my fault. I killed Jace with one phone call. I should have been the one to go. It was my responsibility." Powell has the kindest heart of anyone I've ever met. Of course he would wish he'd gone instead of Jace. And of course he would take the guilt upon himself. But *I* was the one who made the call. *I* was the one who bartered with Jace to get him to go. This is *my* fault. But I have to set aside my emotions and be the strong one. Again.

I grab my brother's shoulders and shake him gently. "No. You did nothing wrong. Don't blame yourself for this." My pep talk won't be effective, but at least I tried. This situation was easier when we thought it was an accident. "Now, come on. Let's go back out there. We need to tell the others."

"You want to tell Devon that his best friend was murdered by some killer who was after me?" Powell looks positively ill at the thought, and truthfully, I feel the same way. This is worse than when I had to call Devon and tell him that Jace died. Finding out about the intentionality behind the explosion is far more trauma inducing.

"No, not really. But they'll find out anyway. Better they hear it from us." There are no secrets anymore, especially when practically the entire world is salivating for details about the great Jace's death.

We return to the former Barons, who are still playing around with their instruments and talking softly.

The news is received terribly, which is not at all surprising. Devon runs from the room to throw up. Xander goes into defensive mode and he starts denying the possibility of any kind of sabotage against anyone. Mason is terrified and asks if the rest of the ex-band is in danger as well. He immediately calls his wife and tells her to increase their home security, as if they weren't already surrounded by armed guards protecting images of the baby.

When Devon comes back from the bathroom, he goes straight to the wet bar and takes out a couple of bottles of Macallan 25. We're going to drink to Jace tonight, and try to drink away the horror of knowing that there is a target on one or all of them.

I'm always careful when I drink. I never have more than two beverages, but Devon tends to overpour, and he likes to top off glasses before they're finished, so perhaps I consumed more than I should have. I wake up with a mild hangover, but I'm not in as bad of shape as the others. The boys are all hurting.

Last night was awful. What started as toasting Jace and sharing memories became a night of four men trying to outdrink each other. And that's never good for anyone involved.

At one point, we were outside by the pool, and Xander announced it was time to go skinny-dipping. And then he told *me* to go first. Of course, my drunken brother thought that was a good time to stand up for me.

"You will never see my sister naked!" Powell shouted directly in Xander's face.

Xander doesn't like being told no about anything, so he snidely informed Powell—and the rest of us—that he could have any woman he wanted, even me. Before I could vomit in disgust, Powell yelled, "Yeah, you can have her over my dead body," and pushed him.

Xander immediately retaliated with "That's the plan, asshole," and shoved him right back.

And that's when the party dissolved into a battle. Powell and Xander were tussling like clumsy toddlers who only know how to slap, while yelling and dredging up old grudges from all the way back to the day a magazine published a caption identifying them as *Powell Corbitt and that secondary blond guy [name??] from The Last Barons of Sound*. We all know that was an editing mistake, but Xander has always been convinced Powell's people were behind it, and he's never forgiven him.

When Mason tried to pull them apart, the scuffling men lost their balance, and all three fell into the pool. Fortunately, none of them had their phones in their pockets, but Xander's dry-clean only clothes were apparently ruined, at least, according to his rants. I expect a bill will be sent to Powell, and it will be returned unpaid.

From the way everyone is holding their heads and stumbling this morning, they're all regretting polishing off those bottles of scotch, and not just because of the petty pool debacle. Fortunately for us Devon has a plan and it's not that hair-of-the-dog nonsense. No, instead two nurses show up with IV stands and electrolyte bags. I've never tried this before but given the pounding in my head and the residual disgust from some of Xander's comments, I'll do anything to restore my equilibrium.

We all sit in comfortable chairs, while the nurses go around and hook us each up. I'm not sure what we're being infused with, other than saline. The woman setting mine up says "vitamins" but doesn't go into detail.

"It's fine, I did the research," Brixley assures me. Had she not been a six-foot-three perfect specimen of grace and beauty, she would have gone to med school herself. She loves reading medical journals for fun, so I'll trust her, especially since she confides that she's done this before, multiple times. Apparently, this is a popular treatment among the celebrity hard partying crowd. Not that Brixley is normally part of that particular crowd, but sometimes fashion show after-parties get wild.

I shiver as the liquid begins to enter my veins, but then I close my eyes and relax. Forty-five minutes later, the bag is empty and I am reinvigorated, feeling better than I have in days. I'm energetic and ready for the enormous breakfast that was delivered while we de-hangovered ourselves. This isn't bad at all. If they had a service like this back home in Scottsdale, Powell might have made his flight. That thought sobers me up even more. Powell was one bad hangover away from death.

"What's everybody wearing to the funeral?" Xander asks over the meal. Everyone glares at him, including the omelet chef standing by the portable stove set up in the corner of the rather ornate dining room.

"Black," Brixley answers for all of us.

"A tie," Powell adds, unhelpfully.

"I may wear shoes, I haven't decided yet," Mason chimes in.

Devon just gets up and walks away, leaving his half-eaten breakfast behind. He's suffering so much more than the rest of us. It's not only the loss of his friendship, his career is also on the line. He never wanted to be a solo artist.

"What about you, Cass?" Xander asks because he is completely unable to read social cues.

"Don't know," I mutter. That's a lie. I packed a somber black dress, the one I wore to a funeral last year, when my mom's close friend lost her battle with cancer. Unlike the others in the room, I have no problem recycling clothes. I'm just going to be in the background of the publicity shots anyway. Powell's bespoke suit is scheduled for delivery later today, and I bet Brixley called up one of her designer friends and they are frantically sewing at this very moment.

Since nobody takes the bait and repeats the question back to him, Xander takes it upon himself to make the bragging statement that was probably the impetus for asking us anyway.

"Are you familiar with the Italian designer Giustiniano? He's been dying to design something for me, so he's doing my suit. It was supposed to be for an award show where I'm presenting, but I asked him to make the cut more funereal. His team should be showing up today for a final fitting." Even when preparing to bury a loved one, Xander has to make it about himself.

"At your house, right?" Brixley asks pointedly. Xander lives fifteen minutes away, there's no reason he should still be hanging around, but he doesn't pick up on the hint.

"I could tell them to come over here," Xander offers. "That way if the rest of you need a hem done or any alterations, they can take care of it." Does Xander not understand who he's with? Does he really think a world-renowned supermodel wouldn't have an entire team of couturiers, stylists, and seamstresses on speed dial?

"Like we don't have our own people?" Brixley raises one perfectly arched eyebrow as she echoes my thoughts. "Xander, you should go home."

"I thought we were all in this together, like in the old days," he protests. "And Cassidy needs me."

"Don't bring me into this," I say, at the same time Powell says, "Leave my sister out of it."

Xander glowers at my brother. I once heard him arguing that since I'm not a blood relative, Powell needs to drop the overprotective act. It's not an act, we're a real family. And even if we weren't, Powell would still protect me from him. And any other creep that came along. Hopefully he'd do a better job of it than the scene I witnessed last night. While entertaining for the rest of us, a drunken slap-fest is in no way heroic. I suppose it was cathartic for them though, since they can't retaliate against the unknown person or entity that killed their friend.

FIVE

The day of the funeral is sunny and bright. I wish it were raining. I wish the skies opened up and wept down upon us, demonstrating that the entire universe is mourning the loss of one of the greatest lights to ever shine upon our poor, dull, Jaceless planet.

Okay, maybe I'm being a tad bit overdramatic.

The funeral itself is not small, but it is private. That's what they call it when access is limited to invitees whose names are on a curated list and every guest there is someone who actually knew the deceased. Jace's personal assistant handled all the details. Making his final arrangements was the last thing she'll have to do for him. I imagine she'll retire now; Devon told me she inherited twenty percent of Jace's fortune, though it hasn't been announced yet.

I ride there in a limo with Powell, Devon, Brixley, Mason, and Xander. Xander tried to sit next to me, but Powell shoved his way in between us, over Xander's protests. Ten blocks from the ceremony site, we start seeing the fans. They're lined up along the sides of the road, some wearing black, others dressed in band shirts from Last Barons or JaDed. Most are holding signs demonstrating their sadness or love or both.

"Lots of people," Devon observes. I think he's on drugs. There's no way he can be so calm otherwise. His face is slack and his eyes are dead.

"He was loved," Brixley replies, resting her hand on his thigh. It's a minor gesture, but for her that's open affection. They are the least publicly demonstrative of any couple I know. Half the time I forget they're even together. They're a perfect match though. Both are beautiful, brilliant introverts who manage their fame well and trust each other. Who needs more than that?

I carefully try to wipe away a tear with the tips of my fingers. Brixley's stylist did my hair and makeup. Everything on my face is supposedly waterproof, but I don't want to run any risk of showing up with streaks running down my cheeks. Powell passes me a silk handkerchief from his pocket.

"Seriously?" I ask. "Why are you carrying this around?"

"I always take handkerchiefs to funerals. Dad taught me, remember?"

I give him a sad smile. Cancer stole his mother when he was a child. According to Hank, at her funeral he was miserable and acting out, as ten-year-old half-orphans are wont to do. In order to distract him, his father gave him a stack of silk handkerchiefs and told him he had the very important task of helping anyone who was crying. If he saw so much as a single tear, he was to pull one out and offer it. The assignment made Powell feel like he was contributing and gave him something to keep his mind off his own loss. Even after all these years, he still thinks that he must continue the tradition at every funeral he attends.

The problem, however, with him distributing fabric to damsels in distress is what the heck am I supposed to do with it afterward? I carefully dabbed at my eyes, now what? I'm not throwing away barely used silk, but what woman has pockets in her funeral dress? Not me. I end up tucking the square into my cleavage, and unfortunately make eye contact with Xander just as I finish, and he winks. Yuck, he had been staring at my boobs.

Security is keeping the media off the grounds of the funeral home, so the limo is able to drop us off at the door without the

Barons and Brixley having to run the photographer gauntlet. People are milling about in small groups outside. I spot our parents, so Powell and I go to greet them.

"How's Devon?" Mom asks right away as she hugs me. She knows how much harder this is for him than for the rest of us.

"Drugged up," Powell replies. "Xanax, I think."

"He'll get through this," Mom says. She is close with all the Last Barons—she was the nurse who traveled with them on their world tour, and she treated them like they were all her sons. Even Xander. Heck, even Mason, and he was the wild one back then. My mom swears he was responsible for half of her gray hairs. The other half, she claims, are my fault. If they even exist. She's been dying her hair for nearly half a decade, so I have no way of knowing.

"We all will, together," Hank adds. He puts an arm around my shoulders, and I lean into him for support. He's the best of all possible stepfathers. I'm so glad he and Mom met, fell in love, and married. My life would have been so much emptier without him and Powell in it.

"Shall we go in?" Powell, ever the gentleman, holds out his arm to escort Mom, and I follow with Hank. We're seated in the front, with the remaining Last Barons and their family members. Mason's parents are missing—they are playing with their new grandbaby on the other side of the world. They did send an enormous flower arrangement and a generous charitable donation though.

Jace's folks are also notably absent. They were estranged after having stolen from their son during the height of Last Barons fame, then suing Jace for more when the first JaDed album went platinum. The lawsuit was dismissed, of course, but the hard feelings were not. No surprise they aren't welcome at the funeral, though I did see them crying their eyes out on television saying how much they missed their beloved son. I'm sure they got paid handsomely for those interviews too.

Devon delivers the eulogy. When it's his turn to speak, Brixley pats his back gently. He stands, and as he walks to the front of the room, a change comes over him. Gone is the zoned-out zombie from the limo. He straightens, squares his shoulders, and by the time he is standing behind the microphone facing the crowd, he is once again a competent superstar, ready to perform for the masses.

"For those of you who don't know me, my name is Devon Malloy," he says to the crowd. Powell snorts out a laugh but tries to camouflage it as a cough. This is a room full of music industry insiders. Everybody knows exactly who Devon is—if they don't, then they're at the wrong funeral.

"I met Jace over fifteen years ago, at the final round of the Last Barons of Sound auditions. Thirteen of us had been flown out to compete for five spots. Jace was the first to perform, and from the moment we saw him onstage, every person in the room knew there were only four spaces left. He moved on that stage like he was born there, and his voice . . . well, you've all heard how *Beautiful and Stunning*"—Oh, no! He's using Last Baron's song titles in the eulogy. Mason is already struggling to keep a straight face. This might send him over the edge.—"it was. And the way he danced, with his *Long Long Legs*, it made everyone's *Heart Beat in Sync*."

That's it, Mason's lost it. Devon made eye contact with him on that last one, and now Mason is rocking back and forth trying to contain himself. Powell offers him one of those ubiquitous silk handkerchiefs, but that's not going to hold anything in.

"Jace was the *Center of My Heart* of all our hearts, really—when we performed in concert. It was a *Devastating Blow* to all of us when we, the Last Barons, decided to *Unchain from the Pain*, and take on *Separate Lives*. We were afraid we'd *Never Dance Sweetly Again . . .*" And now Devon can't keep a straight face either. He puts his head down on the podium, but the microphone easily picks up his chortling.

"I told him not to do that," Brixley mutters. She is an island of calm in a sea of laughter. Mason's face is bright red, Powell has rolled out of his seat, and even Xander seems to have caught on to the humor. As for me? Yeah, I dug that silk scrap out of my bra so I could wipe my streaming eyes. I didn't expect to find any amusement at this funeral whatsoever, so this laugh is cathartic.

"Jace would have loved this," my mother whispers to me. "I think he would have found it *So Bad It's Good*." Now she's doing it too? She's right though, this is exactly the funeral Jace would have requested. He wasn't one for seriousness or sadness.

Then Hank leans around her. "I never thought I'd have a *Rockin' Good Time* on such a . . . hmmmm." Nice try Hank. He's out of songs. He chews on his lip, thinking for a moment. "Never mind. I give up."

"Do you? You don't want *One More Try*?" I ask him. That was a mistake—Powell had almost managed to calm himself and now he might be choking. I slap his back hard, just in case.

JaDed's manager, Ryland, gently removes Devon from the podium and sends him back to his seat, where he collapses next to Brixley and lets out a few last giggles.

"Is everyone finished? Can we continue with the ceremony?" Ryland apparently has no sense of humor. He delivers a much calmer and more depressing eulogy, with no song references or hysterical Barons. I rest my head on my mother's shoulder, close my eyes and listen. I can't open my eyes. If I do, I'll see Jace's portrait up there, and I'll be hit with the pain of his loss all over again. Or, *For A Long Time Coming*, if I want to keep with the cheesy Last Baron's song-titles theme.

When the ceremony is over, my brother joins his bandmates as well as Ryland and the former Last Barons manager, Conrad, as pallbearers. They line up on the sides of the casket, solemnly take a hold of it, and lift it to their shoulders. As they pass us, I tap Brixley and ask what's inside. I assume it's only being used symbolically, but perhaps it contains a tribute of some sort.

"Some teeth and his left hand," she says, far too calmly for someone delivering such horrifying information. I wish she'd lied and told me it was empty. Thinking about Jace's remains makes me ill and even more guilty. I reduced him to nothing but teeth and a few bones. That's what I did to my good friend. I suspect this guilt will be a part of me for the rest of my life.

After the coffin is loaded onto a hearse and we process out of the funeral home, we have to move on to the next phase. It's not a trip to a cemetery—the actual internment will be private and secret later on, when we aren't all being followed by photographers. When the physical memorial is ready, Devon will announce the location. The fans need somewhere to honor their idol, and the crash site is too remote to be practical.

Per Jace's apparent request, there is no post-funeral reception. Instead, most of us go straight from the funeral services to a lawyer's office. Personally, I think scheduling this meeting so soon is in bad taste. But it isn't up to me.

"Why are we doing this?" Mason asks in the limo. He's already opened up the mini-fridge and pulled out a drink. His hard-partying days are long behind him—or so he promised his wife—but I can understand wanting to take the edge off right now.

"Because Jace wanted us to." Devon barely opens his eyes. He is slumped over, leaning against his girlfriend. He must have taken another pill.

"Jace left specific instructions," Brixley adds. "He was quite serious about estate planning. He didn't know it would come into play so soon, of course, but he updated his will every six months. We're doing everything exactly as he specified."

"I wonder what we're all getting," Xander says, earning himself a limo full of dirty looks.

"Don't be such a ghoul." That came from Powell, sitting across from Xander. I'm crushed between him and Mason, and I gratefully accept a sip from Mason's bottle.

"What?" Xander is good at pulling off affronted with a side of innocence. "I just meant that if we're all invited to this reading, then Jace must have left us something."

I swear I see dollar signs in his eyes. Powell was right, he is a ghoul. Or a graverobber. Tension radiates from Powell's leg which is pressed against mine, and I put my hand on his knee to calm him. We exchange a look, and I read his mind. He's wondering if it would be okay if he punches Xander right now. Or, he telepathically communicates, could I maybe do it for him, so he can protect his precious music playing fingers?

Fortunately, before I grant Powell's psychic request, we arrive at the skyscraper housing the law office. We ride the gilded elevator up to the twentieth floor and converge on a conference room with floor to ceiling windows offering a view of the city. I can see the disgusting yellow smog settling over everything. It was the smog that drove us out of LA. My family lived here for a couple of years when I was a teenager, but Powell hated the air quality—he said it damaged his vocal cords—and decided to move back to his home state of Arizona. Believe me, I had zero compunctions about following him.

Belinda, Jace's assistant, is standing awkwardly in a corner. Even though she knows all of us, there's a class issue at play. She looks uncomfortable in this crowd, so I go to say hello. She's celebrity adjacent, like me, but less so, since assistants are a step down in the hierarchy from sisters.

She hugs me tightly because she's a mom and that's what moms do. "How are you holding up?"

"I'm doing okay," I tell her, appreciating her empathy. She lost her job, but her immediate concern is checking on me. "How are you?"

She lets out a long sigh. "Jace invited my son to go with him. He said it might be fun, my kid's first helicopter ride, but I said no. If I had let him go . . ."

I understand how she feels. Relieved, but guilty for it. I am so grateful my brother is still here, I don't know how I could live without him. But I'll never get over knowing that someone so beloved died in his place.

"Nobody told me why I have to be here for this," Belinda continues. "Do you think he left me anything? I'm out of a job now, and my daughter starts college next year." She sighs again. "You must think I'm a terrible person, going on about money at a time like this."

"Jace loved you. I'm sure you'll be well taken care of." This time, I'm the one who gives her a hug. Jace was the type of person who bestowed his largesse on those he cared about, and he always considered Belinda like family. The kind of family member he wanted, not like the evil thieving ones he actually had. Besides, Devon already told me about that particular bequest.

A team of attorneys finally joins us, and we all find our seats. Despite how it's often shown on television dramas, California doesn't require a reading of the wills. I don't mean that they shouldn't be read, but all the purported heirs don't have to gather in a room while a somber lawyer reads the document aloud and wives and mistresses faint or gasp and random unknown children inherit everything.

But even though it's not a requirement, the head attorney for Jace's estate explains the reason for the gathering. He says the disposition of assets will be easier if we're all on the same page before the will is filed with the court and made into public information. Anyone can request a copy at that point, so it's best if we all find out what's included in advance.

Honestly, though, I'm not sure why *I* need to be here. If Jace bequeathed me anything, it's probably a signed picture of himself, as a joke. He always thought things like that were funny. 'To my beloved Cassidy, I leave an autographed photograph of myself. Please, auction it off and buy yourself a special treat, like a pack of gum or a sticker.'

I spot Mr. and Mrs. Monroe sitting near the head of the conference table, backs straight, expectant looks on their faces. They must have entered while I was distracted talking to Belinda. I bet they assume that because they were asked to come, they will be getting something special, as if Jace would have prioritized taking care of his abusive parents over all his friends—his chosen family—who he truly loved. I check on Devon, who is staring at the Monroes and finally showing an emotion: glee. This is going to be entertaining. Watching their expressions is going to be the best part of the whole reading.

Jace was clever. Oh, he was so very clever. His will starts with his parents. Rather than leaving them anything, he announces there is no inheritance for them, due to their outstanding debt. The will goes on to say that the estate will not pursue repayment of the debt, mixed in with a bunch of legalese. The money in question is now nearly ten million dollars, including the interest that accrued over the past decade. Jace spent years trying to recover it, but despite signing agreements promising a high interest rate and a repayment period, he never saw a penny returned to him.

They look confused and disappointed, and Mr. Monroe has the audacity to ask if there's anything else. This is when I fall in love with Jace's lawyer. He's amazing. He eyes them condescendingly and taps his fingers on the fancy teak tabletop.

"Mr. Monroe, I assure you, that's not all. Our client made sure to leave notarized copies of all of the debt paperwork including your promises to repay him. He has kindly included them as attachments to the will."

Obviously, they'd never intended to make any payments, but Jace had made a big show of requesting the money every few years. The lawyer continues with the bombshell. "As required by tax law, the estate is unwillingly forced to forgive the debt due to your refusal to repay, and therefore the notice of such forgiveness will be submitted to the IRS, for taxation purposes." That's the ultimate blow—by forgiving their debts but making it clear that in no way is it an inheritance or gift, the amount they owe is converted into annual income. Jace is forcing them to pay taxes on a huge amount of money. That's going to hurt.

This is the moment we've all been waiting for. Jace's mom starts shrieking that this is ridiculous, she's contesting the will, this is fraud, all the other nonsense greedy people say when their comeuppance is served to them with well-crafted estate planning. Jace hit them from beyond the grave, sinking their finances. There's no way they can pay that off without selling the mansion they bought with their ill-gotten gains.

The parents end up getting escorted out by security while yelling about future lawsuits, so now it's down to the rest of us, the ones who genuinely loved Jace. But there are a lot of us packed into the room, and it's warm and I'm sleepy, so I just hunker down in my seat in the back, not paying much attention.

I jump when I hear the sound of a body hitting the floor. While I was zoning out, Belinda found out that she's becoming a multi-millionaire, and she took it as well as could be expected. Devon, despite his own drug induced stupor, is there to help revive her from her faint and assure her that, yes, it is all real.

"Ridiculous. All that for an assistant?" Xander mutters. Of course he wouldn't understand that kind of relationship. He's never been able to keep an assistant longer than six months, though that could be because he hires based on cup size in lieu of more appropriate qualifications.

As anticipated, most of the estate goes to Jace's foundation, the one he set up years ago to bring music education to underfunded schools. Devon will be assuming the role of a board member and assisting with managing and distributing those funds. Devon also gets control of Jace's interest in their duo's music, and all of Jace's shares of Last Barons royalties. Xander's face turns purple when he hears that. I suspect he thought Jace's share would return to the collective pot and they'd all get one fourth instead of one fifth. He was probably counting on that money. He spends way more than he earns and then has to make desperate and awful appearances at club openings to cover his bills.

Mason is next. Jace left him two Rolexes, with a message: *Use these so you can show up on time for once.* The bequest brings Mason to tears. He's gotten better about being on time over the years, but his tardiness was legendary. I can remember him sprinting down halls and diving on to the stage while the rest of the band glared at him and the crowd was on the verge of violence.

Powell inherits a car. The smallest of smiles briefly makes an appearance on his face before turning into a frown. Powell loves his collection of cars, but he'd rather have Jace than another vehicle. And, from a logistical standpoint, where's he going to park it? He might be forced to sell something else off to make room. Or worse. I can anticipate the loud sounds of construction if he decides to add another garage somewhere on our lot.

Xander's name is called, causing him to sit up straight on the edge of his chair. His hopeful face makes me hate him more than I already do. Jace left him . . . wait for it . . . his closet full of sneakers, mostly unworn. The collection is a massive assortment of limited-edition shoes, so it's quite valuable. Great, right? Especially since Xander has much larger feet than Jace. Disappointment radiates from him, but he laughs anyway. I guarantee those shoes are going to be on AuctionNet soon enough. I'm sure Jace knew how badly Xander needs money, so he set up a posthumous prank to make him work for it.

My name follows Xander's, and the lawyer searches the faces around the room. I raise my hand to show my presence, and he nods and begins to read. Here it comes: my bequest. Given the value of what he left his bandmates, I'm now afraid he's leaving me something expensive but, in keeping with his sense of humor, something frivolous or unwieldy. Like a boat. *Please don't let it be a boat.*

"To the beautiful and charming Cassidy Blaine-Corbitt, the one true love of my life, in honor of what we had together, I leave all rights to my works *First Kiss* and *Holding Back*."

A silence falls over the room, unusual with so many outgoing personalities gathered in one place. They are all looking at me, some with sympathy, most with confusion. And then there's Xander, with outright surprise and envy.

"I'm sorry, what?" I ask politely. I have no idea what that means. It didn't sound like a joke though. But it must be, right? Why else would Jace make such an absurd statement?

Devon leans on the table so he can see me from that end. There's sympathy in his gaze and I sense that he knows what's going on, even if I don't. "Cass, those are the two albums Jace wrote but never recorded. There are some demos though. They're all yours now."

It's hard to know what to do in a situation like this. Nobody wants to celebrate after such a terribly long day, because then we'd be celebrating Jace's death, but we're not ready to go our separate ways yet. When Mason loudly declares he needs a drink, we all troop down the street to a bar. The manager—thrilled at the patronage of the post-funeral Last Barons—kindly lets us take over a side room for some degree of privacy, though plenty of other customers pause in the doorway to snap photos. I'm sure the bar will want to use this for advertising as well, and the manager will come up with a way to discreetly ask for a group picture.

Brixley takes charge of everything. She excels under pressure, and she's been doing an amazing job handling everything for Devon throughout this process. She negotiates with the bartender for bottle service and a dedicated waitress to run back and forth. The waitress, I can tell, is thrilled. After the first round, she disappears for a few minutes and when she returns, she has redone her eye makeup and apparently traded someone for a more revealing shirt. It's working; Xander can't seem to stop leering.

Powell makes sure my glass is full. "What do you think?" he asks as he steers me over to a table in the corner.

"About what?" My mind is still trying to process Jace's words for me.

"Road tripping home, obviously." Powell has clearly already moved past the whole me getting albums thing and is busy figuring out how to transport his inheritance back to Arizona.

"Depends. Do I get to drive?"

He has the nerve to laugh at me. "You drive like a grandmother. You don't deserve to sit behind the wheel of a $200k Lambo. It's wasted on you."

Ha! He should aspire to drive like me. Of the two of us, I'm the one who never jumped a curb, or sideswiped a tree, or had to go to traffic school as a penalty for 'seeing how fast this thing can go.'

"Maybe I'll fly back, then."

He relents quickly. "Fine, we'll switch off. Want to test out the car first? Follow Highway 1 all the way up the coast?"

We've done that journey a few times, most recently when he was depressed after receiving a negative review from a famous critic and needed time to moodily stare at the ocean and ruminate on his failings. That's also the trip when he wrote his popular hate-anthem, *You Can't Judge Me.*

"How about you take Devon instead, do some male bonding," I suggest. I love Powell, but I'm not in the mood. Honestly, I just want to go home, sleep in my own bed, work out in my own gym. Los Angeles wears me down. And a road trip could benefit them both, give them a chance to talk and privately mourn together.

"I'll ask him. That could be fun," Powell muses, but then winces at his choice of words. "Why is this so hard, Deedee? Every time I feel the least bit happy about anything, I'm hit with this guilty feeling that I don't deserve it. I'm the one who should have died."

"*Nobody* should have died," I correct him. I'm still hoping that Ethan was wrong and it proves to be a tragic accident and not a murder.

Devon joins us then, pulling out a chair and dropping bonelessly into it. I've always liked him—there's a kindness about him that is lacking in many celebrities of his caliber. He doesn't ask for credit for any of his good deeds, either. I know for a fact that over the years he has paid for at least forty special needs accessible playgrounds in low-income areas, and he built them all entirely anonymously.

"He was planning to tell you," Devon says. His skin is practically gray from misery and exhaustion. The drugs must have worn off. Given the way he's drinking, I hope they have. This can't be good for his liver.

"About what? The joke he put in his will?" I still haven't figured out the point. Maybe it was an apology for the way he treated me all those years ago, back when he was twenty-two, immature, spoiled, and so full of himself. But we talked everything out later, and I forgave him. There was no need for additional apologies, and I certainly didn't expect a strange tribute like that to be memorialized after his death.

Devon shakes his head. "You're so blind. It wasn't a joke, Cassidy. As far as Jace was concerned, you were the one who got away. He's loved you for years."

My stomach is sinking. That can't be true. Surely he would have told me, right? Jace used to make jokes all the time, but he never *meant* any of them. "When we're married . . ." he would say, or he'd look deep into my eyes, confess his love, and turn away laughing. But those were all *jokes*.

"His music, those songs," Devon continues, "he wrote them for you. About you. He always thought you'd end up together someday."

"That's ridiculous," Powell says. "Jace rejected her." He knows, he spent hours comforting me the night I threw myself at Jace and he mocked me and broke my heart.

"Jace rejected her when she was seventeen. People grow up. He assumed he had another shot. Cass, don't pretend he never tried."

"He didn't. He was always joking," I insist, but I'm replaying some of Jace's frequent flirtations back in my mind, and maybe he wasn't. I stopped looking at him as a romantic option years ago, and that might have colored my interpretations of his actions. It takes two to fall in love with each other, and I don't think I would have gotten there. Perhaps if his initial rejection hadn't been so cruel. Forgiveness is one thing; forgetting is another.

"He told me he was going to ask you to be his date for the reunion concert. He planned to dedicate a song to you and confess in front of the whole world." Devon polishes off his whiskey and signals the waitress for a refill. "I guess he should have tried sooner."

"He did ask me to go as his date, but I assumed it was like all those other times."

"All those other times when he didn't have the guts to tell you how he felt?"

"Wait," Powell interrupts. "Jace could have had anybody—no offense, Cass—there's no way he was sitting around pining for my sister."

I'm not offended. He's right. Jace was world-renowned. He was the sexiest man alive, twice. He did not lack for confidence.

"Jace lacked confidence," Devon reads my mind and corrects my unspoken thought. "Sure, he was famous and loved, but you know about his parents, how those narcissists spent his childhood tearing him down. He never believed in himself, and he never believed he was worthy of any of his achievements. You, Cass, you're so tough and self-assured. He admired that about you. But he had a crippling fear of being rejected, and you're the only one who didn't fall at his feet. You intimidated him. That's why he hadn't told you yet."

"This is absurd." The waitress, fortunately, refilled all our glasses, so I take another swig of mine to wash these thoughts away. "What am I supposed to do now?" With this knowledge, with this music, with this burden of carrying the weight of a dead man's heart?

"Learn to sing, I guess? Release the songs yourself." Devon is not as supportive as I would like, but I suppose that's to be expected. He probably imagined a future of double dates, him with Brix, me with Jace. And he imagined a future with a solid career, shaking his booty on stage alongside his best friend. Probably with me handling the backstage work for my boyfriend, the way I do for my brother.

"How about you record the songs?" I suggest. That'd be the easiest solution for me.

"Forget it. There's a reason we didn't use them for JaDed. They're good, but not my style. Too morose. They'll be worth a lot though. And don't ask this guy either, he can't pull it off." He uses his glass to indicate Powell then downs its contents. I haven't been keeping track, but that's at least his fourth. I should probably warn Brixley she's going to have to hire someone to carry him home.

"Hey! I have a five-octave vocal range. I can sing anything Jace wrote better than you can," Powell protests.

Devon winks at me. "You're welcome."

That's when my brother realizes he's been set up. "Wait! I wasn't volunteering. I haven't even looked at them. Maybe they're horrible."

"You think Jace left me horrible music? I'm offended, Powell." I'm not, really. Anything Jace wrote is sure to be amazing. He had the Midas touch. "And don't worry. I wouldn't ask *you*. I need to find a talented singer, one who can do justice to his work. It's about emotive skill, not vocal range."

Powell points a finger at Devon. "You hear the way she talks to me? *Someone* is about to get fired and evicted."

That's my cue to stand up. I need to get out of here, have some time by myself to think. "If you gentlemen will excuse me for a moment, *someone* is about to log in to Powell's SwiftaPic account and post some embarrassing pictures. And *someone* is going to change all his passwords, too."

Powell's outraged shout and Devon's laugh follow me as I walk away.

SIX

I don't usually like being home alone. The house is too big and empty, and it leaves me with a deep sense of isolation. But not right now. For once, I'm thrilled that Powell isn't here. He's off on his bro-trip with Devon, cruising the highways in Jace's car. I can follow them on social media, just from all their tags. *I spotted @PowellC and @TheRealDevon at a gas station! And OMG @PowellC is on the 101 looking fine in a Lambo! And Hello, sexy! @TheRealDevon is in the traffic jam next to me! Planning on jumping in his backseat!*

I'm glad he's having this time to relax and do some bonding with his buddy, and selfishly, I'm glad I have time off from being his emotional crutch. Ever since Jace died, I've been taking care of everybody but myself. I've been worrying about Powell's emotions, putting on a brave face at the funeral, pretending I'm not aching inside. I'm the strong one, always have been, from the moment Powell and I met.

Well, no, not necessarily from the exact moment. The first time I met him, I was a starstruck twelve-year-old having the most epic birthday ever, and he was the slightly confused sixteen-year-old wondering who was the lady that his dad was flirting with, and why Hank had brought us backstage. But the second time, that's when we bonded.

At that point, Mom and Hank had been talking on the phone several hours every night for a couple of months. My mother's voice murmuring in the living room was the soundtrack to my nights, and I'd grown used to finding her asleep on the couch in the morning, cordless phone still clutched to her chest. Hank and Powell came out for a visit, and Powell and I somehow already understood each other well enough—or maybe we understood our parents well enough—that we knew to give them some privacy.

There was something melancholy I could see in Powell's eyes as we hung out in my room, pretending we didn't think our parents were making out in the kitchen. Sadness radiated from him, and I realized he wasn't really the golden teenage idol everyone made him out to be. No, he was an unhappy tired boy who deeply, painfully missed his mother. He reminisced about her wistfully, and I recognized his pain. I felt it too, for my father. And when he talked about his life and the tour, I realized something else about him: he was lonely. Everybody always wanted to take from him, to use him, but they didn't care about him personally.

Powell needed someone in his corner, someone who didn't want to use him or borrow his fame or trick him into giving away parts of himself with no return. He needed a family. He needed a sister, someone who wouldn't put up with his crap, who wouldn't put him on a pedestal and worship him. And that's the role I've taken ever since.

But it's nice to have a bit of a break. Usually when he's not home—or when he is and he's annoying me—I escape to my gym. Granted, I pay an operations manager to do the day-to-day running of the place, but I still like to spend time there whenever I can, not just for my daily workout. I'm a certified personal trainer, so I fill in when someone needs a sick day, and I occasionally teach a fitness class. And when I'm bored, I like to hang out at the front desk, sell new memberships, and try to get to know some of the regulars.

For the moment though, I have a different focus. I'm attempting to make a pie. There's a potluck tonight for my fellow board members at the local food bank and I've been assigned a dessert. Obviously, I can afford to purchase a professionally made treat from the upscale bakery nearby, but that's not the point of a potluck. This is coming together to share gifts of food we've made with our own two hands, so that's what I'm doing. Also, last time I showed up with something store bought, I got teased mercilessly.

Admittedly, I'm not much of a baker, but I can follow directions, and I've never turned down a challenge, especially one issued by a group of smirking board members who expect me to fail. Making a pie crust from scratch can't be that hard. All the online reviews for this particular recipe say it's easy and delicious.

So that's what I am in the middle of when the doorbell rings. I tap the app on my tablet with my flour coated finger.

"Yeah?" We aren't expecting a delivery, are we? Usually the security guard at the gatehouse would call and inform us if a driver was on their way.

"It's Tanner. Um. Tanner Smythe." Now he faces the camera and I can see him clearly.

"Why are you here?" Yes, I sound rude. But I don't need paparazzi wandering around my property. I haven't seen him since Jace's death. He was particularly helpful that night, not only with the photos, but he also helped tidy some of the mess and made sure the guests kept their glasses full. But I know he had ulterior motives. He was trying to be indispensable, so we'd accidentally open up to him.

"I wanted to talk to you."

"How'd you get past security?" I am going to have to have words with the guard.

"You put my name on the always let through list."

I most certainly did not put him on any such list. Omaha must have messed up when I told him Tanner was the only one allowed through on crash day. But I have to indulge my inner curiosity.

"No, I didn't, but fine, come in. Front door is unlocked." I hit the button on the app to unlock the door and then punch the pie dough with my fist, trying to get it to look the way it's supposed to.

"Hello?" I hear him calling from the front door.

"Back here. Kitchen!" I form the dough into a lumpy mass again and make another attempt at rolling it into a roughly spherical shape. One of these times it's going to work.

Tanner enters, looking different than last time I'd seen him. For one thing, he's shaved the stubble that had highlighted his jaw before. While I like my men scruffy, he still looks good, just somewhat cleaner. Not that I've been checking him out. He's also surprisingly free of bags. No camera, no laptop, none of the tools of his trade. But I'm not stupid. I assume the rectangular bulge in his pants is his phone and it is recording.

"I don't know why you're here, but you have to shut your phone off before I'll talk to you," I say, as I smash the dough again. On the tutorials I watched, they form a ball and then smoothly convert it into a perfectly even disk with a rolling pin. My dough is misbehaving though.

"My phone? Why? Oh, sorry. I'm not recording this. I'm not here on official business." Still, he takes his phone out of his front pocket and makes a big show of turning it off.

"You don't have official business. Aren't you a freelancer?"

"Mostly. But actually, I'm here to talk to you about something else. An *unofficial* business opportunity."

"Forget it. Powell isn't interested in investing anything with you."

"I doubt you have the right to speak for your brother on financial matters, but that's not what I'm here for . . . wait. Stop. Stop right now. What the hell are you doing?" There is an expression of incredulous horror on his face.

"Making pie for a potluck," I say, as I again crush the dough into a vaguely ball-like shape. "What's it look like?"

"Like you're murdering a crust. You're overworking your dough. That's going to be tough and not at all flaky. Do you hate the other guests?" He's staring at me as though I'm torturing a child in front of him.

"It'll be fine if I can just roll it into the correct shape." I don't need his advice. I know I can do this.

"No. Stop. Cassidy, I mean it, leave that alone. You're done." Without permission, he goes straight to the pantry and brings out the flour, and then opens the fridge for butter. "What is all this?" he asks, when he discovers our efficiently organized shelves stacked with neatly labeled glass containers.

"Food," I reply as sarcastically as possible. Then I relent. There is no reason to be rude to this random pap who wandered into my kitchen and insulted my baking skills. Well, there are several reasons, in fact. "Those are the meals Joel prepared for us. He didn't know Powell would be . . ." I slam my mouth shut, but it's too late, damnit! He got me to admit something. Obviously Tanner doesn't know Powell isn't here, or he wouldn't be sniffing around.

"And Joel is your . . . boyfriend?"

I snort. That's a stupid question. Once, in college, I had a three-month long relationship with a cute boy from my dorm. But I dropped out to go on tour with the Last Barons and never had a boyfriend again. "Ha! No, he's Powell's personal chef slash nutritionist. And he's single if you're interested."

"Rich people," he mutters under his breath. "Okay, Cassidy, get out of the way, I'm fixing this mess." He puts down the butter, rolls up his sleeves and washes his hands.

"Don't you need a recipe?" I ask, though his actions indicate he knows what he is doing. He finds Joel's food scale and starts weighing flour. Interesting methodology. I just scooped it into a cup.

"No. What kind of pie is this supposed to be?"

"Cherry. What difference does it make?"

"I was guessing sweet, but wanted to make sure. For a savory pie, there's a secret ingredient I like to use—though you probably don't have any shiitake mushroom powder."

"We might. Joel leaves all kinds of stuff over here." Our pantry boasts a rather impressive spice rack. On the rare occasions when I cook, I sometimes sniff a bunch of the powders from it and add whatever smells good. Unfortunately for my taste-buds, I'm often not successful at creating palatable spice combinations. My childhood food insecurity means I can't bring myself to waste food, so I force down my concoctions, no matter how awful they taste. That's why I prefer to eat Joel's delicious and properly spiced meals.

"Doesn't matter for cherry pie. Where's your vodka?"

"It's not even noon, and I'm not offering you a drink."

"Very funny. It's for the pie. Why don't you start the filling while I make an edible crust?"

"The filling is done." I point to the large can of cherries on the counter. Tanner's blood pressure rises so high I can feel it myself.

"Your plan is to dump canned cherries on my beautiful crust? Why? What's wrong with you? Why didn't you just buy a dessert to share?"

"Everybody cooks," I say, a bit defensively. "That's what a potluck is. Do they not have those where you come from?"

"St. Louis? Yeah, we have potlucks. But people who can't cook bring the drinks or napkins or a bag of chips. They don't show up with inedible pies."

"I didn't know you were from Missouri. I assumed you were from LA. Is Tanner your real name, or did you start calling yourself that when you moved to California?" He doesn't have much of an accent, but then again, I have no idea what a Missourian should sound like.

"I don't live in California." He gives me a strange look.

Ha, a wannabe journalist uncomfortable with being asked questions. This could be fun.

"You aren't a Cali pap out here to harass celebrities?"

"No. Is that really what you think of me?" He seems hurt by the insinuation. But it's not an unreasonable assumption to make about the guy I only met because he was camped out by my gate trying to take a picture of my brother's possible lover to sell to the highest bidder. "I have some connections with a few LA based gossip magazines, but I live here. And what's wrong with my name?"

"Tanner Smythe-with-a-y? Seriously? It sounds like you're trying to be a soap opera character. Everybody changes their name and reinvents themselves when they move to LA. It's a normal thing to do."

"Did you?" he asks pointedly.

"No, but I've never tried to be a celebrity. Jace did. His real name was Stuart. And do you know Devon? He was born a Norbert. For real." Alright, I made that second one up. I'm testing Tanner's Last Barons knowledge to see if he calls me on it. He doesn't.

"And Powell?"

"Do you not do your boyband research? Powell has always been Powell. It was his mother's maiden name. He's been interviewed about it."

"I'm not a paparazzi by trade," Tanner says. "I don't follow that crap. I just show up where I'm told and take pictures." As we talk, he is combining the butter and flour and working them together with his hands. I'm trying not to stare, but . . . wow. His forearms are strong. Not going to lie, if he were anyone other than a nosy photographer, then watching those arms work would be quite a turn on.

I watch in rapt silence as he separates the dough into two meticulously formed spheres and flattens them into disks exactly matching the ones created by the professionals in the tutorial videos. "I'm wrapping these in plastic and putting them in the fridge. They have to rest for about forty-five minutes. Don't touch them," he warns me sternly, shaking the rolling pin at me in a mock threatening manner. "Now I'm going to see what I can do with your cherries."

"Why are you helping me?" I ask. I still don't even know why he came over.

He laughs. "Baking is my stress release. But since I don't have a kitchen, I don't have the opportunity to do it often. Besides, I couldn't let you get away with what you were trying to do, especially if you intend to make other people eat that . . . creation. Nobody would tell you to your face, but it would have been terrible."

"That's not true," I protest, but I know he's right. They would have eaten every crumb with fake smiles on their faces. Or pretended to, while wrapping bits in their napkins and smuggling them into the nearest garbage receptacle. My value as a board member is in my connections to wealthy potential donors. The others wouldn't dare offend me by insulting my food offerings. I guarantee they would talk about me behind my back though.

"You were joking earlier, right? You weren't seriously planning on just pouring in those cherries, were you?" he asks as he digs through the pantry, coming out with sugar, cornstarch, and almond extract. Intriguing. I'm getting excited to try this pie myself.

"But that's what the recipe said." I point to my tablet on its stand. He wipes flour off the surface and starts skimming. Alarm bells go off in my head. Paparazzo looking at my tablet. Who knows what he could do? Plant a tracking program? I snatch it from him before he can start poking through my private files and installing his bugs.

"It said to use canned *cherry pie filling*, which has already been prepped. Not plain cherries. I guess literacy isn't a requirement for the wealthy."

That is totally uncalled for.

"You don't have to be a jerk. You still haven't told me why you're here, and all you've done is insult me." I cross my arms. "I can call security. Or I can toss you over the fence and let the coyotes deal with you. Or worse, I can tell Eduardo you aren't welcome near Powell and cut off his access until he fires you."

"Who's being a jerk now?" Tanner responds. Then he casts his eyes downwards and sighs. "I'm sorry. You're right. Let me finish with this, and then I'll explain my business proposition."

When the properly augmented filling is nicely bubbling on the stove, he turns back to me and wipes his palms on his jeans. "Okay, here's my idea. You own Star Fitness, correct?"

Oh, this is related to my gym. Now I'm curious. I nod.

"I've seen your social media. You can do better. You need better photography."

"And what would that consist of?"

"I think you need ten photos a month, professional ones, carefully selected to really sell your gym. Inspire potential customers, make them want to come in and get buff and have the full Star Fitness experience. Also, your website needs to be updated. The pics online right now are old. You should showcase attractive athletes in the latest workout clothes, outfits that you also sell." So this guy follows athletic fashion trends? And has already checked out the boutique in my gym?

"Interesting idea, but where would I find a photographer?" I ask, though I can guess where he's going with this self-serving idea.

"Me, of course." If he were wearing suspenders, this would be the moment to hook his thumbs under them and puff his chest out. "You've seen my work. I do excellent portraits."

"And how much would this cost me?" He's after money. They always are.

"You'll like this part. I'll do it in exchange for a membership."

"Why?"

"A couple of reasons." He ticks them off on his fingers. "One, your gym is expensive, and has really high-end equipment. Two, I like all that stuff on your social media about building community. I haven't found anything like that out here yet. Three, I'm broke and I need a place to shower daily."

"Your apartment doesn't have a kitchen or a shower?"

"I live in my van." His eyes dart away as he says it, and there is a subtle shift in his body language. Embarrassment? Or is he lying? There's nothing to be embarrassed about. When Mom and I were homeless, we lived in a car, so I'm not in a position to judge him. His van is probably nicer than our old station wagon was. Of course, I'm not going to tell him about that, either.

"You clearly showered and shaved today," I point out.

"Yeah, I went to a bar last night and met this woman . . ."

"And exchanged sex for a shower? You are a repellent person, Tanner." Although really he's just matching my expectations for a man in his profession.

"For your information, we cuddled on the couch and ate Chinese food until we fell asleep, and she let me use her shower this morning. So no, I did not pay with sexual favors."

"You're lying. Nobody eats Chinese food after the bars. If you had said burritos, I might have believed you."

"She lives next door to a Chinese restaurant and had a fridge full of leftovers. Wait, why am I defending myself to you? What she and I may or may not have done is none of your business."

"True. But I also know how much you got paid for a certain photo of Powell, so you can't be broke."

"My agency pays out after sixty days. Plus, after my agent's cut and taxes and paying off some debts, it's not as much money as you might think. But since I won't see it for a couple of months anyway, it doesn't matter. I can't move into a real place until I can pay for it."

Honestly, I know nothing about that sort of thing. I know how to *buy* buildings, I've done it a few times, though always with my stepfather's guidance. But renting? My business manager collects the monthly payments from my numerous tenants for me, and I have zero experience actually renting anything myself. Something tells me I shouldn't suggest putting the rent on a credit card though. Tanner seems awfully prickly about money.

"I'll consider your offer," I tell him. But I'm not sure if it is a good idea. He is a vampire, stealing people's images to feed to the media. How could I trust him around my celebrity members? Maybe he wants to join to get in with them, so he can stalk them better. I don't want to be an enabler.

I end up inviting Tanner to stay for lunch. That seems like a fair exchange for a well-made pie. It's in the oven, baking to a perfect golden texture, so we pull meals out of the refrigerator. Avocado salad for me, some microwavable casserole for Tanner. We eat outside on the shaded patio, because the weather is too beautiful to waste the day indoors.

"This is pretty tasty," Tanner says, digging in happily. He may be proficient in a real kitchen, but I doubt he can make meals like this in his van.

"Surprised?"

"No. This probably costs as much as you'd pay in a restaurant, so I hoped it would be. Do you seriously not know how to cook?"

That's insulting. What, a woman can't make a flaky pie crust and it somehow means she's completely incompetent in the kitchen?

"Cooking regular food and making pie crusts are two different skill sets. I can cook just fine. But it's convenient and not all that expensive to have a chef do the work, especially since he also does the grocery shopping and meal planning and clean up."

"I'm surprised he cleans too. I would have thought you'd have a maid."

"We do; she's here twice a week. You're coming across as awfully judgmental." Honestly, I am starting to get annoyed with him. Why come to my house, ask for a free membership to my gym, but then constantly criticize me? Especially for things that are out of my control, like how my wealthy brother chooses to spend his own money.

"Am I? I can't figure you out, Cassidy. You sometimes seem so … normal, I guess, but you're actually another spoiled pseudo-celebrity."

"No, I'm not. I'm just celebrity adjacent."

He snorts. "And what exactly does that mean?"

"It means I'm outside of fame, but still connected. I'm adjacent to celebrities. I don't share their lifestyle, nor do I want to. But people treat me differently anyway. I get a lot of the benefits, but I also have a lot of the hardships."

"Hardships like living in a mansion and eating fancy meals and having someone clean up after you? You have my utmost sympathy, Ms. Corbitt."

I don't like his tone.

"Blaine-Corbitt," I correct him. I love being Hank's adopted daughter, but I will not allow anyone to erase my original dad. "And yeah, those are some benefits. The negatives are I have to deal with the paparazzi. You show up and creep around and use me to try and gain access to the celebrities next to me. That's what everybody does. I'm more approachable than my brother because I'm not famous. So you and your cronies see me as the easy path. Instead of directly accessing Powell, you take the side route, through me."

"No wonder." Tanner looks down at his plate, scraping his fork around the rim without spearing any food.

"No wonder what?" I ask, when it's obvious he's not going to continue whatever insult he was struggling to come up with.

"No wonder you treat me like I'm trying to get something out of you. Is there anyone in your life you do trust? Don't you have any friends?"

His remark stings. Of course I have friends. One fewer, thanks to a helicopter explosion, but I have them. "I have plenty of friends. Don't act all snippy with me just because I don't trust vultures like you. And aren't you here because you want a gym membership? I'd call that trying to get something out of me."

"I was suggesting we barter for a service you need. I'm not exploiting you. Cost-wise, I'd charge a lot more for ten pictures a month than the membership is worth. And also, you're really rude! I'm not a vulture, I'm a serious photographer. So what if I do pick up extra cash by taking some human-interest shots that happen to be of famous people?"

"You picked an interesting way to describe your 'career.'" Yes, I used sarcasm quotes with that one. "You camped outside my house, hoping to catch my brother cheating on his girlfriend. That's not human interest, that's an invasion of privacy."

"Your brother needs people like me, so he can stay in the public eye."

At least he admits he's one of them, rather than a 'serious photographer,' whatever that means. I know hundreds of paparazzi who are extremely serious about their work. One of them climbed up on our roof to take a shot through the skylight. He's the reason we had to upgrade our alarm system.

"I'm aware of that, which is why I called you after the helicopter crash. But just because we have a symbiotic relationship doesn't mean I have to like it."

"I've been wondering about that night. Why me? You must know tons of photographers, and I saw how you acted with those local reporters too. You're on a first name basis. Why would you offer the shot to me, knowing what it was worth?"

I clasp my hands together and lean forward. "That must have been rather upsetting for you."

His brow furrows in confusion. "Why would it upset me? Pictures like that put my name out there. It was a boost to my career."

"No, that's what you said to me. When I told you about my lawsuit against the tabloid that accused Powell of sleeping with me."

"And I stand by it. That was a horrible thing for anyone to go through, especially a teenager."

"Yes, I know. And that's why I called you. You're the only one outside of my immediate family who ever expressed any empathy. Everybody else who hears the story tells me how lucky I am, like I won some kind of lottery. It was traumatizing for me. It's the worst thing I ever went through, but everyone acts like I gamed the system."

"I can understand why they say that. Some folks only focus on dollar signs. But in my line of work, I've learned to see people for who they truly are. And I could tell you were hurting."

"Your line of work? Stalking?"

"I told you, I'm a serious photographer," he says defensively. "I shoot portraits. Family pictures, engagements, other important moments in a person's life. I used to have a successful business built up, but I lost it when I moved out here. I'm cobbling together whatever work I can while I rebuild my customer base."

"Why'd you move here?" I ask. He briefly puts his face in his hands and rubs his temples.

"I followed my girlfriend."

"Does she know about your Chinese food affair last night?"

"Doubt it. She moved here a few weeks ahead of me. We were starting fresh after my divorce . . ."

"Wait, what?" My mental picture of him is changing rapidly. "How old are you?"

"Twenty-eight."

"How does that happen? You and I are the same age and you've already been married *and* divorced? I knew we had different lives but that's . . . that's . . ." I am unable to come up with the words to express my surprise. At this point I haven't even dated anyone longer than a season, and he's had an entire marriage.

"We do have different lives." He gestures with his hand, encompassing the pool area, the view, and our chef-prepared meals. Touché. "My girlfriend and I wanted to start over, far away. She was offered a transfer to her company's Phoenix office, and we both thought it was a great opportunity. I stayed behind to finish up some things and by the time I got here, she had met someone else. She thrived on drama, and I wasn't as interesting once I wasn't married anymore."

"So you're a cheater?" Makes sense for someone with such a sleazy career path to also have a sleazy romantic past.

"Only on paper. My wife and I were emotionally separated for years."

I've heard that one before.

"Did your wife know that?"

"Of course she did! She dated other guys too. She even moved one of her lovers in for a while. Look, we were incompatible as a couple. We got married straight out of high school because she needed an escape from her cultish family. Marrying me meant they couldn't marry her off to the much older man they had picked out for her."

"So in this not-quite-believable scenario, you're some kind of hero?"

"Yes, actually I am. And it's true." I can't tell if his defensiveness is because I implied that he's lying, or because he's telling the truth and is sensitive about it.

"What did you get out of the deal?" I refuse to believe that a conniving photographer runs around rescuing women from forced marriages out of the goodness of his heart.

He shrugs. "Does everything have to be a transaction? Marianne was my closest friend and an awesome roommate. Do you seriously not have someone in your life you'd do anything for? She needed me. As long as we were married, her family left her alone. They sorta hate me."

"Why bother getting divorced then? Sounds like you had everything working out so well." At least, as well as can be in a loveless marriage.

"We lived in Kansas City, but my wife was offered her dream job back home in St. Louis. We couldn't keep up the charade if we moved there, and she really wanted the job, so we decided to quietly and amicably end it. Unfortunately, her former cult also doesn't approve of divorce and when her parents came to save her soul, they walked in on me and my girlfriend. Suddenly I wasn't just the daughter-stealer, I was the evil degenerate cheater."

In my head, I'm casting the movie version of this ridiculous drama. If Tanner sells his life rights, Powell's going to jump at the chance to write the soundtrack. This is just cheesy enough for his kind of music. The ending, where Tanner and his new lover ride off into the sunset—in the opposite direction as Marianne and her extremely attractive new husband who also has a hobby of saving women from cults—will have a lovely acoustic ballad about starting over. We'll cut to credits before Tanner's heart is mercilessly discarded by his manipulative drama-loving girlfriend, and if box office numbers are high enough, that will be the start of the sequel in which he learns to love again.

"Then you moved out here and got dumped. That sucks. Why didn't you just turn around and drive home?" This information may be important for *Tanner Smythe: Hometown Hero part II, New Beginnings*.

"There was nothing left for me there. My ex's family made sure to trash my business—I couldn't even get a job taking passport photos. Most of my so-called friends weren't particularly supportive when all that was going on, and I never had a good relationship with my parents and siblings. None of my family members follow me on SwiftaPic, if that tells you anything. My van and my cameras are all I have left of my previous life."

I consider it for a moment. His life is somewhat paralleling my childhood. After my dad died, my paternal relatives tried to steal me from my mother. She had to flee with me in the middle of the night, we were homeless for a year, and crushingly poor for another couple of years. I remember what it was like to lose everything. And I remember having a membership at the YMCA, so when we lived in our car we had a consistent place to shower. Tanner is asking for the kind of help my mom needed. How can I turn him down, especially when it doesn't cost me anything?

"Alright, you've convinced me."

"Of what?" He's suddenly confused, as if he's already forgotten the reason he's here and telling me this whole thing to begin with.

"Your sob story has swayed me, Tanner. We have a deal. Welcome to the gym."

"That wasn't a sob story," he objects, but he smiles when he says it, revealing that adorable dimple in his left cheek. It's too bad about his profession. I think I'd like him if he wasn't a pap.

SEVEN

I HOPE UR READY FOR THE PERFORMANCE OF A LIFETIME.

I stare at my phone, trying to interpret the text from Devon. Powell left yesterday to join him and Xander in Los Angeles, where they are auditioning dancers for the upcoming show. Is it going terribly? Am I getting called in? I do know the dances and reluctantly performed in two of their videos, but there's no way I'm getting on a stage and doing that in a concert being broadcast to millions. No way.

Before I can send a strongly worded objection with some middle-finger emojis, I receive a second, clarifying message: JACE'S WILL HAS BEEN FILED. BE PREPARED FOR A MEDIA STORM.

Crap, that's much worse. All court filings are considered public information, which means anyone who requests them will be granted access. Once some gossip site does that, everyone will know what Jace said about me, and there will be questions.

I've been dreading this moment.

The way I see it, I have two choices: I can either pretend to have actually been the love of Jace's life or I can deny it. If I admit to being Jace's great love (and lover?) I'll have the sympathy of the media, while they simultaneously tear me apart for not having been in a steady long-term relationship with him and judgmentally compare me to all the other names he's been romantically linked with in the past. If I deny it, if I make his love unrequited and unreturned, I'm the selfish succubus who broke Jace's heart and left him lonely. And if it ever comes out that I'm the one who put him on that helicopter, then they'll think I'm also the one who murdered him. Conspiracy theorists and bored gossips will wonder if perhaps I wanted to get rid of him, if I sent Jace to his death intentionally.

Powell is media savvy, and his advice has been to admit but deflect. Oh, Jace, how I loved him, but the timing was wrong. We'd always thought we'd have forever. Sigh. Wipe a tear. Then I can advise Jace's fans that if they have someone special in their lives, tell them, please tell them now before it's too late. Repeat sigh, wipe another tear, stare mournfully into the distance.

Now I regret not going out to California with Powell. The potential media storm would be so much easier to manage while reclining on a chair next to Devon's pool with Brixley and a cold drink at my side. They could have told reporters they were sheltering me, guiding me through my heartbreak and loss.

Maybe I should head over to my parents' house, hide out there? No, that will never work; we live in the same neighborhood and if I'm not home it's the first place the paparazzi will check.

So there's only one thing to do: shut my phone off and get a good night's sleep. I'll deal with the madness tomorrow. That's not me avoiding my problems, that's me gathering my strength and engaging in self-care so I can face them head on. Or so I'm telling myself.

I wake up ready to face the inevitable.

No, not really. But I've resigned myself to my fate. After a workout in my home gym—I won't risk making an appearance at Star Fitness—and a large breakfast, I turn my phone back on. It takes two full minutes for all of the notifications to load.

I keep an alert set up for mentions of my name in the media, and . . . yeah, it's out there. The big headline is "Who is Cassidy

Blaine-Corbitt and How Did She Steal Jace Monroe's Heart?" Another: "Jace Monroe's Long-lost Love Revealed in His Will." And another: "Jace and the Woman Who Broke His Heart." That's hurtful. Why do they assume his heart was broken rather than full to bursting with love in our clandestine relationship?

My inbox is filling up with interview requests. The dozens of texts are either supportive or irrelevant. My parents send me encouragement, Mason sends a picture of his baby (he probably missed the will announcement—baby pictures arrive daily), Powell sends a reminder to have Hank take my car for an oil change, and Brixley sends virtual hugs.

And then there's a message from Tanner. That's not unusual. In the weeks since cherry pie day, he's texted often. Usually it's with a random question: WHAT KIND OF CACTUS IS THIS? CAN YOU RECOMMEND A DENTIST? WHERE CAN I BUY FRESH CHILES?

Once it was THERE IS A SPIDER IN MY VAN! DO YOU HAVE A FLAMETHROWER AND CAN YOU RESCUE ME? THIS IS NOT A JOKE! That particular text was accompanied by a picture of the tiniest, cutest little baby tarantula, and I ended up driving way out into the desert to coax it out of his vehicle for him. He repaid me with drinks at a dive bar, where he tolerated my teasing about his arachnophobia, and I let him beat me at shufflepuck to assuage his ego.

This latest message is short and to the point: CAN I TAKE A PICTURE OF YOU, PRETTY PLEASE?

At least he asked nicely. I call him. "How much were you offered for a recent photo of me?"

"Enough that I was willing to ask you for one."

"What do they want?"

"You sobbing about your lost boyfriend. No, just kidding. They're hoping for a pic of you out partying, so they can show what a heartless shrew you are, celebrating your inheritance."

"I'm not big on partying."

"I figured. For the record, I don't think you're a heartless shrew either. So, how about it? Can I come over?"

"Seriously? Are you asking permission to ambush me?"

"By definition, if you know I'm coming, it's not an ambush. Come on, Cass. It's a beautiful day and you have a heated pool. Let me take your picture, and then we can swim. I'll bring margarita mix."

"You're trying to get me drunk so you can take a terrible photo to humiliate me in the press."

"Nope. I'm a professional. I haven't taken a terrible photo in years. And why would I want to humiliate you? I'm trying to help. I promise, I'll take the picture first, let you approve it before I send it off, and then we relax and drink margaritas poolside. Please?"

Hmmm. He's shown himself to be an excellent photographer—his work on my gym's social media proves that. I do appreciate getting the final say on the image he uses. And, truthfully, I enjoy his company. Hanging out with him is better than being by myself right now.

"Fine, come over. But don't show up with margarita mix. I have better stuff here."

Tanner arrives an hour later, laden down with camera equipment, a bag of tortilla chips and a covered bowl.

"You said not to bring margarita mix, but I couldn't show up empty handed," he says, giving the bowl to me.

"Salsa?" I ask, peeling back the lid to peer at the contents. "Is it homemade?"

"Van made, technically." He flashes his cheeky grin. I hate when he does that. It makes me like him more, and I don't want to like a paparazzo.

Out of habit, I take the bag of chips and read the ingredients.

"They're organic." There's a defensiveness to his tone. "I figured someone like you would be picky about those sorts of things."

"Someone like me?" Is this another rich people dig?

He seems to realize he came across as rude. "I meant because you're super health conscious."

"I was checking for peanuts," I explain. "We can't let anything into the house that was even processed in a factory that also processes peanuts." Fortunately, the chips are clean. Otherwise, I would have sent them back out to his van. Even when my brother is out of town, we don't take risks.

"You're allergic?"

"Powell is." Tanner must be the absolute worst paparazzo. After being in our home a couple of times and meeting my brother, he's still done absolutely no research. Powell's allergy is common knowledge. He's appeared in multiple allergy awareness campaigns. He's also been hospitalized twice, though not in the time I've known him. I'm militant about policing food products. There will be no anaphylaxis on my watch.

"Good to know. You ready to start shooting?" He's starting to collapse under the weight of his equipment. He brought fancy lights and everything.

"Of course." I'm kind of offended he asked. Has he not looked at me? I'm wearing a tasteful modest dress in a solid color that will photograph well. My hair is brushed smooth, and I've put on some light makeup. Not much, but enough to cover the zit on my forehead and make my eyes stand out. What more does he want me to do?

"You look nice," He gives me a belated compliment and adjusts the load in his arms. "Did you decide what you want?" Oh, I can choose the pose, too? I'm not sure if this makes him good at his job, or bad at it.

"Follow me." I lead him into the dining room. I've gotten every printed picture of Jace and me and fanned them out over the table. They go back years. Some are framed. Some just came off the printer in the past half hour. Some are cut out of magazines, like the full page spread from the time I went as Jace's date to the Kid's Vote Awards. That one conveys the illusion of couplehood, the way Jace is whispering in my ear, and I'm laughing. Our stance looks intimate and loving, though in truth he was telling me a long-winded story about some backstage shenanigans that ended in Devon covered in the contents of a shrimp platter.

Tanner lets out a low whistle upon seeing the layout. "So the rumors are true then? You are Jace's long lost love?"

"You sound like you didn't believe it before. What, you don't think someone like him could fall for someone like me?" I'm bristling a little. I've heard all of those types of insinuations already, every time I ever went out in public with Jace. Yes, I know basic internet rules: never read the comments sections. But sometimes I can't help myself, and then I'm reminded of how many hateful trolls there are in the world.

"I didn't mean to imply that. It's just you're so ... so ..." he hesitates and runs a hand through his messy hair. It's not intentionally stylishly messy either, more like someone who's been in a van all morning.

"So what? So not good enough?"

"That's not it at all. You're ... you are definitely good enough. I meant that even though you say you prefer hiding out in the background and avoiding attention, you're not a wallflower. If you wanted Jace, you'd have had him. You wouldn't let a chance like that pass you by."

He's right. If I'd ever thought Jace was serious, and if I'd felt the same way, I would have jumped on the opportunity. I didn't love him like that though. But if I ever admit it, I'll be destroyed, I'll be the monster that coldly smashed Jace's heart. I owe it to his memory to pretend. Better to be the pining lost love than the emotionless robot I fear I might be.

"Jace and I were close friends, and I did love him."

"You did?" Tanner studies my face with those luminous green eyes. I'm beginning to suspect they're his natural color.

"Jace left me his music. He said what he wanted to say. Can we leave it at that? I don't owe anybody an explanation of our relationship. It was what it was, and we were both content with how things worked out." Well, one of us was.

Tanner looks like he doesn't agree with what I'm saying, but he doesn't have to. He just needs to shut up and take the photo. Then we can finally jump in the pool, which is where I really want to be right now.

"Alright, I'll take your word for it. Now, let's see what we can do." Tanner goes into portrait photographer mode. He adjusts the curtains to optimize the light coming in, he rearranges the chairs. He even gets some props from the living room to make the space appear softer—in his words—and homier. I have to sit at the table, staring into the distance, surrounded by pictures. I know whoever buys this from him is going to blow the image up and analyze everything visible in the scattered photos, so I make sure the best ones are closest to me. It's not that I'm vain, but I do know what internet trolls target and want to minimize their criticisms.

Afterward, he loads the images onto his laptop and starts moving through them until he finds what he wants. I'm floored by how stunning it is. My expression appears haunted and sad, yet somehow hopeful. I'm not sure how he did it since I'm quite certain I don't actually look like that. He's a magician, I guess.

"Let me send this to my agent, and then we can relax," he suggests. He's been casting longing glances out the window toward the pool.

"I get a cut, right?"

He frowns. "I hadn't thought about that, but it seems fair. You did a lot of the work."

"Donate a portion to Jace's foundation, and we'll call it even." I don't need Tanner's money; I just wanted to find out how greedy he was with it.

We change into swimsuits—after I make sure Tanner stows his camera gear—and head out. But we barely make it poolside when he receives a text from his agent. They want more. Numerous sites are trying to schedule interviews with me, but my phone is off again, and Tanner is the only one who can reach me.

"This is insane," Tanner says as he skims through the messages. His phone keeps beeping with new notifications. "They think I've got an in with you, and they want me to cash in on it."

"Who does?"

"Everybody, even ones I've never heard of. *Celebutante* offered me $10k if I can get you to spill your guts to their reporter. They want me to trick you into going to a restaurant tonight, where she'll be lying in wait."

"Forget it. I hate that site." But I do appreciate that he told me about it instead of suggesting we go out for dinner.

"The Snarky Gossip is offering me money—oh, only $5k—if I can convince you to take a phone call with them."

"Pass."

"Eduardo says he knows I'm with you and for $8k he'd like to send someone to your house for an exclusive."

"For you or me?"

"The $8k is for me to persuade you and take pictures. Your payment is a bit more." He shows me his phone. Nope, not enough. For either of us, actually. Eduardo does not respect Tanner's skill. He keeps undercutting him on price.

"No thanks."

"You seriously don't want a piece of this action? When Jace died, you were all about it."

That's an asshole thing to say. And a total misinterpretation of my motives.

"Jace's death was less than an hour from leaking anyway. I know him, and I did exactly what he would have wanted me to do. You haven't figured out the importance of spin control yet?" Truthfully, the decision was out of my hands. Jace didn't have any family and was on the verge of firing his publicist. That left Devon as the best option to take over the announcement, but he was too distraught and begged me to leak it for him. Putting the news out through a gossip blog took the pressure off Devon and was the easiest way to get it out there without all the hassle of the press conference that Jace's former people were trying to set up. Making Eduardo pay for it was just a bonus.

"Spin control, yeah, I get that. But would he really have wanted you to profit from his death?" Tanner is skeptical. He clearly doesn't know me at all.

"Information costs money, especially when the person who wants it is a soul-sucking vampire who only cares about website hits and not the actual human beings involved. But that doesn't matter anyway because I didn't keep a penny of that blood money. You're the only one who profited."

"You didn't?" He's apparently surprised by that. I'm rather offended now.

"I spent it all on insulin."

"If you're diabetic, why'd you suggest margaritas?" he scoffs. He's acting like he caught me in a lie.

"I didn't. You're the one who suggested margaritas. I just agreed to them. And anyway, it wasn't for me. Do you have any idea how much insulin costs every month? I went on Please-

FundMe and found all the posts where people were asking for money for insulin, and I funded them all. And a few kids' insulin pumps as well. Jace would have approved." Jace did that sort of thing anonymously sometimes. One of his hobbies was getting drunk and paying for strangers' healthcare.

"I can't believe you did that." Now he's staring at me like he's never seen me before.

"I can't believe you assumed I spent the money on myself. Now I know what you really think of me."

He runs both hands through his messy hair, like he always does when he's thinking or agitated or about to insult me. "I don't know what to think of you. I can't figure you out, Cassidy."

I'm not comfortable with his probing. "You don't need to figure me out. But like I said, you're the only death profiteer."

"I don't look at it that way. I was doing my job, and you have to admit I took a gorgeous picture. But I wouldn't want to . . . I wouldn't want to exploit you. You're trusting me right now, and I would never take advantage of that."

I study him for a moment. He's serious. He's not going to secretly text some journalist.

"So what do you think I should do?"

"Me?" I can't tell if he's surprised or flattered that I'm soliciting his opinion.

"You're the only person who stands to benefit from this interaction. You've got tabloids offering you money for access to me. Tell me what to do."

"I think you should make a pitcher of margaritas and we should jump in the pool," he suggests. "You don't owe them anything. Keep your private life private." That's an unexpected response. I thought he'd choose whatever offer made him the most money. Maybe I've misjudged him, too.

"Alright, sounds like a plan. Turn your phone off and put it inside." I don't trust him that far. For all I know he could be trying to record our conversation and sell that. I'll have to watch out for him asking anything about Jace or our history together. Maybe that's why Tanner wants to drink with me—he hopes I'll loosen up.

As he does so, I move to the outdoor bar and pull out the blender and ingredients. We're going with prickly pear today and using the expensive tequila. I rim the pool-safe plastic cups with salt because I'm a conscientious hostess, fill them with sweet icy deliciousness, and then I wait. He takes longer than he should, making me wonder what else he's doing in there. I can always review the feed from the interior cameras later. I don't usually leave them on when I'm home, but I didn't want to take any chances with a snoop like him in my house.

"I messaged all of them back saying that I'd left you and you weren't answering my calls," he says. "And I turned mine off."

"Great." I carry our drinks over next to the pool, so he has to come to me. Then I set them on the ground.

"Why'd you do that?" he asks as he stoops to pick one up. That's what I was waiting for. Before he touches the cup, I give him a quick shove into the water. He comes to the surface sputtering. "What the hell, Cassidy?"

"Just making sure you didn't have your phone on you. I told you I want electronic privacy today," I say. He pulls himself up to sit on the edge and reaches for his margarita again, this time while carefully watching me. I'm tempted to fake like I'm going to push him again and see if he flinches.

"Good thing I'm not a liar. My phone is off and inside. You can go verify if you don't believe me."

"Don't need to now. You'd have pulled it out immediately to check the damage if it had been in your pocket." I pick up my own beverage. "Cheers."

"I'm learning never to cross you. Cheers." He grins as he taps his cup against mine and we both drink deeply. And as soon as I set my margarita down, he slips back into the water, seizes my legs, and pulls me off the side. I go under and come up laughing.

He surprised me, and I don't actually mind. The phones are off, we're not talking about Jace, and I love to swim.

Tanner spent the night last night.

No, not like *that*.

We swam until we got hungry, then we ate way too much food from the fridge meals. Joel had left this weird meaty stew that Powell likes, and Tanner ended up devouring both servings, while I finished off some vegetarian risotto. Our personal chef is the only one I've ever met who is able to make risotto that still tastes delicious warmed up in the microwave.

Then we drank some more. Not to get drunk, that's never been my goal. But there's something so pleasant about sitting outside all evening, sometimes in the hot tub, slowly sipping a beer, and just talking.

I was careful though, as always. I listened to Tanner's stories from art school, and all about his photography business, but I kept myself back. Not that I acted completely reticent, but I limited any sharing to what he could find out with an internet connection, knowledge of keywords, and a few minutes' time.

At one point, he said he was glad that I was finally opening up to him.

"I'm not telling you anything you couldn't have already read in the tabloids or learned in the unofficial Last Baron's documentary."

He seemed hurt by that, but I'm not stupid. A paparazzo, coming to my house, pretending he's my friend?

"I've never watched that and I don't intend to. Cassidy, I'd prefer to get to know you in person instead of stalking you online."

"I'm hard to find online," I told him, which is not quite true. I have a social media presence, but I don't make public posts. My online existence is restricted to following famous friends, other people tagging me, and of course, my gym account. But that's work, not pleasure.

"I know. I looked," Tanner said, directly contradicting his previous statement about not wanting to stalk me online. I raised my eyebrows at him, and he blushed. "I mean . . ."

"It's fine, you're just doing what everybody does, and now you're trying to manipulate me so you can get a more in-depth story." I knew he was a wannabe journalist, despite his prior 'serious photographer' claims.

"I'm not. I'm trying to be your friend. But you don't let anyone in, do you?" He stared off into the distance like his feelings were hurt. He'd probably be a pretty good actor.

That effectively ended the conversation, but I couldn't kick him out. He wasn't drunk, but he'd had too much to drive, and I didn't want him sitting in his van in our driveway, so instead I took him to the media room, made popcorn, and we settled in to watch a movie. Based on 'serious artist' claims, I expected him to be one of those hipster snobs who only watches foreign films, but it turns out he's really into crime thrillers, which happen to be my favorites as well. It's nice to not have to fight over movie choices—Powell likes slapstick comedies.

And afterwards, I escorted him to a guest suite, wished him sweet dreams, and set the house alarm.

Yes, I switched on the interior sensors.

I didn't entirely trust Tanner not to creep around, looking for some way to exploit us.

That's why I'm pleasantly surprised to wake up on my own at eight thirty. By on my own, I mean of course, by waking from sleep of my own accord rather than because of blaring alarms. I'm not surprised to be *alone*. Tanner might be a sneaky paparazzo, seeking to ingratiate himself to me as part of a nefarious hunt for a story, but I do trust that he's not the kind of guy who would appear uninvited in a lady's bed. That's more of a Xander move, and if I thought he was anything like Xander, I would have made him sleep on the patio. The chaises out there are comfortable.

I get dressed and turn off the interior security and head to the kitchen. Since I have a guest, I'm feeling inspired to cook. I make a fabulous breakfast casserole. My mom and I used to make them on Sunday mornings and heat up leftovers the rest of the week. It was a quick and easy meal. Cheap too, because the dollar store near our apartment sold bags of the frozen hash browns that we used for the casserole base. Nowadays, I use hash browns from the organic grocery, and cage free, cruelty free, possibly hand fed chickens with biographies printed on the carton. Today's eggs come from Clucky, Bertha, and Peckster. My guess is that those names are all made up, but who am I to argue with their marketing techniques?

Tanner stumbles out of the guest wing, bleary eyed, just as the food comes out of the oven.

"You're baking?" he asks in surprise.

"I felt like making breakfast."

"But in the oven?"

Oh, I get it. He thought I was only capable of reheating one of Joel's microwavable concoctions. That's a fair assumption, given that Joel's meals are all I've served him so far.

"Are you assuming I can't cook just because I don't make a perfect pie crust like a fifties housewife?"

"Ouch. I'm not a fifties housewife. If anything, I'm the perfect modern man. I have a job, I'm fiscally responsible, and I can bake anything. And, in case you haven't noticed, I'm kind of cute." He winks, and I laugh. Truth is, he is kind of cute. He has that dimple in his left cheek that only appears sometimes, and when it does . . . yeah. He's cute. Too bad he's also a spy. Or something like that.

"Right. Sit down, I'll get the plates."

"And coffee?" He looks around hopefully, as though a steaming mug will magically appear in front of him. I point to the espresso machine, which, as it turns out Mr. Modern Man doesn't know how to operate. So much for perfection.

As we're enjoying our breakfast—after I fixed the espresso machine and he cleaned up his mess—he decides to ruin everything.

"So when does your brother get back?"

There it is. He did hang out after the shoot hoping to elicit information. This wasn't about me at all; it never is. He fooled me with his willingness to pass up money for setting up an interview with me, because he had bigger fish to fry.

"Why do you ask?" I'm going to give him a chance to tell the truth.

He glances down at his plate. "I was just wondering if he was going to walk in and see us. I don't want him to get the wrong idea." It's a clever lie; he's fast on his feet.

"Like what?" Now I'm intentionally needling him.

"I don't want him to think I heard about your relationship with Jace and tried to move in on you while you're grieving over losing the love of your life."

"Jace wasn't the love of my life," I correct him automatically. Oh no! He did it! He got me to say that out loud. Wonder how much money my little slip up earned him? *Newsflash: Cassidy Blaine-Corbitt didn't love Jace. She led him on! He died broken-hearted because of her!* I can't wait for all the hate mail that gets me.

"Sorry. Anyway, whatever your relationship was, lovers, friends, whatever, you are in mourning, and everybody wants to harass you for details. I don't want you or your brother to think I'm like that too."

See what he's doing? He's slithering in like the snake that he is, hoping to trick me into revealing more. I was expecting this, but it still hurts, especially after all the fun we had yesterday. This is yet more evidence that I can't trust anybody.

"Maybe you should go."

He laughs, like he's not taking me seriously. "Why? Is Powell on his way home?"

"Maybe you should go because you're exactly like everybody else. You're trying to worm your way in so you can ask about Jace too."

"No, I'm not!"

I've said it before, he's a good actor. He pulls off a plausible show of looking offended by the insinuation when all I'm doing is describing his current behavior.

"You are, you're doing it right now. 'Whatever your relationship was,' like that's not fishing for more information."

"I'm not, I only care because . . ." He pauses and his eyes shift away. "Never mind. It doesn't matter. You're clearly not someone who trusts, and I doubt you're ever going to believe me, so I won't bother defending myself."

"Good, because there's no defense for your behavior." I cross my arms and glare at him. He continues to eat, as though we're having a discussion rather than a battle.

"Cassidy, I want to be your friend. But you aren't the kind of person who has friends, are you? You don't let anyone get close to you, and when they try you push them away. You must lead a sad, lonely life." He forks his last bite of food into his mouth and gets up and walks away. I hear him gathering his belongings from the dining room.

Part of me is disappointed. We had been having fun, until he ruined everything, twisting the conversation to Jace like that. I stay in the kitchen, finishing my breakfast, and listen to him leave without saying goodbye. The front door closes gently behind him—I bet that annoyed him. I'm going to view the exterior security footage later and see if he tried to slam it but was foiled by the soft close latch Powell had installed. He claimed the door jarred the equipment in his recording studio if it slammed too hard. It makes storming out far less satisfying.

EIGHT

"Did I see you dancing to old pop songs?" Whitney asks. She's the new assistant manager at my gym. She's worked for me for a couple of months now. I like her—she's calm, efficient, and determined. And not usually nosy.

"Hmmm?" I half-answer. I'm at the front desk with her, trying to get in touch with my IT guy. We've been having issues with our computer system lately and he is not responding to my increasingly annoyed emails. I'm typing up a particularly angry one reminding him about contractual obligations and the need for having functional security cameras.

"In the class studio? I walked past and I heard the music."

Alright, I'll deal with IT support later. I should probably take some time before I send anything I regret. I don't want to burn bridges with someone who has access to my system.

"Yes. I was," I admit. "But not by choice." Powell is back, and he's entering full-on prep mode for the upcoming reunion concert. And, despite my numerous protests, I have to help. He has a dance coach who works with him, but Powell's Last Baron's stage positioning was always second from left, so he likes to rehearse in between two others. As someone who knows the dances and is in good enough shape to keep up with him, I've been conscripted as one of his brackets, filling in for Mason. His coach takes the position Jace used to occupy. Jace was the centerpiece of the group; I don't know how any of them are going to manage the tribute concert without being able to follow his lead.

I'll never admit this to Powell, but I don't mind rehearsing with him. The workout is fun, intense, and heavy on the cardio. I'm even considering offering an exclusive class to my members. It might be popular: *Burn calories by dancing to hits from the Last Barons! Special appearance by Powell Corbitt!* Of course, I'd have to get him to agree to that. But he probably would; my brother always did like showing off.

Whitney opens her mouth like she wants to ask more questions, but she thinks the better of it. And that's when my nemesis appears, walking past the desk post-workout and heading straight for the doors without looking at me.

Okay, fine, Tanner isn't my nemesis. But he sure is acting like it with this avoidant behavior.

"Thank you for coming to Star Fitness, sir!" I call out as loudly and cheerfully as I can. "Have a wonderful afternoon!"

He pauses mid-step before turning to look at me. "I thought we weren't on speaking terms."

Wait, he's blaming his sullen attitude on me? Excuse me?

"The last thing you said to me was that I didn't have any friends and I lead a . . . how did you put it? A sad and lonely life? Was I supposed to reach out to you for some reason?"

"I . . ." Tanner flushes. His cheeks darken into a purply shade of red. "Well, that's not what . . ."

I like seeing him all flustered. I raise an eyebrow and wait for him to come up with an apology, which is what he owes me. But he suddenly recovers and doubles down.

"Fine, you're right. You don't have to have any friends at all to live a full and rewarding life. You're doing just fine."

Then Whitney, my newly discovered defender, pipes up behind me. "Why would you say that? Everybody loves Cassidy and she has tons of friends. Heck, she and I are friends. We're going out for drinks tonight. We'd invite you along, but it's ladies only."

Tanner glances from her to me. I feel like I'm back in middle school, but this time I have someone to stand up for me against my bullies. Thanks, Whitney.

"Have fun I guess," Tanner mutters, and heads out the door, still without expressing any remorse for his conniving ways and unnecessary insults.

"Sorry about jumping in there. We don't actually have to go out for drinks," Whitney apologizes when I turn back to work. She busies herself with rearranging some fliers. I think she worries she may have overstepped, since I am her boss and we've never spent time together outside of work before. But hitting up a happy hour sounds nice, and not just to rub it in Tanner's smug face. Though that is an added benefit.

"It'll be fun," I assure her. "I'd love to grab a drink."

And that's when the door opens, revealing Tanner's return. What is with that guy? Except he's not coming over to the desk, and he's not doing another workout. He's carrying his laptop bag over to a table in the lobby and settling in like he's in his own personal office space. Does he think this is a coffee shop? The tables and chairs are set up so members can enjoy a post-workout snack or meal, not so they can hang out and annoy my employees and take advantage of the free wi-fi.

"He always comes back in here to work," Whitney informs me.

I try to tamp down my irritation. Would I be mad if someone else did it? No? So why worry about Tanner, even if it seems like he's spitefully working here to distract me? I'll be the better person; I won't complain at all. Just like I haven't told him that I know he parks his van in my back parking lot some nights. I'm considering his presence a security advantage since the cameras keep malfunctioning.

I'm not *watching* him, but I am glaring at him, so that's why I notice when Tanner begins frowning at his screen, drumming his fingers on the table, and blinking rapidly. He keeps darting glances at me, which I pretend to ignore. The drumming becomes more and more agitated, and he starts and stops typing multiple times. Finally he gets up and approaches me.

"Did you do this?" He is strangely antsy. "Did you give my name to *Matters Magazine*?"

"Why would I do that?" I'm not denying it though. And I'm a little amused by his reaction.

"Why else would they contact me out of the blue to shoot a feature? I've never worked with them before."

I shrug. "You're pretty talented. Maybe they saw your picture of Powell. What's the story they offered?"

His mouth twitches and that damned dimple makes its appearance. "You know. You gave them my name."

I shrug again. "If I'm going to be in a magazine, I want to look my best. It was a professional decision, not a personal one."

He just shakes his head and gives me a rueful smile. "I'm never going to figure you out."

I return to the gym to pick Whitney up after her shift.

"Wow, this is a fancy car," she says as she gets in, and I immediately regret it. I should have driven one of Powell's 'hiding in public' ones, something less flashy, instead of my sporty little yellow Boxster.

"Thanks, my brother bought it for me for my birthday a few years ago." I don't want her to think I am the rich one, which is the image the vehicle conveys. Of course, she knows I own the gym, so she probably already suspects I have *some* money. She's also aware of my familial connections. It's no secret amongst my employees.

"Your brother is a lot more generous than mine. For my last birthday, he gave me a Target gift card with $4.12 on it."

"Does that number have special significance?"

"Yeah, my aunt gave us each a $25 gift card for Christmas, and he bought about twenty bucks worth of stuff with his."

We laugh together and it feels good. *See, I can be social. In your face, Tanner.*

I let her control the music, and when she opens to the center console to access a port to hook up her phone, she pulls out the EpiPens. There's a set in every car, one in my purse, and six of them in strategic locations throughout our house. Powell is single-handedly propping up the EpiPen industry.

"What's this?" she asks, studying the packaging.

"Peanut allergy." I don't elaborate, even though she'll likely assume they're mine. Doesn't matter, I avoid peanuts anyway, so I don't bring any potential contamination home with me.

"You too? I heard about your brother . . ." she stops abruptly as if worried she may have said something wrong.

"Everybody's heard about my brother. He's kind of famous." I'm making a joke to lighten the mood. My gym employees know better than to try and access Powell through me. Several other local celebrities work out there as well, and staff members freaking out like super fans is a fireable offense. It's in their contracts.

"Sorry, I just meant I was told that the reason we have those bleach wipes all over the place is because *he* has a peanut allergy and he's paranoid about it." Her statement is mostly accurate. I'm actually the paranoid one who does most of the Powell's-going-to-touch-this cleaning. I love my brother. I'll do anything to keep him safe.

"Peanut allergies are deadly," I say, as if that explains it all.

"Yeah, and Powell . . . I'm sorry, I'm not fangirling, I promise. I didn't even like the Last Barons. I was a You4Me fan."

"Those guys are hacks." That particular quartet was always chasing the Last Barons up the charts and falling short. As they should have—their lyrics were the literal worst. Even Xander could write better songs than they could. But they were entertaining to hang out with. And I may have made out with one of them once. Or twice.

If popular culture has taught me anything, it's that at my age, I'm supposed to be part of a solid foursome of fabulous females. We're supposed to regularly get together for cocktails and discuss our love lives. Every once in a while, we take a spin class or barre class, or whatever trendy fitness routine is popular at the moment. One of them is promiscuous, but in an empowering way, and she would encourage me to frequently seek sexual partners. One would be a somewhat conservative romantic, and the third would have a series of failed relationships before ending up with a woman. I, of course, would be the emotionally stunted one who never dates, but fully supports my friends as they do so, plus I invite them to a bunch of fun parties where wacky things happen.

That's the way it's supposed to be if life mirrored marketing. But instead, I have mostly acquaintances and industry contacts rather than regular let's-hang-out friends. I mean, I have Powell, of course. And Brixley, though when we're together we don't go out much—she likes to avoid the spotlight when she's not being paid to stand in it.

No matter what Tanner says though, my lack of intimate non-celeb friendships doesn't reflect poorly on me. Or at least, it shouldn't. I learned early on that because of my celebrity adjacent status, people would use me for access. Nobody wanted to be friends with me, Cassidy Blaine. They wanted to be friends with Cass Corbitt, Powell's sister. They wanted passes to shows, they wanted to meet him, or sneak away from slumber parties to attempt to climb into his bed, or casually post pictures on various social media platforms claiming some of Powell's fame for themselves. *Dinner at the Corbitts with @PowellC. Hanging with Powell. Just another musical evening, thanks @PowellC.* I would go untagged, because they wanted the illusion of being his friend, not mine.

They taught me a valuable lesson: people can't be trusted. They all want something, and in my case I always know exactly what that something is.

But sometimes I can set all of that aside. I can shove it all deep down inside and plaster on a smile and pretend things are different. Pretend there are rare exceptions who like me for me and I can enjoy their company. Like right now with Whitney, for example.

She and I bond over a big platter of appetizers and a couple of martinis. It's sort of fun, to be out with another woman, masquerading as friends. She's my age and we have a lot of common interests, so perhaps we could do this more often, maybe even form a superficial real-life friendship, not merely a temporary proving-Tanner-wrong one.

At one point the conversation turns serious. "I really like your parents," she tells me. "Especially your father. He's always so friendly and kind when he visits the gym." Hank comes in often, and not always to work out. My gym manager was his best friend in Hank's pre-stage dad life. Hank likes to sit in his office and shoot the breeze with him. I assume they chat about how much happier they are now than when they worked eighty-hour weeks as real estate developers and had no lives outside of their jobs.

"He's my stepdad," I correct. "My bio dad passed away when I was six."

"I was seventeen," Whitney replies, and I'm about to tell her our age difference can't be that great when I realize she is talking about her own father.

"I'm sorry," I automatically respond. All of us half-orphans understand the anguish and sorrow of losing a parent, so more words aren't necessary.

"Ten years ago, but time doesn't heal the loss." She stares into the distance for a moment. "What happened to yours?"

"Hit by a car while riding his bike." Since we're bonding over a shared experience, I don't mind telling her. If I didn't, she could just look it up. It's not a secret. My father was in grad school at the time, painfully close to finishing his dissertation. He was on his way to campus to meet with his advisor when a woman who thought applying mascara was more important than paying attention to the road crashed into him. My poor mother was doing her nursing clinicals at the same hospital the ambulance took him to, so at least she was able to hold his hand while he passed. I don't like to talk about that day. "What about your dad?"

"Suicide." She says the word flatly, but I hear the pain. That's so much worse.

"Oh, no, I am so sorry." My repeated apology sounds weak. I imagine parental suicide is much harder to deal with than accidental death. No matter the actual reason, the child probably interprets it as *I don't love you enough to stick around. I don't want to watch you grow up. You aren't enough for me.*

"He lost his job and his self-worth. He felt like a failure and that we would be better off without him. We weren't, of course. We—my brother and I—were better off with him."

"How awful." I'm not a writer like my brother or Jace, so I don't have the right words to express my sympathies. I can't imagine how terrible it would be to go through a tragedy like that. My dad didn't want to die. It wasn't his choice. If he'd had his way, he and my mom would be happily together, and me and my never-born younger siblings would visit them often. Maybe the hypothetical little brother they were always planning to try for would still live at home, and we'd share weekly dinners and group chats full of silly jokes.

"It caused me to eat my feelings." Whitney holds up one thin muscular arm. "I used to be five times this size. That's why I have all these stretch marks. I did nothing but eat for a couple of years. Then I woke up one day, looked in the mirror and hated myself. And after having a long cry and seriously considering following my dad to his grave, I came to the realization that I was hating the wrong person. I should hate the one who took my father away.

"That's when I started working out," she continues. "I lost the weight and got stronger. I feel better now, like I can do something about my father's death. Because it wasn't his fault, not really. He was lied to and manipulated, which cost him his job. Without a job, he felt like he couldn't take care of us, especially since he'd been blackballed in his industry. The selfish monsters who did it to him not only got away scot-free, but they have these amazing awesome lives built on my father's blood." There is such bitterness in her voice, it's almost frightening. I don't think this is a healthy obsession.

"Have you ever contacted them?" I've thought about doing that myself. I won't admit it to Whitney, since it makes me seem as obsessed as her, but I've looked up my dad's killer on social media before. The $175 fine she was given for 'failure to yield' had no affect on her life. She posts pictures with her grandbaby and shares those obnoxious memes about happiness and positive energy and being *#soblessed*. It makes me *#soangry*, that she gets to go on and do all the things she took away from us.

Whitney shakes her head. "Contact them? Ha. I plot revenge from afar."

"What are you going to do? Wait, are you actually going to do anything?" Anything I could think of would be illegal.

She studies me, eyes glittering. She looks like she's trying to decide if she trusts me enough. *Please don't,* I think. I don't want to be an accessory to murder—they serve jailtime too. Her smile is toothy and fake. "Of course not. I just like to imagine it sometimes."

Something about her tone gives me pause. I suspect she's lying. Maybe this whole go-out-and-make-friends thing was a bad idea. But I won't admit that to Tanner.

"Well . . . good." I don't really want to have this kind of conversation. I have no interest in being a co-conspirator, and this isn't the sort of thing that two people who are barely acquaintances should get into at their first happy hour. "Cheers, then, to moving on." We clink our glasses, sloshing a little bit of martini on the table. These might be a little stronger than I'm used to. I suspect I'll be ordering a Ryde car to get us both home.

NINE

When singer-songwriter Jace Monroe passed away in a tragic accident, he left behind an unexpected gift: two unrecorded albums. Even more unexpected was the message that accompanied them: they were written to honor his one true love. Despite earning accolades as the World's Sexiest Man, Jace was always discreet, or as some would say, standoffish regarding his romantic relationships. In interviews he insisted on privacy and never mentioned his love connections. That's why it was such a shock to learn that there had been a woman who stole his heart: Cassidy Blaine-Corbitt, the younger stepsister of his former bandmate.

Powell looks up from the magazine. "This article is tripe, but the photos are exceptional."

"I know, right?" I'm not thrilled with how I'm portrayed, though it's far more flattering than things I've found online. Some members of Jace's fan club are vicious. I'm going to chalk up their reactions to jealousy, but the vileness of their comments still hurts.

"I'm glad you wore the blue dress. It photographs well."

"Tanner suggested it, actually."

"Yeah? What's going on between the two of you?" Powell asks. He's shifted positions, one ankle resting on the other knee, magazine clasped loosely in his hands. This is his casual pose, one he uses in television interviews. It's too practiced to be natural, so I'm suspicious as to why he's using it.

"Nothing. He's the photographer they hired, and I thought he'd have some insight on what would work."

"Hmmmmm." Powell studies me intently. "I didn't know he contracted with them."

"I guess he does."

"Hmmmmm." Powell's getting annoying with the way he's staring at me and pretending he isn't performing an inquisition. A subtle inquisition, but I know him well. I wait him out, and he breaks first. "How exactly did Tanner suggest it?"

"The usual way?" I don't understand my brother's reaction. "He looked at a few and picked this one."

"You let him into your closet?"

Ah, now I see. "Yes. I don't have a sliding rack."

"How come he's allowed in your closet and I'm not?"

"Because you once knocked over an entire shoe rack trying to demonstrate a dance move, and you didn't help me clean it up." Against my better judgment, I did grant Tanner temporary access to my closet. I had to endure a couple of comments about how it was larger than his van, and some snide remark about how the closet reflected my personality better than my bedroom did. *This is who you are. Perfect outer shell, chaotic interior. Zen-like room, messy closet.* It was almost enough to make me cancel the entire shoot.

I'm glad I didn't cancel though since the whole thing turned out to be kind of fun. Not fun enough for me to invite him to stay for dinner afterwards, but enough to break down some of the mild animosity between us. That's all on his end, not mine, of course.

"I would've picked up your shoes if you weren't yelling at me," Powell mutters sullenly, apparently still miffed that part of the house is off-limits to him. He studies the magazine again. "What's this crap?" He starts reading out loud:

> "It was just never the right time for us," Cassidy admits, tears sparkling in her sapphire eyes. She runs a hand through her thick brown hair, a self-soothing gesture she exhibits almost every time Jace's name is mentioned. "I did love him very much though." That may not be enough assurance for Jace's fans, some of whom blame Cassidy for his lonely life. 'Jace deserved happiness' is a common refrain on websites devoted to the superstar's memory.

"When did you develop self-soothing gestures? What are you, a toddler?"

"Right? I kept touching my hair because it felt weird. Their stylist put in too many products." I reflexively pat the strands again because I'm thinking about it, and Powell smirks.

"And Jace deserved happiness," Powell repeats the line so often found on the Jacedom, a website dedicated exclusively to loving and honoring Jace. "Obviously he did. But he was happy. He was the happiest guy I knew. Sometimes I hate that he's gone and I'm still here." Pain flashes across his face.

I hate that Powell feels that way.

"You've got survivor's guilt. Neither of you should have died," I remind my brother. He's right though, it hurts to read these kinds of things. I'm still struggling with my own guilt from making the call condemning Jace to death. I'm glad my role has not been publicized. This article would have denounced me, and I would be getting more hate mail than I already do. Fortunately, over the years I've developed a thick skin.

Cassidy invites me out into her backyard. It is evening, and as the sun sets, the lights of the Phoenix valley twinkle like stars. She sits in an Adirondack chair, legs curled under her, looking very much like the vulnerable young girl she was when she first met Jace.

"Jace didn't remember that meeting, of course. I was just another kid, brought backstage to meet the band. They had dozens of fans like me coming through every night. He had no way of knowing that he'd ever see me again, or that we would develop such a deep friendship." Back then, she was an awkward pre-teen, and Jace was shooting to fame as one of the most popular heartthrobs from the Last Barons of Sound, still on their first major tour. As fate would have it, Cassidy's widowed mother began dating Hank Corbitt, whose son Powell was also a Last Baron.

At age fifteen, Cassidy embarked on tour as well, joining the Last Barons as they went back on the road. Her mother was employed as a nurse, her new stepfather acted as Powell's manager, and she sold merchandise at the nightly shows.

The labor was backbreaking, carting around boxes of T-shirts and interacting with screaming fans desperate for souvenirs. Still, despite the hard work, Cassidy loved traveling with the band, especially hanging out backstage with her stepbrother and his friends.

"Jace and I had our first kiss on that tour," she reminisces, her fingers gently tracing her lips in memory of Jace's touch. "He was too old for me, so it never went beyond that. But that kiss did change our relationship."

However, circumstances conspired against her. Four years later, the band broke up. Jace went on to found JaDed with his fellow Last Baron, Devon Malloy. Cassidy was hired on as Powell's assistant and followed him to Arizona where he based his solo career. Now they were separated not just by age, but by distance.

"We saw each other as often as we were able. There's a guest room in our house that we still refer to as Jace's. He used to text all the time. Sometimes I still check my phone, looking for new messages. I haven't adapted to his absence yet." Her voice takes on a dreamy quality as she speaks, and the ghost of a smile drifts across her face. "I miss him every single day. But it was just never the right time for us."

"I thought they spent an entire day with you. You'd think they'd get some better quotes. Didn't my publicist give you some tips?" Powell expresses the same annoyance I felt when I read the preliminary draft of the article.

"She gave me the 'never the right time' line. I thought that was pretty good." I don't mean to be so defensive, but where was Powell while I was doing the interview? He should have been here to help out. He's much better at acting cool and suave than I am. I'm annoyed at the way the interviewer makes me sound like a two-dimensional character who exists only to sigh sadly about lost love. But it's better than contradicting Jace's will. I'd rather be portrayed as heartbroken than heartless.

"And now that's over with, what's your next step? With Jace's music, I mean?" Powell is the billionth person to ask, but I don't mind the question coming from him. There are so many factors to consider. I want to do Jace's memory justice. The writer quotes me as saying "I need to find the right voice to share Jace's words with the world." But the truth is, I have no idea how to go about handling this. Numerous musicians' agents keep leaving me messages, but I haven't returned any of their calls.

"Do you want to sing them?" Wouldn't that be the easiest solution?

The same puppy dog eyes he uses on me do not work on my brother. He shakes his head.

"Nope. I only sing my own songs now. That's the joy of not being in a group anymore." Powell's smugness is well deserved. The fact is, he's talented. And he writes catchy music. It's not deep and soulful, but he has a gift for creating choruses that stick in your head forever. *One heart, two hearts, never beat apart* gets stuck in my head at the most inopportune moments. The song isn't even good, but for some reason it's an earworm.

"Your music is kind of . . . juvenile and cheesy," I inform him. "Jace was profound and meaningful. His songs are above your skill level anyway."

Powell doesn't rise to the bait. Instead, he laughs at me. "My songs pay your salary. Tell you what, I'll record one as a tribute. I'll release it as a single, and all the profits can go to Jace's foundation. That ought to get people off your back for a little while."

I love my brother.

"Thank you!" I give him a hug, almost making him drop the magazine.

"No problem. I suppose it's the right time to do something like this." He waves the pages directly in my face. "The right time for us."

"They say that a dozen times. Shoddy writing."

"I like the concept though. The idea of the pieces having to fall into place. Finding the right time." He closes his eyes and begins to hum. I recognize his expression: this conversation is over. I've lost my brother. I find the nearest legal pad—he keeps them scattered throughout the house in case of a lyrical emergency—and set it down in front of him. Then I walk away. He's gone into writing mode. He'll emerge later with either a new hit or a bunch of drivel. Or, honestly, it could be both.

TEN

"I'm not going," Powell says as soon as I open the door to his basement recording studio. He doesn't bother to turn around and look at me. All of his attention is on Allison, his favorite sound engineer, as they hunch over the sound board together. She moves toggles up and down, and he holds his headphones over his ears, listening intently.

"I like this take the best," Allison tells Powell, without acknowledging my presence at all.

"Powell," I protest. I know, he's doing this for me. He's kindly recording *If You Were Here* by the late great Jace. But still, he could take a break to do a *different* favor for me.

"Too much bass," my brother ignores me completely. "What if we try this . . ." He moves some other toggles. I'm not entirely sure what any of those things do, but they both sit back with tilted heads and quizzical expressions.

"POWELL!" Now I shout. He looks over his shoulder in annoyance.

"I said I'm not going."

"You're the one who agreed we'd go out for dinner with Xander tonight. Please don't make me suffer alone." I still don't know what Xander wants to talk to us about. A big and important announcement, he said, and it must be if he flew all the way out to Scottsdale and offered to spring for an expensive meal. He enjoys bragging about his wealth, but he also likes to hoard it by making others pay for things for him.

"Take someone else. We're onto something here." Then he and Allison start talking again, throwing around words like 'reverb' and 'bus compression.' This is not an area of the business I pay much attention to—I like the finished songs, not so much the process to create them. And I'm not a fan of being dismissed so easily, especially since that means having to deal with the most annoying man I've ever met without a buffer.

But I can think of someone to call.

"Am I underdressed for this?" Tanner belatedly tucks in his long sleeve T-shirt and attempts to smooth his thick mop of hair. Cafe Mariposa, while having a casual-sounding name, is an iconic restaurant known for its elegance and exclusivity. They are reservation only and always fully booked months in advance. I don't know exactly how Xander managed to secure a table for three on a Friday night, but I assume name-dropping was involved. Most likely Powell's.

"Yes. But we're eating with Xander, so your outfit doesn't matter. People bend over backwards for celebrities, even if their hangers-on look like they just wandered in off the street."

Tanner isn't offended by my teasing.

"Don't you mean just rolled out of a van?" he asks with a wink, while still doing something ineffectual to his unmanageable hair. "Anyway, I doubt Xander is still considered a celebrity." He has a point. Xander is the only one of the Last Barons to still be capitalizing on old fame rather than trying to make a new name. That's why the others (with one tragic exception) are doing so much better than him these days.

"To be fair, he probably promised them my brother would be here." That wouldn't surprise me. Everybody loves Powell. Xander is an ass. For one thing, he's one of those C-list celebs that believes his autograph is a sufficient tip. That's the reason I have a wallet full of cash in my purse right now. I won't let him get away with that kind of crap if he does follow through with his offer to pay. I wouldn't be surprised if he 'forgot' his wallet though. To counter that possibility, I also brought my black card. Well, technically, it's my brother's. But my name is on it, so that counts.

Xander is already at a table waiting, and his reaction to seeing us is one of surprise. I had told Powell to text him and tell him I was bringing someone else, but I'm assuming that didn't happen. When my brother is in his studio his head is in a different world, one in which mundane tasks and common courtesies don't exist.

"Where's Powell?" he asks as we approach. "And who's this guy?"

"Xander, I believe you've met Tanner before," I say, but Xander's eyes skim over him without a hint of recognition. He's an asshole.

"I don't think so." He rises to his feet and there is a brief awkward scuffle as both men try to pull my chair out for me. Tanner steps back and lets Xander have the honor, and I scowl at him.

"I work at her gym," Tanner explains, which, albeit sort of true, is a rather odd introduction. I guess he doesn't want to remind Xander of their prior meeting and out himself as a pap. Xander only pays attention to the cameras, not the people operating them.

"I see." Xander frowns. He has no interest in associating with anyone who has to do actual work for a living. "I thought Powell was coming."

"Something came up. He's busy with Allison . . ." I bite my tongue. I'm not sure he knows who Allison is, but he has always been prickly about the rest of them continuing to succeed in the music (or, in Mason's case, Bollywood) business.

"That's alright, as long as you're here," Xander places his hand on mine possessively, and I pull it back. Perhaps I should keep both hands in my lap at all times.

"Cassidy invited me, saying it would be a shame to waste the reservation," Tanner interjects smoothly, reminding Xander of his presence. "This place looks amazing."

"I live in LA; this is nothing." Xander dismisses the restaurant rather prematurely, as one does when one is a complete snob with few redeeming qualities. "I've ordered the tasting menu for us. Don't worry, Cassidy, yours is vegetarian. But Chandler, if you like, I can ask if they have a children's menu instead."

"It's *Tanner*. And why would I need that?" Tanner is more amused than annoyed at Xander's attempt to antagonize him.

"In case a fine dining restaurant like this is too much for you. Maybe you need a burger or mac and cheese." I don't know why he's being a pretentious prick. Well, yes I do, he always is, but there's no reason to insult Tanner, especially in such a childish manner.

"You're the one who puts ketchup on everything. Remember when we were in Japan?" I smile as I make the subtle dig, referencing Xander's request for American condiments at a sushi restaurant while on a world tour. Admittedly, he had no experience with raw fish before, but making a big scene about how they should accommodate him—*because he was a star, damnit!*—and then demanding they fry the sashimi before he would try any was a cultural disaster. There was a mocking write up in the Japanese press and some rather humorous news reports back home.

"People change, Deedee."

"Don't call me that," I snap at him. My nickname is personal and the right to use it must be earned. Xander has earned nothing and never will. Tanner raises one of his bushy caterpillar eyebrows at me. He's probably not heard that name before, but I'm not going to explain it.

Fortunately, the wine arrives—and Xander makes a big show of tasting it before pronouncing the vintage 'adequate'—so we don't need to keep talking about nicknames or embarrassing food memories. Though I do have a few other stories to bring Xander down a notch or two, if necessary.

The first course—an intriguing sweet pea tart for me, a bruschetta involving lump crab for the omnivores—is delicious, to those of us at the table who aren't trying to impress everyone with gastronomical snobbery. Apparently, Xander has sampled all of the finest restaurants in the world, and they are far superior to anything produced in our dusty little desert town. Or so he claims. All that restaurant sampling must have taken place in the past couple of years, long after the Last Baron's tour where he tried to limit his explorations to American chains on foreign soil.

"If this is such an inferior restaurant, why did you invite us here?" I finally ask. I'm getting desperate to find out why I'm being forced to sit through a meal with him.

"I have exciting news. I wanted to share it with Powell, but it's important for you too, and for our future," Xander says, and I physically force myself not to go through with an instinctive eye roll.

"What future?" Tanner asks innocently. He sees what's going on just as well as I do. He has also, I've secretly noticed, been letting Xander play footsie with him for the past five minutes. Xander hasn't caught on that he's toeing the wrong person.

Xander ignores him and taps out a drumroll on the tabletop before making his announcement. "Cassidy, it's time to make my comeback. I'm going to record a new album."

"How nice for you." I try to make my tone as condescending as his has been. I can already see where this is going. He's going to ask to use Powell's recording studio, probably for free. And Powell's mixing skills. And whatever else he can exploit. I bet he wants Powell playing uncredited back up as well.

"So you'll give me one?"

"One what?"

"One of Jace's albums."

Oh. Well that was unexpected. And absurd. There is no way I'm going to sully Jace's legacy by gifting his music to such a pompous jerk. Xander has a beautiful voice. If he didn't, he never would have made it through the Last Baron's grueling audition process all those years ago. But quality of vocal tone and range is irrelevant when I'm in charge of casting.

"I don't think that's a good idea," I tell him politely. I refrain from adding that Jace's music would cost him a heck of a lot more than a fancy meal for three, especially when that meal also involves spending time with him.

"Why not? It's perfect!" He reaches across the table to take my hand, which I immediately pull away again. "Cass, think about this logically. Jace was my friend and your lover. You give me the album, and I'll dedicate it to you. The press will go crazy—Jace's music as performed by the man who took his place in your heart. It lends an air of romance to the whole thing, since they're love songs written for you, right?"

There are so many things wrong with that idea, I don't even know how to begin to correct him. Maybe I should start with the worst and most disgusting assumption of all: "What do you mean the man who took his place in my heart?"

He flutters his eyelashes at me. Yes, Xander is a grown man who bats his eyelashes like a flirty teen girl. "Cassidy, stop playing around. You and I both sense this attraction. Isn't it time we finally move on it?"

"I have a boyfriend!" I say loudly, backing my chair up and jumping to my feet. Xander's eyes widen as he realizes that if I'm standing, the feet under the table must belong to the smirking man across from him. Tanner winks and I tightly purse my lips to keep from cracking up.

"A boyfriend?" Xander repeats skeptically. He's aware of my lack of romantic history. And yes, I'm lying, but this is the only thing that will work on Xander. He's one of those misogynists who won't back off, who won't accept any excuse from a woman—not even a straight up "I don't like you"—but will respect another man's territory. Or at least he will in front of other men. If I were alone, it would be a different story. He'd be trying to grope me and saying things like "he doesn't have to know" or "I can keep a secret if you can," all the smarmy lines sleazeballs like Xander use.

"Yes, a serious boyfriend." I sit back down and give Tanner a pointed look. He reacts quickly.

"Cass, my darling, I didn't think we were telling anyone," he says and puts his arm around my shoulder. His body gives off a pleasant amount of heat. I lean into him. He smells like cinnamon, again. He must have been baking today. I wonder whose kitchen he used? Not mine, so he must be a kitchen tramp.

"We weren't, but maybe we should now." I flutter my lashes in an exact imitation of Xander's earlier failed flirtation.

"You're dating a gym rat?" Xander asks in disgust, proving that he genuinely did not recognize Tanner. I had thought it was an ego or superiority thing, showing he was too high above to acknowledge a lowly photographer. "He's using you, you know. Probably angling for a promotion."

"I doubt that. *Tanner* is not manipulative."

"And I don't need a promotion," Tanner adds.

"Whatever." Xander makes it clear he is no longer interested in discussing my fake relationship. He changes the subject to his preferred conversational topics: himself, how much money his possessions cost, and degrading gossip about others in the industry. Tanner and I are a quiet captive audience. The food helps; every course is extraordinary. I hope Tanner takes inspiration from the fabulously decadent dark chocolate delice served for dessert and asks to borrow my kitchen to replicate it.

At the end of the meal, while signing the receipt and writing a big fat zero on the tip line, Xander makes one last appeal. "Please, Cass, give me one of the albums. My lawyer drew up the paperwork, all you need to do is sign."

Wow, presumptuous much? I'm not surprised he assumed I would so easily bend to his will and hand over the music. But that's never going to happen. Xander barely deserves to be a footnote to Jace's life story. Jace was a wonderful man and his songs should be sung by someone who will honor his memory, not just do it for the publicity.

"Absolutely not. You should write your own music instead," I encourage Xander. I'm going to have to tell Powell I suggested that. He'll think it's hilarious. Xander has stage presence, he can sing, he can dance, but his writing skills . . . they're a bit lacking. I've heard some of his work before—he has a penchant for making every line rhyme. Lyrics don't need an ABAB pattern. I could write better songs than him and I don't have a creative bone in my body.

"I'm working on that too," he says. "But having Jace's name on this project . . ."

And there it is. Sometimes I dismiss Xander as a little bit dumb, but he's not. He has poor social skills, but he understands the vagaries of fame. And he knows if he wants to be successful again, he needs to find some coattails to ride on, and what could be better than jumping on Jace's posthumous ones?

"If Jace wanted you to have the music, he'd have left it to you in his will." I want those words to stab Xander right in the heart. I've checked out his page on AuctionNet; he's already started selling off the shoes Jace bequeathed him. He's making decent money too, because Jace's fans are buying them up.

"I'm sure that was because he expected you to do the right thing, Cassidy." Xander sounds annoyed now. "Come on, you know how close Jace and I were. What better way to memorialize him than to let one of his brothers sing his songs?"

"Oh, you were brothers?" Tanner interrupts. "I don't really follow former teen pop stars, so I didn't realize you were related. I'm so sorry for your loss." I want to high five him right now. His words visibly cut Xander deeply.

"We were close like brothers." Xander glares daggers at Tanner, and they are now sworn enemies. Xander will definitely recognize him on their next encounter. "It would give me such joy to be able to give voice to his words." That's a great line. He probably came up with that days ago and has been saving it for this moment. But I would never give Jace's music to Xander, for one simple reason: I don't like him.

"This is not up for discussion," I inform Xander, glad that we finished the dessert course and can escape now. All of my enjoyment of this fine food has been ruined by the company.

On the way out—after finding the waiter and slipping him an exorbitant cash tip as an apology for having to deal with our dining companion—I take Tanner's hand. If we're going to claim to be in a relationship, we need to make it appear realistic.

When we reach the parking lot though, he looks down at our clasped hands and drops mine aggressively. "Fun game for you, Cass?" he snarls.

"What? Putting up with Xander?"

"No, this bullshit with pretending you like me."

That's quite an assumption. I'm fairly sure I only claimed to be *dating* him, I said nothing about *liking* him.

"Excuse me? I told Xander I had a boyfriend. You chose to jump in and pretend to be him."

"What was I supposed to do?"

"I don't know, nod and smile? I could have been referring to someone else." Truthfully, I had hoped he'd jump in on the act, but he didn't have to. He could have said he met my boyfriend before or merely confirmed said boyfriend's existence. There are lots of ways to lie to Xander.

"Cass . . . I don't get you. You use people. You used me in there."

"I did not . . . oh, no. He just came out the door. He can see us. We can't look like we're fighting." I don't want Xander to get the idea that my fictional relationship has a crack.

"Fine." Tanner puts his palms on the sides of my face, pulls me closer, and kisses me.

Tanner kisses me.

He does, he seriously, deeply kisses me.

And I totally melt.

I've been celibate for an awfully long time. I have battery operated boyfriends, of course, but they do not kiss. They do not have warm hands and tongues and a firm body to press up against.

The kiss lasts maybe thirty seconds. When he releases me, my knees are weak and my head is spinning. I stare at him, trying to catch my breath and wishing we'd driven his van rather than my backseat-less vehicle. I check over his shoulder.

"I think he's gone." Maybe we can move on to a more intimate location.

"And that's what matters, isn't it?" Is that contempt in Tanner's voice? "I hope that worked. I hope we made him sufficiently jealous."

"I don't want to make him jealous," I correct. That was never my goal. "I want to make him leave me alone."

"Right. Rich, successful superstar, and you want him to go away? You'd rather slum it with someone like me?"

At the moment, that is very much what I want. My fingers, of their own accord, start to reach for him, but I hold them back. This is *Tanner*. I can't let myself get involved with a paparazzo, no matter how skilled he is at kissing. What is wrong with me?

"I'm sorry," is all I can say. Sorry I can't actually throw caution to the wind and jump into his arms and wrap my legs around his waist and . . . yeah, none of that. This was a mistake. A huge mistake.

"You're a user, Cassidy. I'm not going to keep doing this."

Doing what, exactly? I want to ask, but he walks away. I guess he forgot I drove us here. Fine. He can walk off his pouty attitude. I don't know what his problem is anyway. He's the one who kissed me, not the other way around. If anything, he's the user.

ELEVEN

I arrive home in a sour mood, which worsens when I see who is sitting at the kitchen table with Powell. No, thankfully, it's not Xander, who I'm sure is off to the most exclusive club he can find, where he can treat waitresses like servants and pick up lonely fans to take back to his hotel. Instead, it's Ethan, the investigator from the NTSB. If he is here, he can't be bringing good news.

"Sit and have a drink," Powell suggests.

There are three whiskey glasses on the table. The one in front of Powell is empty, the one in front of Ethan is half-full, and a full one waits in front of an empty chair. I feel like a very adult Goldilocks.

"After the evening I've had, I probably shouldn't." I sit, but I don't touch the glass. Tanner has got me all twisted up inside. I hate this feeling.

"Xander being Xander again?" Normally Powell would make a joke, but his mouth is set in a grim line and furrows are etched into his forehead—he might want to talk to somebody about those before they become permanent.

"Among other things. What's going on? Is there an update?" I realize that's a stupid question. There's no other reason an investigator from the NTSB would be sitting in my kitchen. This is clearly not a social call.

"I came here because I thought this news was best served in person," Ethan says. The glance he exchanges with my brother tells me Powell already knows. Maybe I do need whiskey for this. "We've determined the cause of the crash."

"Do I want to know?" I ask. *No, please, I don't.*

Ethan sighs. "This is important. There was a small bomb hidden on the underside of the console. Overall, the device was rather unsophisticated, but they cleverly used an altimeter as the trigger. Once the helicopter reached a certain altitude, it detonated. The explosion wasn't capable of bringing the chopper down by itself, but it destroyed part of the control panel and incapacitated the pilot."

"So someone targeted Jace?" I don't want to think that, but the alternative is more horrifying.

"No. We believe it was meant for Powell."

That's precisely what I didn't want to hear. They'd suspected it before, but I held out hope that they'd find a mechanical failure or pilot error. I down half the whiskey, feeling the fiery liquid burn my throat. It's not strong enough to burn away the pain.

"You can't know that for certain." I say this as a declarative statement, as though loud denial will erase the horrifying possibility.

"Your phone call to Jace occurred about four hours before the flight. The bomb was placed earlier that morning."

"How can you tell?"

"We've tracked down the person who installed it. He was a mechanic who worked for the heliport."

"Why don't either of you seem happy about this?" I look from Ethan to Powell, both of whom have frowns on their faces. "He's in jail, right? Powell is safe now?"

"He's not in jail. He died under mysterious circumstances a few days after the incident."

"But that means it's over, doesn't it? If he's dead he can't make another attempt." I'm sure I sound naïve, but I am going for hopeful. I don't want to spend my nights lying awake and wondering if someone out there wants my brother dead, someone who doesn't care how many innocent victims he has to take out to kill Powell. Jace, the pilot, the two videographers, they were all collateral damage.

"The mechanic wasn't the mastermind. Someone wired him money. A lot of money. The FBI is trying to trace the origins of the deposit. But no, Powell isn't safe." Ethan stares deeply into my eyes, a serious expression on his handsome face. "And neither are you, Cassidy."

"Me?" I don't see what I have to do with it. I'm not the famous one.

"You're his roommate. If the killer wasn't concerned about the other people on the helicopter, there's no reason he'd be averse to killing you if you happen to be nearby."

"I've contacted a security company," Powell tries to reassure me. "We'll be protected. Finish your drink." Before I can pick it up, he tops off my glass and pours another for himself as well.

Drinking when I'm upset is a bad idea. Drinking when I'm shaky from all that happened tonight—fending off Xander, Tanner kissing me, me liking it, and now finding out my brother is being targeted by a killer—is a worse idea. I'm becoming fragile and needy, and I don't like being in that state.

Powell reacts differently than I do. Whereas I want companionship, he wants to be left alone. He abruptly swallows down the rest of his whiskey and disappears to his music room to pound out his sorrows on the piano. That's his way of dealing with frustrations and fears—I expect he'll be playing angry music tonight.

But I'm still in the kitchen with Ethan, and I'm starting to feel warm and lonely and craving human touch.

"Do you think your brother is okay?" Ethan asks, looking in the direction Powell went. He's not aware of my brother's habit of wandering away from conversations.

"He'll be fine." And I know he will, partially because he sort of drifts through life, expecting everything to fall into place around him, and it always does.

"Do you think he's coming back?"

"Probably not."

"Good." And then Ethan leans in and kisses me. That's two different men in one night—definitely a record, but not one I'm going to brag about. The moment feels surreal, because I both want this and I don't. He doesn't make me feel anything, but the whiskey does. The whiskey makes me want to be in the comfort of someone's arms. The whiskey makes me want to forget the world and all my problems for a little while.

When the kiss ends, I pull back from Ethan. "What was that for?" I'm curious how far he expects this to go.

"I need to tell you the truth. I could have given you all the information about the bomb over the phone, but I wanted to see you again."

"Me? Why?" Don't get me wrong, I did immediately find the man attractive when we met, but I never expected to act on that attraction. I'm very selective when it comes to my flings.

"When I met you in California, you were so tough under pressure. You were strong, and in control of the situation, and I just . . . wanted to find out if you were always that way."

In response, I kiss him. He thinks I'm in control, and this is like what Tanner said to me once before, I'm a woman who takes what I want. And right now I just want . . . *something*. I'm lonely, I'm tipsy, and I want some kind of physical connection. So, yeah, an attractive man comes all this way for me, I'm going to kiss the heck out of him. Why not?

"Cassidy," he breathes into my ear. "Shall we take this to your chambers?"

His phrasing is peculiar, but his intentions are clear. And we're in agreement. I certainly don't want to continue this make-out-and-possibly-more session in an area where my brother might find us, so I invite him to my bedroom.

He pauses in the doorway.

"This is your room? I thought it would be . . . darker," Ethan says as he surveys my personal space. That's an unusual observation, but he's not here for his interior decorating advice.

I lead him inside, where we begin making out desperately, driven by alcohol and trauma and fear. And for a moment, I'm enjoying myself. Clothing is coming off, hands are exploring bodies, and we're nearing the bed.

"Am I a bad boy?" Ethan asks as he's biting my neck.

Um, what?

"Sure."

"Tell me I'm a bad boy."

Oh, no. I seem to have found myself a dirty talker.

"You're a bad boy." I'll follow along with this game briefly and hope he soon occupies his mouth with other things and shuts up.

"I am, I'm so very bad. How are you going to punish me, mommy?"

Well, that's a real record scratch moment.

"What did you call me?" I shove him off and back away. After the night I've been having, I'm surprised it was able to get any weirder. I thought I'd already reached peak oddity levels.

He's panting heavily. "Come on, Cassidy, I know what you're like. I could tell from the moment I met you. You're tough, you're fierce, you need someone to dominate." He drops to his knees in front of me, holding his arms up, wrists together as though tied. "I'm ready for my punishment."

"You called me mommy." The sudden queasiness in my stomach has nothing to do with how much I drank.

"Do you prefer mistress? Did I do something bad? Spank me, mistress. Spank me hard." He crouches on all fours now, fully expecting me to grab the closest paddle—which apparently, he assumes I have. This has gone far enough.

I wake up slightly headachey and fully regretful. Ethan is worse for the wear. I told him his punishment was to sleep on my bathroom floor, and for some strange reason he obeyed, directly on the cold tile. He didn't even put a towel down, nor did he accept the blanket I offered. I bet he thought that at one point I would decide he had been sufficiently punished and would allow him to come to bed and service me. If he were a smarter man, he would have figured out that it was never going to happen and stayed in a guest room instead, but I guess that doesn't fit with his kink.

"Is there anything else you'd like me to do, mistress?" he asks hopefully when I wake him up, and now I want to drive my hungover head through the wall.

"Let's go eat breakfast and you don't act like this in front of anybody else."

But of course, Powell is already up—why didn't he sleep in today?—and is in the kitchen when we emerge. Ethan is wearing a pair of my sweatpants and an old t-shirt, which he was only too happy to put on. I may let him keep them; I don't think I want those clothes back.

The smirk my brother gives me says it all: I'm never going to hear the end of this. Fine. After what I went through last night, I deserve his teasing, even without him knowing the real details.

Powell is eating with his newly arrived bodyguard, and I'm relieved to discover he's hired Mike Ochoa. Mike can be summed up in one word: awesome. At first glance, nobody would ever believe he is a bodyguard. He's nerdy and wears glasses, and if he were to be typecast in a movie he'd be the quiet unnoticed accountant in the background. I suspect his glasses aren't real, and they probably conceal weapons. Tiny poison darts, or knives, or a lock pick set.

If anyone made it past Mike's nondescript exterior to really study him, they'd notice his forearms are ropey with muscle and when he moves his neck little bits shift beneath the skin, muscles that don't exist on most mortal men. He's fast, too, and smart. Also, he's an expert in five or six different kinds of fighting, and he carries a gun concealed so well you'd never know it was there until he's pointing the barrel at your head. Powell couldn't be in better hands.

"Morning, Cass," Mike greets me cheerfully. He and I get along well. He was head of security on Powell's last tour, so we shared a bus for a several months. That's how I learned not to play poker with him. Or any card game. I don't like losing.

"I'm so happy to see you," I reply, hugging him. I'm not merely giving him a friendly welcome; I'm secretly trying to see if I can find any weapons hidden under his shirt. Other than the muscular guns in his sleeves, of course. "Do I get a bodyguard too?"

Mike is about to answer, but Ethan interrupts.

"You aren't in any danger, and if you were, I'd protect you." A couple of problems here: for one thing, he's heading back to wherever he came from today, so no, he's not going to be around to protect me. And what's with saying I'm not in danger, when before he said I was? Was that a line? Oh. Oh, it was, and I fell for it too. Bad Cassidy.

"This is Ethan, he's one of the investigators in Jace's murder," I introduce my disappointing almost-lover to Mike, and the horror of that again washes over me. Someone murdered Jace Monroe, my dear friend, and worse, it was a case of mistaken identity because they were trying to kill the person I love most in the world.

"You'll be fine, Cass, I'm keeping eyes on you, but nobody thinks you're a target. Powell isn't going anywhere without me until this is resolved." Mike makes the proclamation with confidence, but it doesn't assuage my fears.

"So what's the plan now?" I ask. I assume some kind of security upgrade to our house. Maybe defensive turrets, mounted guns, an entire entourage of Mike's highly trained personnel moving in. Sure, he said I don't get my own bodyguard, but I wouldn't turn one down.

"We start with home safety. I've already taken care of the perimeter. This morning my men are examining all the windows, and I need to check your panic room, make sure it's fully stocked."

"It is," Powell assures him. "I always keep it prepared."

Mike's skeptical expression means he's going to check anyway which he should—I know what Powell thinks *prepared* means.

"So, what food did you put in there?" I ask my brother pointedly because I already know the answer. I was in the panic room that connects our closets last week, switching out books. I keep my to-be-read stack in there, so if we get trapped I have something to entertain me. The only food I saw was my candy stash and a bottle of merlot.

"Food? What for? How long do you think we'd have to hang out in there? No, I have my cello and an electronic keyboard. That's all I need." Basically, music is life, is what Powell is saying. This is why he has staff to take care of him. Or, rather, this is why he *needs* staff to take care of him.

"Why a cello?" Ethan asks. His interest in the conversation piqued when the panic room was mentioned. I bet he's picturing it as a dungeon, the way he imagined my bedroom.

"It took up too much space in the music room. Made it look cluttered."

"And that's why I'm in charge of security," Mike informs him. "You can have your cello, but you're also going to have forty-eight hours' worth of actual supplies, just in case." Ethan nods along with this pronouncement, as though being an accident investigator gives him some insight into the world of personal security. Though I suppose it's possible that, like Mike, he is ex-military. I really don't know anything about him besides his job title and his humiliation fetish.

"Whatever, we'll deal with that later. What I'm more interested in is when the FBI gets here." Powell's voice is way too enthusiastic. You aren't supposed to be excited when killers are after you, even if it does give you the apparently exciting opportunity to meet real FBI agents. "They'll be here any minute."

I've watched the movies, so I know exactly what to expect from the FBI. We'll have a whole team here, and they'll bring computers and establish a command center in our living room. They'll connect to everything, our security cameras, the neighbor's security cameras, they'll likely hack some satellites so they can look down from above.

Our case will be assigned to two agents. One will be younger and sexy. He'll have short hair and a chiseled jaw, and I'll be able to tell by looking in his eyes that he's seen some *things*, some hard and difficult things. He'll be single, of course. They all are, because relationships don't survive the job. But he and I will form an instant powerful connection, beyond just sexual chemistry, though that will initially predominate. The other agent will be an older, wiser man, bald and with a bit of a gut. He's been on the job for a long time and he's familiar with the criminal syndicate that is targeting my brother. We'll trust his smart grandfatherly vibe, and he'll share pithy words of wisdom while tracking down the perpetrator, the one Agent Sexy will bring down in a firefight. I might be as excited as Powell about this.

But when the doorbell rings, it isn't who we expect. No, it's Tanner, because somehow the gate guard can't get it through his head to stop letting that man through without checking with us first.

Mike answers the door and lets him in because Powell says so. He doesn't ask me, or I would have sent him away. Well, maybe not, since he's carrying a box of donuts.

"Cassidy, I wanted to talk to you . . ." he begins, but then he notices Ethan perched on the kitchen stool next to me. "Oh, sorry, you're obviously . . . busy."

"This is Ethan"—crap! I don't remember his last name!—"from the National Aircraft Safety Board."

"National Transportation Safety Board, babe," Ethan corrects me. So I've transitioned from mommy to mistress to babe, all in a twelve hour period? Does he think we've reached the faux relationship level of him calling me pet names in front of others? What's with every guy getting so possessive over me lately?

Tanner's eyes meet mine and his lips press into a grimace. Disgust? Disappointment? Whatever it is, it makes little tiptoes of guilt creep up my spine, even though I should have nothing to feel guilty about. "I brought you some breakfast. But since you have company, I'm going to head out." He sets the box down on the nearest counter and walks away.

"Tanner, wait!" I chase after him, catching him right outside the front door, but he jerks his arm out of my grip.

"I came by because I thought we should talk about what happened last night," he says. "But after what I just saw, I don't think we have anything to talk about after all."

"That wasn't what you think."

"I'm sure it wasn't. I'm sure pink sweatpants are the standard uniform of the NTSB."

"Ethan only came here to give us an update about the helicopter explosion."

"This morning?"

"No, he was here when I got home last night, but—"

"So it is what I thought. Cass, you don't owe me an explanation. You don't owe me anything at all." And apparently that's the end of the discussion. He does an about face and strides off angrily toward his van. Seriously? He won't stick around long enough to listen to me? How immature.

Fortunately, his window is down as he drives away, giving me the opportunity to have the last word.

"Those pants aren't pink, they're fuchsia!"

He doesn't acknowledge hearing my shout, which is an extra layer of irritation on an already irritating morning. Screw him. I'm going in, I'm eating a donut out of spite, and I'm getting rid of Ethan.

Unfortunately for me, by the time I return to the kitchen, Mike has wrapped the donut box in plastic and disposed of it.

"Sorry, Cass. Don't know that guy, not taking any chances. I haven't verified whether that shop is peanut free." Friggin fantastic. I really wanted one of those. At least he didn't discard the offering in front of Tanner, that would have made this whole situation much worse. *Thanks for the apology food, we're trashing it now.*

So, I was wrong. Deeply, disappointingly wrong.

Soon after Ethan leaves—which he thankfully does without asking to be punished first—two FBI agents show up, but that's all. No big team of hackers. And the agents are both women. I'm not complaining. Women are equally as capable as men, if not more so. I'm just disappointed. I mean, one of them is kind of attractive but I don't swing that way. All my fantasies involving Agent Sexy dissolve instantly.

Agents Benítez and Johnson sit down with all of us at the dining room table so we can have a frank discussion about Powell's enemies. Except the problem is, we can't come up with any. Don't get me wrong, the guy is not universally loved. Every celebrity gets the occasional hater, whether it's a disagreement with the 'politicization of music videos' (yes, that's a real complaint he got when he shot *Live Free* outside of a marriage equality rally), or someone who just hates the celebrity's fashion/hairstyle/eating habits. But those haters manifest as anonymous online trolls who hide behind keyboards and would wet themselves if they had to have an in-person confrontation. I imagine most of them aren't old enough to drive, much less old enough to get a job and save enough money to pay someone to blow up a helicopter.

Eventually, they separate us for individual questioning. I expected this, based on my history of being interviewed by the NTSB back when we thought this was an accident. I briefly wonder if we should invite Powell's lawyer over here, but he's in California and does contracts, not criminal investigations. And it doesn't matter, as we aren't suspects—or at least, we shouldn't be.

Agent Benítez and I go into the sunroom. She tells me to call her Yasmin, which I'm not going to do. I immediately recognize it as a tactic to make me comfortable, so I'll be more open. It doesn't work on me; I'll be open anyway, without creating the illusion of false friendliness. Why wouldn't I tell her everything? I want the perpetrator to suffer. I'm not inclined to forgive the person who killed Jace, robbing the world of a phenomenal talent. Plus, they tried to kill Powell, and may try again.

"You and your brother seem pretty close," she says. It's not a question, but I still give an answer.

"We are. He's my best friend. And I work for him."

"But you didn't meet until you were twelve?"

"That's correct. I spent my formative teenage years as his sister. We bonded." We were both hurting after losing a parent, and it was one of the first deep conversations we had. I think that's why Powell took me under his wing. He took care of me because we had a shared pain. Besides, he always wanted to be a big brother. He asked for a baby sister for Christmas every year until his mother's cancer diagnosis. I'm his much-delayed gift, or so I often remind him when we're arguing. *You wanted a sister, buddy, you deal with the consequences.*

"And you were close with the other Last Barons as well?"

"I worked on their tours, first as a merch girl and later as a production assistant. We spent a lot of time on buses together."

"Did you ever date or have sex with any of them?"

Wow, that's an invasive personal question, and quite the sudden jump. I recognize what she's doing here, she's trying to catch me off guard. I read police procedurals, I know the tactics, or at least the tactics in gritty worlds where the heroes are always attractive but emotionally scarred and the criminals always pay.

"Of course not. We were like a family. I knew them too well to have any interest in sleeping with any of them." One was completely off the table, Devon was always taken, Mason was way too experienced (and I suspect disease-ridden) for me, and Xander was—and still is—to put it politely, gross. And Jace, well, he turned me down.

"According to news reports, you were the love of Jace's life."

"According to Jace's will, I was." I wait patiently for her to ask more questions, because I'm certainly not going to elaborate on that. None of this should be relevant.

"But you were never in a relationship with him?

"No. It was never the right time for us." Yep, I trotted out that tired old line. "He made it clear in his will how he felt about me. He didn't necessarily make it clear in life."

"So, no sexual relationship with Jace. What about Powell?"

"Excuse me?" She'd better not be asking what I think she is asking.

She looks down at her notebook. "I understand a few years ago there was an article published outlining a certain intimate encounter between you and Powell."

I swear my vision darkens and I have to clench my hands into fists and take a few long slow breaths before I can answer. "That was a lie. There has never been any sexual contact between Powell and me. We sued the tabloid into oblivion for publishing that."

I've never regretted anything more than I regret staying in Powell's hotel room that night. Not that I had a choice. He was babysitting my drunken self, rescuing me from my own stupidity. It was the same night I decided I was ready, willing, and able to lose my virginity and tried to hand my v-card to be stamped by the oh-so-hot Jace Monroe. And after he rejected me and broke my heart, I reassessed my plans for the night and gave up the virgin drinks instead.

I remember nearly passing out on a couch and creepy Xander suggesting he could take care of me. And then Powell came from out of nowhere, punched him in the face—Xander's black eye was a huge hassle for the makeup artist—scooped me in his arms and carried me away. He took me to his room, cared for me as I was sick, gently wiped the vomit from my face and held me as I shook with embarrassment. My brother softly soothed me and assured me that I was beautiful no matter how snidely Jace had laughed, no matter how cruelly he had mocked my advances.

That entire article was based upon Powell being seen carrying my barely conscious body away from the post-show party and me being spotted sneaking out of his room the following morning, still in my clothes from the night before. Some made-up source claimed Powell bragged about it, with the falsest quotes I've ever heard. I guarantee my brother has never used the term "deflowering" in his life, and he's never been one to kiss and tell. Or cheat, and he had a girlfriend at the time. But I was still forced to submit to an exam as part of the proof for both the lawsuit and a criminal investigation against my brother. The first person to ever touch my private parts was a sexual assault nurse examiner. While she was very professional and considerate, it was still traumatizing, and made worse by the fact that all of the "evidence" had to be handed over to the opposing party. My suffering earned us our eventual settlement and the destruction of that awful lying tabloid.

But I'm not going to share any of those details for this investigation. I'm not going to talk about the way Jace looked at my naked teenage body when he found me waiting in his room, or the way his words, *go home, little girl, you think I'd be interested in a child?* seared into my soul. How I was questioned afterward about my drinking as though my drunkenness was an ongoing problem, rather than a first-time event. How Powell was my rock through that whole time, even while dealing with the tarnish to his golden image in the media, constantly having to defend himself and my overnight presence in his hotel room.

Benítez stares at me as though she's analyzing my response and waiting for more. She's using silence to try to make me uncomfortable so I start babbling and accidentally reveal all my secrets. Unfortunately for her, that won't work on me. I'm comfortable with silence.

"Did the rest of the band believe the rumors?" she finally asks, when it becomes obvious I'm not going to offer any further details.

"Of course not! They knew both of us. Mason was there the night it supposedly happened. He was deposed—is that the right word? Depositioned? Whatever they call those interviews to gather evidence." He was the one who gleefully provided me with the alcohol and laughed at my increasing intoxication. Mason's involvement didn't damage his wild-child reputation. If anything, it enhanced it.

"What about Jace?"

"Jace was aware that the tabloid story wasn't true," I say. "They all were, Jace, Devon, Xander. How does that old rumor have anything to do with what's going on now?"

"I'm just trying to cover everything. That was the most negative publicity he ever got, and my understanding is that it led to the break-up of the Last Barons."

"No, they broke up two years later, and only because they were all ready to move on. Boybands don't last forever. You have to go out on a high note and start solo careers while still on top. It was a marketing decision, really." Marketing, and a tiny bit of animosity and jealousy developing amongst the singers. But that had nothing to do with me, and everything to do with Xander and his desperate need for attention.

"Did any of the other band members have enemies?"

"Probably. Ask them," I say. How should I know? I didn't even know Powell did and I live with the guy. I'm still not certain that he does. Although I suppose he must if someone is trying to kill him. Good friends and admirers don't do that sort of thing.

"We're wondering if they've been targeted as a group," Benítez says. She leans forward. "Is there anyone you can think of with a collective hatred for them?"

"You think the bomb was just the start?" If I'm understanding correctly, she means Powell wasn't targeted for himself, he was the first of five. The bomber might have been thrilled to kill Jace and is now going after the others as well.

"It's possible. It's possible the mastermind behind the attack only knew about the presence of a Last Baron on the flight without knowing which one." That makes sense; it was booked by their production company. We already know Jace wasn't the intended victim, since the only ones who knew he was there were me, Powell, and the people who died with him.

"Have you contacted the others?" My immediate concern is for Mason. He has a brand-new baby, he needs to be aware of the threat. And Devon is off "finding himself" somewhere isolated, so he's an easy target, for anyone who can afford the travel. I'm fairly certain *isolated* refers to a private tropical island.

"They're being interviewed as well. And they have their own security teams."

When my interview concludes, I am invited to join Powell's. We spend hours with Agent Johnson, combing through his mentions on every social media site and cataloging the haters and trolls making nasty comments. Nobody jumps out as the sort of person who would plant a bomb on a helicopter. In the weeks leading up to the bombing, most chatter about him was whether he'd bring back his signature Last Barons haircut for the reunion concert (No! No, he will not! That style is dead and buried and should never be brought back).

And whoever it is can't be someone we know in real life—we certainly don't know anyone capable of making any kind of explosive, or even learning how to do it. Honestly, Powell's friends aren't all that internet savvy. They can post on social media, because keeping in the public eye is part of their jobs, but they can't access the dark web and learn how to make things explode. They lack the skills, and hopefully, the inclination.

"He thought it was a bug," Powell says, hanging up the phone. I'm sitting in the kitchen eating an unfamiliar pasta dish Joel left in the fridge. I freeze with my next bite halfway to my mouth. A bug? Is he talking about this food? Last time he was over, our chef did tell me some long story about the health benefits of meal worms.

"I thought it was a mushroom." I carefully examine the brown bits on the tines of my fork. It looks like a mushroom. Joel knows I'm a vegetarian, and bugs should count as meat.

"No, the mechanic."

"What mechanic?" Sometimes I have to pry details from him. Powell lives in his head most of the time, so he has a bad habit of continuing conversations that I wasn't a part of.

"The helicopter mechanic." Powell sighs impatiently. "The guy who attached the bomb to the console? Remember?"

"Of course I remember his existence, but you need to use details in your stories if you expect people to understand what you're talking about. You have a personal mechanic, too."

"Yeah, and did I tell you he said he may have found a way to . . . never mind, car talk." I guess he noticed my eyes glazing over. "Anyway, like I was saying, the helicopter mechanic. He was paid to place the bomb, but he thought he was installing a listening device from some gossip magazine. He did it for the money, obviously, but he had no idea anybody would die."

"How do you know?" I ask through gritted teeth. I wish there were a way to teach Powell how to start stories from the beginning. It would save a lot of time and questions.

"That was Agent Johnson who called. She said they interviewed the guy's wife. He confessed to her after Jace died. He was trying to decide what to do. He wanted to come forward and help the investigation, but she encouraged him not to, because she was afraid he would go to jail. Then two days later, he was killed in a carjacking."

"That's not a coincidence, is it?" This situation is getting scarier. Carjacking is a more hands-on type of murder.

"Nobody thinks so. The wife called the FBI because she's terrified. Unfortunately, she doesn't know who it was or how they contacted her husband. But at least the FBI has a lead to follow now."

"You're enjoying this, aren't you?" It's an uncharitable thing to say, but Powell does seem rather excited. He immediately switches into his serious interview face, the one he uses when he's talking about charity work or celebrity tragedies.

"No, Deedee, of course not. Somebody is dead. But isn't it starting to sound like a mystery? We can solve it. We'll call ourselves the Corbitt Siblings Detective Agency, and we'll buy a hypo-allergenic dog and matching hats."

"Yes, brilliant idea. And what happens when we're inevitably captured by your enemies? This is real life, Powell. They'll kill you. It's not like the movies where the bad guys take twenty minutes to give every detail of their evil plan and the good guys save the day at the last minute. Mike's not going to jump in front of a bullet for you."

"He'd better. That's what I pay him for."

"No, you pay him to keep you from getting anywhere near the bullets in the first place."

"True." Powell sighs and then helps himself to some of my pasta. Gross, I don't need his unwashed hands reaching into a meal I'm suddenly suspicious of anyway. I'm no longer entirely sure it contains mushrooms.

"You finish this." I shove the plate at him, but he only picks at the food, though thankfully with a fork. Something must be wrong. "How are you holding up?" I finally ask.

"I'm scared," he admits. "Someone killed my friend, and they may still be trying to kill me. I have no idea who they are, and I don't know how to protect myself or even if another attack is going to happen. Mike wants me to stay inside all the time."

"Our windows are bullet proof, right?" He'd paid a lot of money to re-do all the windows when we moved into this house. Back then he was worried about stalkers, because one of his movie star friends had been shot. That case ended up being a hoax; the movie star had been irresponsibly playing with a gun and made up the stalker story, but there was still a rush on sales of bullet proof glass among the rich and famous crowd.

"Yeah, but not bomb proof."

"I think they'd try a different method next time. If there is a next time." I don't know why I'm giving false reassurances to him like this; I have no idea how mad bombers think. Also, *they'll try another way to kill you* probably isn't as comforting as I'd intended.

"I'm sure the investigation will turn something up. We'll be fine." Powell's always been an optimist. That's why he needs me around. Someone has to be a realist and occasionally remind him that everything doesn't always work out in the end.

TWELVE

I'm working out at my gym when Tanner walks in. I haven't seen him in almost two weeks, since the disastrous night out with Xander and the even more disastrous donut delivery. I kind of want to talk to him, clear the air. It's not like I meant to "use" him, as he claimed.

He takes the stationary bike right next to me, even though there are two others open. But he doesn't say anything, he puts in his headphones and starts pedaling. I wait a few minutes, but he doesn't glance my way at all. What a dramatic baby.

"You're exactly like everybody else, aren't you?" I finally say. He takes out an earbud and looks at me, one furry caterpillar eyebrow raised.

"Did you say something?" he asks, even though he knows damn well I did.

"I did. I said you're exactly like everyone else. You're petty and stupid and you don't stick around."

"That's . . . rather insulting. You're the one who—"

I raise my hand to cut him off. "I'm not the one who did anything wrong. You keep saying you want to be my friend, but that's all fake. You don't listen; you don't care. But I guess that means my first impressions were correct, and you're nothing but another scheming paparazzo."

While perhaps he doesn't necessarily deserve it, I'm lashing out because: 1) Tanner was right, it did seem like I was using him; and 2) he kissed me and I liked it and then he got all weird and I ended up making out with a guy who called me mommy and asked me to paddle him. Okay, maybe I'm somewhat responsible for that last part. Maybe.

"I told you, I'm a serious photographer! And I *thought* we were friends, but you invited me out to dinner just to make some other man jealous. That's selfish and lousy, Cass." His brow furrows in anger and he aggressively speeds up on his bike. I find myself pedaling harder as well.

"That's not why I invited you! I asked you to come with me because we *were* friends, and I thought you'd appreciate a free meal at an expensive restaurant. Powell came up with a last-minute excuse, and if I have to deal with Xander, I'd rather not do it by myself."

"Then maybe you should have warned me in advance! Xander was incredibly obnoxious," Tanner says. He's broken out in a sweat and he's breathing hard now. Ha! This is nothing to me. I up my speed because I like to show off sometimes.

"He's the worst," I confirm. "But you've met him before, so you knew that. It's not like I lied and told you we were meeting up with somebody else."

"The food was good," Tanner admits. He's slowing down.

"It was." I think I've won. But I go a little faster, just to rub it in. Behold my superior physical condition and weep, Tanner.

"You seriously weren't trying to make him jealous? I thought maybe you liked him or something."

"What is this, ninth grade? No, Xander is terrible. I only have to put up with him because he's Powell's ex-bandmate. Even Powell doesn't like him very much."

"What about the other guy? Pink sweatpants guy?"

"Fuchsia, and I told you, it wasn't what you thought."

"What was it then?" Tanner's pedaling is slowing even more. He's at a child's walking pace now.

"I can't tell you because if I did, you'd die laughing and I don't want my staff to have to haul your dead body out of here or deal with towing your van."

There it is! I saw a brief flash of dimple.

"Would you tell me over drinks?"

"Depends on the drinks."

"Whatever you want. The money from the Powell photo landed in my account today, so it's my treat. Are you working out much longer?" Ah, no wonder he was so easy to tease into a better mood. That, and he's a gracious stationary bike race loser.

"I'll be finished soon, then I need a quick shower. Maybe meet out front in a half hour? We can take my car." That's not altruism, I'm just not interested in riding around in his crappy van.

After Tanner walks away—after the shortest cardio workout ever—Powell and his ever-present human shadow come over to say hello. Mike is wearing a baggy sweatshirt, which creates the illusion that he doesn't have the world's most powerful body. If I were him, I'd show it off, but he prefers discretion.

"They let you out?" I ask. Powell gives Mike the side-eye.

"Temporary reprieve. I like using your studio to practice. He let me come in for a rehearsal and now I want to go out for Mexican. Can we trade cars?"

"Depends. Are you getting your food to go? I don't want my car to stink." I know his usual order; I don't want that meaty smell permeating my custom vegan leather seats.

"No, eating in. We've already had the restaurant checked out." Mike is not Powell's only security goon, he's just the only one visible at all times.

"Which car did you drive?"

"The Phantom Drophead Coupe."

I blink at him, like I don't recognize the name. It always irritates him when I act like I can't tell his many vehicles apart.

He sighs deeply, annoyed at my disinterest in his hobbies. "The blue Rolls-Royce convertible that you call a pretentious land yacht but everybody else likes it."

"Oh, that one. Sure, as long as Mike is doing the driving. Wait, why are we trading? What's going on?"

"Nothing, Mike's just paranoid. He thinks someone was following me."

"So I should trick them into following me instead? You're setting me up?"

"It's not like that, I promise," Mike assures me. "It's a convertible, so you leave here with the top down, everyone knows it's you. You won't be followed."

"But someone was following you earlier?" I press. This is scary for me, mainly because I love my brother and I don't want anything bad to happen to him. But also, I don't want to be collateral damage.

"I'm not sure," Mike says. "I thought I saw someone, but it could have been a coincidence. None of my men spotted anything. You'll be fine. I've got eyes on you, and you're not a target."

People keep saying that, but it doesn't mean I'm not at risk. Whatever, I'll have Tanner with me. Not that he's some kind of bodyguard, but he's very obviously not Powell. And he'll stand up for me if anyone confronts us. It might have been a harmless stalker following them earlier anyway. One of the legions of female fans hoping to engineer a meet-cute and make Powell fall in love at first sight. That happens more often than one might expect. The attempt, that is. Bumping into a rich and famous person and having them instantaneously fall in love with you is limited to romantic fiction.

Tanner is waiting for me in the parking lot. He cleans up nicely, though his hair is doing its own thing, as usual. He waves and asks where my car is. I point and click the key fob to make it flash its headlights at us, and his jaw drops.

"You traded up."

"It's Powell's."

"Can I drive?"

"Nope." We get in, and I lower the top for the benefit of the potential stalker. Tanner touches everything, runs his hands over the leather seats, starts hitting buttons. I watch in amusement. "What are you, a five-year-old?"

"This is the fanciest car I've ever been in," he says, almost in awe. Any second now I expect him to pull out his phone and start taking selfies for his SwiftaPic followers, but he doesn't.

Since he's so impressed and the bar we're going to is so close, we decide to go for a short drive first, a scenic detour. We head toward the mountains, music playing, wind in our hair. It's a perfect evening for a drive like this.

"I can't believe Powell works on his own vehicles." Tanner slides his fingers over the dashboard reverently. I didn't realize he was such a car guy.

"He doesn't." I can't imagine Powell getting his hands dirty. He loves *washing* his cars, he'll spend an entire weekend doing that, shirtless, of course. But when it comes to tinkering with their internal engine bits, he uses the mechanic he keeps on call. He likes to watch over the mechanic's shoulder and talk about what the guy is doing, but he doesn't dare assist. My brother is paranoid that heavy metal bits might slip and break his fingers, which would destroy his piano and guitar playing.

"That wasn't him?"

"Who?"

"I saw someone's legs under this car in the parking lot earlier tonight. I assumed it was someone fixing something or checking out the engine."

His words set off alarm bells in my mind. I pull over so fast the brakes squeal, which may get me in trouble with my brother, but he's the least of my concerns right now.

"Get out."

"What? Why, what'd I say?"

"Just get out of the car, now." I've already undone my seatbelt and grabbed my purse. "Now, Tanner."

I'm out the door and walking away quickly, pulling my phone out to call Powell when I hear the pounding footsteps of Tanner running after me.

"What's going on? Cassidy?" He grabs my shoulder, but I ignore him.

"Powell!" I shout as soon as my brother answers. "Someone was messing with your car in the gym parking lot."

"Are you sure?" he asks. "Let me put you on speaker."

Mariachi music blares, followed by Mike's voice.

"Cass? It's Mike. Describe exactly what happened."

"Tanner saw someone under the car back at the gym," I tell them, and Mike starts to swear.

"Where are you? Where's the car now?" Powell asks, but I can't answer. I am blown off my feet by the explosion.

THIRTEEN

On television, when a car explodes, the nearest by-standers—usually the heroes, because explosions are fatal to villains—are thrown in the air. They windmill their arms, land together, stagger to their feet and immediately afterward check to make sure that the other is okay. They can do that because they've hit the ground in the same place, and they, of course, are uninjured, except for artfully placed smears of dirt or soot.

That's not how it happens in real life.

In real life, the shockwave does send you flying through the air. In my case, instead of performing the movie hero maneuver of propelling my arms as though swimming, I let go of my phone and instinctively protect my face. I feel like I'm diving, forced through supercharged air by heat and fire and bits of metal that burn my skin.

When I land, it's not so much a crash as it is a skid, my body violently sliding across the asphalt. My arms bear the brunt of the injury, leaving my right shoulder and both forearms shredded and bleeding. I might be screaming, but it's hard to tell. I just know I hurt and the world is suddenly silent.

Someone grabs me, rolls me over. It is an older man in a dark green polo. For some reason all I can fixate on is the little logo on his shirt. *Hello, crocodile.* He is shouting at me, or so I assume by the way his mouth is moving, but I can't hear anything at all. Maybe I'm in shock. Where is Tanner? He was right next to me, but now he's gone. I attempt to turn my head and look for him, but the man stops me, prevents me from moving. A gray-haired woman kneels beside me, pats my head, and wipes something off my cheek. She is on the phone, probably with the police. Red and blue lights are filling the sky now, though no sirens pierce the silence.

Paramedics lean over me. One puts an oxygen mask over my face. I try to fight it off, but they restrain me. My arms are stinging with pain, my shirt is torn and bloody, and my whole body is tight, like I strained all my muscles at once. As they load me into an ambulance, I finally spot Tanner, or presumably, it's him. Nobody else was on the road with us. They're putting him on a stretcher face down. Something must be horribly wrong. But at least they aren't covering him with a white sheet.

The paramedic is mouthing words at me, but I can't respond through the mask. I finally manage to pull it off and tell him, "I can't hear you." He nods as if he already knew. Maybe that's normal.

"Can you call my brother?" My phone is missing. I have a vague memory of dropping it. "Call my brother, please," I plead. I'm shaking now, I don't know why. Is it cold? I feel cold. The paramedic injects me with an unknown substance, and my eyes are closing of their own accord. I fight to stay awake. I need to know what's going on.

I wake up in a hospital bed. Someone has cleaned me up. I'm in one of those awful flimsy gowns, and the bloody wounds on my arms have been scrubbed and bandaged. "Hello?" I call, and then I notice a doctor standing nearby holding a chart. Was she there before? She smiles and her mouth moves, but no sounds come out.

Then she pulls out a notepad and writes *You've been in an explosion. Do you remember what happened?*

I accept the offered pad from her and write *I can't hear any-thing*. Writing is difficult; my bandages catch on the edges of the paper and my hands are sore. It's hard to grip the pen.

She laughs and takes it back. *Yes, that's common. You don't need to write; I can hear you.*

"Sorry. Where's Tanner?"

Was that the man you were with? I nod. *Don't worry, he's going to be fine.*

Her words do not give me solace. Don't doctors often lie to patients about bad news during the healing process? Tanner could be just fine, or he could be dying painfully.

"Will my hearing come back?" I ask, which is my other big concern at the moment.

Most likely. Your eardrums are damaged. We're trying a new treatment that is used on soldiers in war. I'll bring you a pamphlet.

I'd rather she wrote it all down for me now, so I can get myself in the right headspace to process a possibly silent future. My life revolves around my brother's music, so I have to be able to hear it. Otherwise, how can I critique him in a harsh yet sisterly manner?

Your family is outside. Can they come in?

"Yes, of course!" I'm so relieved they're here.

If you'd like to permit me to discuss your medical condition with them, I need you to sign these forms. She gives me a clipboard with HIPAA paperwork, and I eagerly but clumsily grant permission for her to tell them everything, though I think it's rather insensitive of her to focus on bureaucracy at a time like this.

Mom is the first one through the door, and the first to navigate through the tubes of my IV and the monitor wires in order to give me a careful hug. I can't hug back very well. Despite what I presume are painkillers traveling down my IV line, my arms ache, and they're completely wrapped in gauze bandages. I don't even want to imagine what the torn-up skin looks like underneath.

Hank doesn't try to maneuver around the medical equipment. He stays at the end of the bed, but his comforting hands briefly squeeze my foot. I can't tell the words he's saying, but I think he's conveying love and relief.

And then there's Powell, with his ever-present bodyguard. He comes to the side opposite my mom and is slightly less careful than her when he leans in to embrace me. He squeezes me much tighter too, and when he pulls away I can see the absolute sorrow and guilt on his face. His mouth is moving, and *I'm sorry, I'm so sorry*, is what he had better be saying.

"I'm deaf," I announce, and Powell recoils in horror. That might be his worst nightmare. For himself, I mean, not for me. I don't know what he would do if he lost his music.

Mom starts typing into her phone. THE DAMAGE ISN'T PERMANENT. YOU'LL BE ABLE TO HEAR AGAIN SOON.

I certainly hope so. I reach up to touch my ears for the first time and discover a thick wrapping covering both of them.

Powell is typing furiously, thumbs flying. He passes me his phone. I'M SO SORRY I DIDN'T KNOW THERE WAS A BOMB, I SWEAR I NEVER WOULD HAVE TRADED CARS WITH YOU.

"It was a bomb?" I shouldn't be so surprised, but obviously I'm not thinking clearly. What else could it have been? I told Powell the killer would try a different method; if I wasn't injured, he'd be teasing me for being so wrong.

THE FBI IS INVESTIGATING. THEY'VE BLOCKED OFF THE SITE OF THE EXPLOSION AND THEY WANT TO QUESTION YOU AND TANNER.

"Have you seen Tanner yet?" I ask, and they all shake their heads. Hank, who is always the last choice for a charades partner, makes a series of odd gestures that I optimistically interpret as an offer to find Tanner, so I send him off. I need to make sure he's okay, and I trust my stepfather to tell me the truth, even if the news is horrible and scary. I owe Tanner a huge debt of gratitude. If he hadn't mentioned what he saw, we would have been in the car when the bomb went off. "Powell, Tanner spotted a person under your car. If he hadn't said anything, I would have kept driving."

Why'd you get out? Powell asks via text.

"Seriously, Powell? *Someone was under your car*, doing something to it. There are only two possibilities, tracking device or bomb. Either way, I didn't want to be anywhere in the vicinity." Since I can't hear myself, I can't tell what I sound like, but apparently I should be more careful with my tone: I've made my mother cry.

I'm so glad you did, Mom writes as tears pour down her face. I couldn't bear it if something happened to you. I hope she never finds out how close it was. A few seconds later, they would have been picking up pieces of me, if I weren't completely vaporized. I don't know how powerful the blast was, but based on the parts I felt, there couldn't have been much left from the interior of the car.

Hank returns, followed by our FBI agents. I hope they like writing. But before I'm willing to interact with them, I ask my stepfather what he's found out. Some of the tension leaves my body as I read the message he hands me:

> *Tanner says he's going to be okay, though they're monitoring him for a possible head injury. He seemed more worried about you. No broken bones, no major injuries, just thousands of cactus spines from landing in a prickly pear. A couple of interns with tweezers are torturing him right now, but it's for his own good.*

Poor guy. He hasn't lived in Arizona very long; I bet that's his painful initiation to the injured-by-cactus club. I've been a proud member since the day Powell and I went house hunting and a teddy bear cholla proved not to be as soft as it looked. In my defense, my brother touched it too.

Agent Benítez waves to attract my attention and says words I cannot hear. Whatever it was, it caused Hank, Powell, and even Mike to clear out of the room but triggered an argument with my mom. It's like watching an old-time silent film, especially with my mother's exaggerated gestures. Finally, Benítez throws her hands in the air, and my mom takes a seat at my side, smiling triumphantly. She types a quick message on her phone: THEY TOLD ME TO LEAVE THE ROOM. NOT HAPPENING. I'M HERE FOR YOU DD.

I reach out to grasp her hand, grateful for the strength and support she provides. Only the last two joints of my fingers are exposed, but I'm able to curl them around her palm and take comfort in her closeness. Part of me wants to peel back these bandages and examine the extent of my injuries, but I remember seeing a lot of blood, so perhaps I should leave them alone.

"The doctors warned you I can't hear, right?" I ask. Both agents nod, and Benítez holds up a note pad. Yay. This is not going to be fun. "Can I start by telling you everything I remember? Maybe reduce the number of questions you need to write down?"

When they agree, I fill them in on the full story, although there's not much to it. I drove a car, it went boom. Their follow-up interrogation revolves around why Tanner and I evacuated when we did.

"Honestly, it was instinct. Tanner told me he noticed legs sticking out from underneath the car when it was in my parking lot. Powell—this is off the record—doesn't fix his own cars, no matter what he claims. Don't tell him I told you. Okay, back on the record. When Tanner said that, I got concerned because I knew it couldn't have been Mike either, because he would have told me if he'd placed a tracker on the car. That's what I assumed it was because he'd mentioned someone might have been following them earlier. I was afraid the person might show up with guns or something, and I didn't want to be kidnapped or murdered. My instinct was to get away from the vehicle. I called Powell so they could send one of Mike's people to pick us up and arrange a tow truck so that the security team could check it out."

I slump against my pillows. That barely coherent speech exhausted me; I don't have the energy to continue this questioning. My fiercely protective mother is now glaring at the agents for doing this to me, and they are trying to ignore the fire burning in her eyes.

Your instincts saved two lives tonight, Benítez writes, with a cautious glance at my mom. *You were lucky. The bomb was on a timer, set to go off fourteen minutes from when you started the ignition.*

I close my eyes and consider that for a moment. "The drive home from the gym takes about eighteen minutes. If I'd have been going home . . ." I wouldn't have stopped. Anyone following Powell would already know our address; I wouldn't have been concerned about someone tracking me to my house, because they wouldn't get past our gate guard. If I hadn't been going out for drinks with Tanner, I would have died in my neighborhood. And if he hadn't told me what he saw, we both would have been blown to bits in the car. And if he hadn't been so admiring of the car, we would have gone straight to the bar, and the explosion would have happened in a crowded area rather than an isolated road. More innocent people could have been killed. Through sheer luck and a photographer's observation skills we avoided an entire series of deadly possibilities tonight.

The agents clearly have more to say, but the second Johnson opens her mouth, my mom crosses her arms and frowns. I recognize that look from my teenage years. Her expression is the sort to freeze you in your tracks and make you confess all of your sins. Johnson sighs and passes me one last message, assuring me that this incident is staying out of the news, so I won't have to worry about the media harassing me. That's a relief. There's only one member of the media I want to see right now, and he's not able to leave his bed.

The hospital decided to keep me in for "observation," which is a fancy way of saying they did a wallet biopsy and want to extract what they found. But after all the tests, mostly to make sure I didn't hit my head and sustain brain damage, they tell me that I'm fine. Minus the temporary deafness and the dozens of stitches holding the skin on my arms and shoulder together, of course.

While waiting on my discharge paperwork, I insist on visiting Tanner. They only agree to let me if I ride there in a wheel-chair, because apparently having a morphine-addled deaf person wandering the halls is too much of a liability.

He's nearby, only a few doors down. I wish I'd known that before; I would have snuck over without the help of a nursing assistant. When I make my grand rolled entrance, he's lying on his stomach with his head looking toward the door. His eyes light up when he sees me, but he can't sit up to greet me. Rumor has it—or rather, Hank reported—that he was thrown into the prickly pear sideways and somehow managed to roll onto his back, making him into even more of a human pincushion.

"How are you doing?" I ask, before I remember he can't hear either. We're bandage twins right now, as his head is also wrapped to protect his damaged ears.

He answers by extending an arm and giving me a thumbs down. I stand up from my wheelchair, ignoring the aches in my body and the nursing assistant's annoyed gestures. My hearing loss provides a convenient excuse for my intentional disobedi-ence.

There's enough room for me to sit down on the foot of Tanner's bed. He can't see me well from that position, but I can see enough of him—he's wearing nothing but a hospital gown that opens in the back. Nope, I shouldn't sit here. This is an inappropriate view, so I move to stand awkwardly next to the bed instead. If I weren't so injured, I'd drag a chair over, but I don't want to hurt my wounded arms and my surly escort doesn't appear inclined to help.

Tanner is trying to ask me something, but I point to the thick padding wrapped around my head. Supposedly I should start hearing again soon, but all I can make out right now is a distant roaring. Then he exaggeratedly mouths "How are you?"

Oh. I should have guessed that's what he would ask. I point to myself and give a thumbs up, then to my ears and give a thumbs down. He responds, but I can't read his lips sideways. This visit is pointless. We can't hear each other, and with the way he's positioned, he's not capable of communicating via writing.

So I pick up the pad of paper from the bedside table and scribble a note:

I'm so sorry this happened. And I'm so grateful you saved my life. They're letting me go home today. Text me when you get out.

He reads it and moves his head in an approximation of a nod. There's nothing else for me to do, so I plop back into my wheelchair for the short trek back to my room.

FOURTEEN

When I left the hospital, I didn't go home. As the injured survivor of a terrible explosion there is only one place suitable for my recovery: my parents' house. Sometimes a girl just needs her mother.

Also, I'm here because my mom is less annoying than Powell. It's been a week, and he shows up every single day with his set of tuning forks and a pitch pipe. He tests my hearing with a series of questions that he keeps repeating over and over again: *Can you hear this? What about this? Identify the note. Is it sharp or flat? Why are you walking away from me? Hey, give those back!*

Fortunately, after this morning's hearing test, Powell flew out to Los Angeles to do press for the concert. Poor guy is going to be stuck filming promos with Xander. I'm not sure which of us has it worse right now. Probably him, since he's dealing with an overgrown man-child while I'm surrounded by loving support and being coddled. My wounds are at the stage where I have to leave them uncovered so they can heal properly, but mom is monitoring them and rubbing them with salve. She is also making sure I take my steroids and antibiotics on time and providing me with delicious homemade milkshakes as a reward for choking down all the pills.

If my body didn't still ache so much from being blasted through the air onto the hard ground, I would kind of enjoy my current lifestyle. It's nice having someone take care of me, for once.

At the moment, I'm on the living room couch, watching an old black and white detective movie from Hank's collection and picking at my healing lacerations. I know I'm not supposed to, but the stitches are dissolving, and they itch. All I want to do is pull the thread fragments out.

The doorbell interrupts my DIY de-stitching and movie watching, but since it's not my house, I don't have to move. I lay there, like a scabby damaged log, until my mom comes in and claps her hands loudly, the slightly rude method she's been using to get my attention lately. I look up, and immediately jump to my feet. Tanner!

As usual, he gives a good hug, though this time it's slightly tentative due to our injuries. His body is warm and firm and somehow always smells faintly of cinnamon. Could it be something he eats for breakfast? Or his deodorant? I will solve this mystery someday, possibly with my partner in the Corbitt Siblings Detective Agency and our hypothetical hypoallergenic dog. I could just ask, but that would take the fun away.

The hug may have gone on a moment too long because I realize what I'm doing and take an abrupt step back.

"Can you hear now?" I ask.

"Yes. You?"

"Yep."

"Good."

And now we're staring at each other like idiots.

"Go sit down and catch up. I'll bring you a drink," my mom offers. "Tanner, coffee, tea or soda?"

He requests water instead, and we go back to the couch. I move my blanket and pillow and pretend I haven't left a Cass-shaped dent from lying stationary for days.

"I'm glad you came. You never texted me or anything," I reproach him. I assumed that meant he was fine and busy, but it could have equally meant that he'd developed a raging infection from all his puncture wounds and slipped into a coma.

"My phone was destroyed, I only just now got a new one, but I don't have any numbers in it yet. *You* could have texted *me*."

Okay, he makes a valid point.

"Did Powell get it for you?" I ask, but only because he pulled it out of his pocket and it's the exact same not-yet-released-to-the-public model that my brother bought me. Maybe I'm not as special as I thought.

"Well, yeah." Tanner seems a bit sheepish. "He felt bad about his car almost killing me, so he replaced my phone. He offered to buy me new clothes too. Mine were cut off in the ambulance." I bite my lip so I don't laugh at the image of his clothes being sliced off his body. I guess it was the easiest way to get them off, because of all the cactus spines.

"Did he send you to Ramón?"

"Yeah, and that was awkward. When he gave me the address and appointment time, I assumed it was his favorite salesclerk at a store. I didn't know he was sending me to a tailor."

"Powell doesn't buy off the rack." My brother's wardrobe consists of two types of clothing: the faded old comfortable things he wears around the house when it's only us, and the made-exclusively-for-him couture that either arrives in a curated box from his stylist or is created by Ramón. Before Tanner can make another of his "ugh, rich people" comments, I continue, "If you have any other bills, I'm sure he—or his insurance—will cover them."

"We've already worked those details out. Can I see your arms?" He carefully takes my left arm and examines it. "Wow, that had to hurt." He tentatively brushes a finger on the skin between scrapes, and I break out in goose pimples.

"Not as much as landing in a prickly pear." Little raised spots still coat the back of his hand. He's in a long sleeve shirt, but I can imagine those bumps continue upward.

"Yeah, that kind of sucked. They couldn't get all the spines out, so I have to wait for them to work their way through to the surface. When there's enough poking out to grab, I pull it out with tweezers. Everything itches now." He tugs at his sleeve. "That's why I'm wearing this shirt, to keep me from scratching."

"Doesn't the material snag on the pokey bits?" I gently lift his hand and run my fingers across the back until I find one of them, a tiny sharp spike. I've gotten cacti in me before, but never quite so much.

"Sometimes. It's not been pleasant. But I survived an explosion, so when the FBI finally grants us permission to talk about it, at least I have a cool story to share."

My mom interrupts with a tray carrying our drinks—she generously got me a water too—along with chips and fresh guacamole. As she goes to set it down on the coffee table, I catch her eyeing my search for cacti bits, and I immediately drop Tanner's hand. I don't want to give her the wrong impression, but maybe it's too late, because she retreats back to the kitchen with a knowing smile.

After we've enjoyed a few handfuls of chips, he says, "I have a serious question for you. How did we survive?"

"Distance from the car," I respond. He couldn't figure it out for himself? We were close enough to get injured, but far enough to avoid most of the blast and shrapnel.

"Yes, obviously, but how did you know there was a bomb? In the note you wrote me in the hospital, you thanked me for saving your life. Did I shield you or protect you somehow? All the details are hazy to me."

"I didn't know specifically, but I knew something was wrong, because you said you saw someone under the car. Powell doesn't work on his own vehicles, and even if he did, it wouldn't be in the gym parking lot. He doesn't own any clothes he's willing to get that dirty. If you hadn't said anything, I'd have kept on driving."

"And the bomb was on a timer." We are both silent for a moment. We owe each other our lives. "Cassidy, who did this? Was it the same person who killed Jace?"

"Most likely." That's what the professionals seem to think, and who am I to argue?

"You know if you're in danger, you can come stay with me." He manages to make the ridiculous offer with a straight face.

"Oh, great, thanks. I'd love to. Do I get to sleep in the passenger seat or the driver's seat?"

"My van has a bed. It's more spacious than you realize. Plenty of room for two."

"Excuse me?" Is he using this opportunity to hit on me?

His face slowly reddens as he realizes what he suggested. "Not that I think we should . . . I mean . . . I was just thinking no crazed bomber is going to look for you there."

"True, nobody would."

"Yeah, who could ever think you'd be hiding out with someone like me," he mutters under his breath. He's awfully prickly sometimes. Literally and figuratively.

"Relax, Tanner. You don't need to worry about me, I'm perfectly safe. My brother is the target, not me."

"You live with him, and you've already almost been killed once. Next step, the bomber blows up your house." That's a sobering thought. But we have security cameras and Mike. Nobody can get on the property without us noticing. But what if it's a package bomb? Or another one of those car bombs? Has Mike checked Powell's other vehicles? I take a deep breath. I'm the strong one. I can pretend everything's fine, the way I always do.

"Tanner, I'm well protected. The FBI is involved, they'll find the guy soon enough." I project a confidence I no longer feel.

"Or girl. The bomber could be female. An obsessed fan, maybe."

"True. Or perhaps this was unrelated to the other case and they were after you. Maybe your ex-wife is holding a grudge."

"I'll provide her name to the FBI. She'll appreciate that. Or better—I'll tell them I suspect my little brother. He could use a good scare."

We laugh together, and it's so good to see him that I don't even object when my mom invites him to stay for dinner.

FIFTEEN

Three days later, I move back to my own home. I'm healed enough that my mother's fussing has started to become annoying and anyway, Brixley is coming out to check on me. She's not being totally altruistic; she's doing her monthly hide-from-the-media while she's on her period. Something about a bloated belly and not wanting pregnancy speculation.

I'm excited about her visit, our first chance to spend time together since right after Jace's funeral. She and I have been close friends ever since she was cast as *Love Interest #1* in a Last Barons video many years ago. The two of us (me being cast as *Girl in Crowd, second row*) hit it off on set. Not as well as she and Devon did, of course. While it wasn't quite insta-love, the two of them have built an amazing relationship based on mutual respect, a desire for privacy, and a shared love of esoteric knowledge. Seriously. Those two beautiful nerds set up their media room so they can watch all of the lectures the Massachusetts Institute of Technology makes available via their online OpenCourse. That's what they do for fun.

So maybe Brix and I don't have that much in common, but we enjoy each other's company.

"I brought you magic scar remover," she says when she breezes in, handing me a bag from a company with a name I can't pronounce. "All the girls swear by it. And so does my dermatologist." Her dermatologist is actually her father, and back when she was Brianna Oxley, she planned to follow in his footsteps, dreaming of medical school and one day examining other people's disgusting skin conditions. But on a fateful afternoon when she was fourteen, she went to the mall and was discovered. That's right, at the age when the rest of us are gawky and knock-kneed, with zits and braces, she was so beautiful that a talent scout chased her, pressed his card upon her, and begged her to let him call her parents right then and there. If she had kept walking, she would have led a vastly different life.

"Tell your dad I appreciate it," I say, accepting the gift. She's right, I will have terrible scarring on my arms if I don't take care of them properly. Right now my beauty regimen is aloe vera gel and avoiding the sun.

Brixley has been traveling for almost a full day, and is exhausted, so we head out to lounge poolside. I put on sunscreen to protect my fragile new skin. Brix is not only wearing SPF 80, she's also fully dressed in a loose long-sleeved shirt and pants. And she's hiding under a huge sun hat, even though we are in the shade. Her pale skin is integral to her "look," so she can't risk adding any color to it, especially with an upcoming shoot for a multi-page swimsuit spread.

As we're out here, my phone beeps, signaling someone ringing the doorbell. There is exactly one person who has developed a bad habit of dropping by unannounced, and there is exactly one person who has somehow managed to consistently convince the security guard at the gate to grant him access.

"What are you doing, Tanner?" I ask through the intercom. I love this app, I didn't even have to get up from my chair.

"I need a favor. Can I come in?"

Of course he needs a favor, and since he did save my life recently, I'll indulge him. "Fine, walk around to the back, we're at the pool."

"Who was that?" Brixley asks.

"Be warned, it's our local pap."

"I thought this was a safe place," Brixley sighs, adjusting her hat and licking her lips to make them shiny. I feel sorry for her sometimes. She always has to be on.

"I thought so too, but Omaha has been surprisingly lax where Tanner is concerned."

"Don't be too mad. Omaha is trying to be helpful. He warned me about the government spy satellites overhead. And have you heard his thoughts on chemtrails?"

"Yeah, those are part of his latest conspiracy. And don't worry about Tanner. He's at least courteous. He won't shoot you without asking permission."

Tanner comes around the side of the house. He's wearing jeans and a short-sleeved shirt. That's a positive sign—he must not be having as many problems with the cactus spines if he's willing to expose his forearms.

"Sorry, I wasn't aware you had company," he apologizes.

"It's fine. Tanner, meet Brixley."

His eyes widen when he recognizes her famous face. "Wow! I know who you are. Graham Baxter photographed you with a Siberian Tiger."

"Yes, I remember that," she says coolly. She doesn't respond kindly to fans fawning over her. *Aloof* is the defining characteristic of her public persona.

"Wow," he repeats, awed. "That shot was iconic. I was lucky enough to see it full sized in a gallery. What that man can do with natural light is amazing. He's my idol. Cass, you should check out his work, he doesn't use any digital manipulation whatsoever. Do you know the one I'm talking about? I aspire to achieve that level of magic."

Um, yeah, I'm familiar with the photo. It is, as he said, iconic. Everybody in the world has seen Brixley, in all her pale glory, with a live—but tranquilized—Siberian tiger covering up all the naughty bits. Besides, I happened to be there for the shoot, while visiting Brix for a mini vacay. I'm most amused by Tanner's enthusiasm. Only he would be so focused on the photographer and not the supermodel right in front of him.

"It's famous, obviously I know it. Tanner, why are you here?"

"Oh, yeah," he recovers from his excitement at meeting someone who worked with the great Graham Baxter. "I need a huge favor. There's this contest I want to enter . . ."

"Powell's not here."

"It's got nothing to do with him."

"What do you want a photo of this time?" I ask, in a long-suffering voice.

He looks confused. "What? No, not that kind of contest. You know the Rusty Mug, the bar I like?"

"The one down the street from the gym? Yeah." We almost went there together once. Almost.

"They're having a cookie contest. The entries have to go well with beer. I want to make super fudgy pretzel cookies to pair with dark ale, but I don't have a kitchen and you do . . ." he raises his eyebrows and looks at me expectantly. Oh my god, he is sometimes so cute. I hate that about him.

"Go ahead. Do I need to call for a grocery delivery? We probably don't have the ingredients on hand."

There's his dimple producing grin. "I was counting on you to say yes. My groceries are sitting by the front door, all peanut-free. As a thank you, I brought enough to make a batch for you too."

When he heads into the house to start baking, I turn to see Brixley staring at me, one perfect eyebrow arched. "Intriguing. He's cute. I'll make a deal with you. I've got tweezers in my bag. When he comes back out, you hold him down and I'll deal with that eyebrow issue."

"I like his eyebrows," I protest. Sure, they're unruly, but they make his face more interesting. And they distract from that adorable dimple.

"Do you? Good, because he likes you. Maybe I should head back to Cali and let him be the one to nurse you back to health."

"Very funny." It's obvious he's not interested in me. He just comes around because he can make money off us. "He's the guy I told you about, the one who was in the explosion with me. Maybe you should be taking care of him instead."

"Oh?" Now both eyebrows are raised. "Were you on your way to a press event?"

"No, we were going out for drinks."

"You didn't tell me you were on a date! Cassidy! How long has this been going on? And why have you kept it from me?" Brix is way more enthusiastic about her misinterpretation of my relationship than she should be.

"It wasn't a date, just drinks. We're friends," I protest, but she waves my words away.

"Just drinks with a guy who can't take his eyes off you. Seriously, did you not see that? It's the first time I've been ignored. It was refreshing." She relaxes back onto her chaise, a smug smirk on her face. She's wrong, but if I correct her she'll think I'm hiding something by protesting too much.

When Tanner emerges from the house, he's carrying a tray with an artistically arranged plate of cookies and two small glasses of beer. I bet if I pull up his SwiftaPic feed I'll see them posted already. And knowing him, he's crafted a bunch of silly hashtags. *#cookiemadness #chocolatefordays #voteTanner #betterthankCassforherkitchen*

"Okay, you need to try these." He sets the tray on the small table between our lounge chairs. "Wait, I should have asked, Brixley, you eat, right?"

"Everybody eats," she says. He flushes.

"I mean, no gluten intolerances or anything. I assumed you consumed food." I suspect he's backpedaling because he's embarrassed about making assumptions based on her career. But she doesn't seem to mind.

"I eat carefully, but I do eat. And I do like chocolate." She winks at me, leaving off the unspoken *especially at this time of the month*. Me too, sister. Me, too.

"These look delicious," I tell him honestly as I reach for one. He can borrow my kitchen anytime, as long as there are planned leftovers.

"Wait, you have to take a sip of the beer, then try the cookie. And be honest with me. If they don't go together, I'm going to lose." He's watching us, anxious to read our expressions. I'm trying not to laugh at the way he's nervously running his hands through his already tousled hair.

"Is there a prize?" There has to be a reason he's so concerned.

"Bragging rights and a bar T-shirt."

"You're going to a lot of effort for a Rusty Mug shirt. What are they usually, ten bucks?"

"Did you miss the bragging rights part? Those are priceless. Come on, eat." Tanner is practically vibrating with impatience, so Brix and I take sips of beer and chase them with bites of the cookies. And holy baking skills, that man knows what he's doing in the kitchen.

"These are perfect!" Brixley, who has been served pastries on plates of gold from the world's finest chefs, is effusive in her praise. "I'm not kidding. You could open a bakery and sell nothing but these!"

"Nah, baking is my hobby. If it became a job I wouldn't enjoy it anymore," he says. "But I'm glad you like them."

"Are you on SwiftaPic? What's your handle?" she asks, reaching into her bag for her phone and a selfie stick.

"Seriously? It's @TannerTakesPics. But let me get it for you; with this light it needs to come from over here." He takes her phone and moves until he's in the proper place, repeatedly looking at the sky and making slight adjustments to his position before finally taking the shot.

"Lovely." Brixley approves of the image and starts typing an update to her millions of followers.

"Really?" I ask, looking at what she just posted. *OMG! @TannerTakesPics can bake! #chocolate4life*

"Watch your subscriber count go up," Brixley tells Tanner. "If you make another batch and dip them in ganache, I'll even post a selfie with you."

Sure enough, Brixley's offer provided the right incentive. Tanner disappears into the house and returns later with a fresh batch of ganache coated cookies. They are so decadent they almost make my toes curl and my eyes roll back in my head. If I believed in love, I would fall into it with a man who bakes cookies like these.

"Alright, you earned this," Brix pulls out her selfie stick again and gestures for Tanner to get in with her. This could be huge for his career. He needs clients, and hanging out with a popular supermodel is a fantastic way to bring them in. If he has enough people hiring him for portraits, he won't be forced to do contract work for the gossip blogs anymore.

"You too, Cass," he tugs me over next to him. "I couldn't have done it without you."

So even though I hate having my picture taken for social media, I allow it. And then I eat two cookies, because I'm supposed to be taking care of myself, and chocolate has magical healing properties.

After Tanner leaves, Brix opens up her SwiftaPic feed to show me. *Now with ganache! I think I'm in love! #nobodytellDevon @TannerTakesPics @CassBC*

"Very nice," I say, relieved I don't have a ridiculous expression on my face, though as my friend, I'm sure she wouldn't have posted it if I did.

"Look at Tanner," Brixley encourages. "Do you see that?"

"See what?" I scan the image, hoping he has a glob of chocolate on his teeth. That would make me happy.

"See how his head is tilted toward you, not me? It's an indication of interest, and it proves my theory that he's totally into you."

"Stop teasing me. He's just a pap trying to stay on my good side so he can maintain access to my brother."

"I think you're wrong. You know what we should do? We should go to that bar tonight and help him win."

"You actually want to go to a public place, without Devon? Or a bodyguard?"

She waves dismissively. "We'll be fine. Your brother's security constantly has eyes on you. Besides, if anything happens, Tanner will protect you."

"He's not as tough as you think," I point out. If my body still aches from the explosion, I'm sure his does too. Especially since he sleeps in a van. That can't be conducive to healing.

But somehow, I still let her talk me into it. Alright, tonight instead of curling up in the media room with a bottle of wine, we're going to a bar cookie contest.

All the air gets sucked out of the Rusty Mug when we enter. Opening the door creates a vacuum effect that leads to everybody turning, staring, and getting pulled toward us with their mouths gaping open.

But Brixley is used to it. She ignores all the gaping mouths, all the excited whispering, and strides in, head held high. I walk next to her, keeping my face impassive. This is no different from going out with Powell. Actually, no, it's a little different. When I'm with Powell, I have to fend off horny young women from my brother, but men don't bother with me, unless they want me to pass their demo along. Seriously, I've been slipped so much terrible music over the years. With Brix at my side, we run the risk of getting hit on by packs of men who are absurdly confident that up until this very moment, the only thing that's stood in the way of hooking up with a supermodel has been lack of proximity.

Tanner is at the bar raising a glass to his lips, but he almost drops it when he spots us. Then he scans the room, as though wondering who we're here to meet. I give him a little wave thinking *yes, you ridiculous fool, it's you. You made us cookies, so we're here to cast a vote.*

He jumps from his stool to greet us, and Brixley smoothly leans down and hugs him. Tanner is taller than me, but even he looks like a child next to her towering height, augmented by her favorite six-inch heels. Then he wraps an arm around my shoulders in a friendly hug without spilling his beer. As always, I am hit with the faintest odor of cinnamon. Perhaps he's an alcoholic who constantly guzzles Fireball or some other cinnamon liquor. That's my current working theory.

"I didn't know you ladies were coming," he says, with a huge grin on his face. His arm is still draped over my shoulders, but I don't shake him off until I see the corner of Brix's mouth quirk. I shouldn't encourage her outlandish theory. "Let me buy you both a drink."

"Don't drinks come with the cookies? When does that start?" It's sweet of him to offer, but I don't need him to spend money on me.

"In about twenty minutes. You can buy your contest tickets over there." He shepherds us over to a table where a dark-haired young woman is selling the punch cards. For fifteen dollars, we get to choose five cookie/beer combinations. Apparently, this is an annual fundraiser. There are twenty entries, so it's expensive to try them all. I don't necessarily want to scarf down twenty cookies, but I am willing to split things with Brix and try twenty *half* cookies.

The ticket seller is trying to be cool and calm, but she's shaking from excitement. It takes her three tries to swipe Brixley's credit card, and she almost drops it as she hands it back.

A whispering crowd is already surrounding us, and several people are pulling out their cell phones to take pictures. I don't enjoy this, but I do know how to stand—if you slump your shoulders even the tiniest bit, your belly sticks out and the tabloids speculate as to how far along your pregnancy is. *Is Jace Monroe having a posthumous child?* Or *Moved on already? Jace is dead and his true love is having another man's baby! Details inside.* Maybe I should have worn shapewear like Brixley did—though she claims it's only because the pressure of tight binding helps relieve her cramps. I think she just doesn't want pictures with any hints of bloat.

"Don't mind us, we came for the cookies," Brixley announces to our spectators. She is like Moses. The crowd parts around us, and Tanner and I follow her to the bar, where she orders him another beer and two vodka tonics for us. "Low calorie, since we're going to be indulging soon," she tells me. No surprise, the bartender says the drinks are on him. Also no surprise, she drops a fifty on the bar. She has the same view on tipping as Powell: spread the wealth. He's been known to buy an ice cream cone with a hundred-dollar bill and tell them to keep the change. I once saw Brixley write a three-thousand-dollar check to a waiter Xander tried to stiff. A picture of it went viral, and she had to switch banks.

"I can't believe you came out tonight," Tanner repeats as we try to find a table. This place is packed, and newcomers are arriving every minute. I suspect some of them have motives other than noshing on homemade cookies.

"It may have been a bad idea," Brixley concedes. She's surveying our surroundings and checking the location of the bouncers. Maybe I should call Mike. He's out of town guarding Powell, obviously, but I suspect he has someone clandestinely following me. Maybe I can get my possible hidden bodyguard to reveal himself, so we all feel safer.

"I'm surprised you don't have security like Powell," Tanner says. "He's got a guy who follows him everywhere."

"You knew Mike was security?" I ask, somewhat surprised. Tanner claims that, as a "serious photographer," he's able to read people well, but I didn't realize he was observant enough to see past the accountant exterior. I'll have to warn Mike his cover was blown.

"The guy who aggressively questioned me in the hospital? Yeah, I kinda figured it out." He tilts his head sideways and sheepishly adds, "It helped that he gave me his card." Oh. Yeah, that's a giveaway.

Brixley looks up from typing on her phone. "I have a team coming. I'll have to buy them all cookies. Meanwhile, that table just opened up." She leads us to the high-top, the whispering crowd falling silent as she passes. The group who was sitting here gave it up for her; I know this because they are now standing two feet away, pretending they aren't taking pictures, selfies with a certain supermodel "accidentally" in the background.

Brix takes the stool closest to the wall, to prevent people coming up behind her. She gets ambushed sometimes by wannabe influencers trying to sneak photos with her. Since the advent of social media, an uncountable number of candids, taken without her permission have been posted all over by strangers.

"Is it always like this for you?" Tanner asks. He should know, he's usually holding a camera and being part of the invasive crowd.

"Only out here," Brixley casts her eyes over the not-so-discreet selfie-takers. "Back home people are used to seeing celebrities, so they don't trouble me as much. Tourists though, that's another story."

"It's different out here with Powell." Tanner's nonchalant comment throws me off. Has he been stalking us? Has he been secretly watching my brother when he goes out in public?

"How would you know?" I ask pointedly.

"We went out for steak last week," Tanner says, which is shocking new information to me. Powell never mentioned it. Maybe Tanner is lying.

"You did?" Brixley asks, probably because she can see I'm about to do some Mike-level "aggressive questioning."

"I ran into him when I went to pick up my clothes from the tailor and he asked if I wanted to hang out. He said he was craving a big slab of red meat and since Cass is vegetarian, he needed someone else to go with him. But he didn't have people gathering around staring at him. They treated him just like anybody else."

First of all, Powell isn't supposed to be having big slabs of anything with his pre-concert training diet. Second of all, why wouldn't he tell me he'd been getting friendly with a pap? Now I have another person to aggressively question.

"Of course they did, that's the difference between local celebs and visiting ones. Powell lives here, he tips well, and having him patronize a business increases their popularity. You remember the time you accosted me at Mama Nina's?"

"I didn't accost you! That was a friendly conversation."

"Don't rewrite history, Tanner."

"I'm not! I just wanted to talk to you about the pictures."

"The ones you took of my ass?"

Brixley lets out a gasp. She's been watching us, head moving back and forth as though she's at a tennis match. "This is better than reality TV! What pictures? Mason needs more details." I should have known she was live-texting this. Brixley might be a super genius, but even brilliant minds need escapism some-times, and she's a fan of trashy television programming and real life over the top drama. Ask her about the modeling world, she'll gleefully fill you in on all the sordid details and hot gossip.

"Why does Mason care?" I ask, because I don't want to get too far into this.

"He's pinned down under a napping baby and needs entertainment. Ordinarily, I'd tell Devon, but in his words, he's 'eschewing personal electronic devices' in favor of 'living in the present analog moment.'" Brixley's rolling eyes tell me exactly what she thinks about her boyfriend's neo-luddism.

"When did that start?" Devon is still active on SwiftaPic, though it's entirely possible all of his new postings could have been made by an assistant. Most celebrities outsource such things.

"Nice try changing the subject. Mason already knows about Devon, he doesn't already know about"—Brix waves her hand to encompass Tanner and myself—"whatever is happening here."

Since she's not going to let me redirect the conversation, I may as well tell her. "Tanner and I met because he was crouching in our bushes trying to get shots for a gossip blog. It was . . ." I hesitate. It was the day Jace died, and I don't want to bring that up and dampen the mood.

"It was a mistake," Tanner supplies, picking up on the importance of not bringing up such a sad topic. "And maybe I shouldn't have approached you, but if I hadn't, we wouldn't be sitting here today, would we?"

"Ohhh . . . valid point. Counterpoint, Cassidy?" Brix is enjoying this far too much.

But I don't get the chance to make any kind of counterpoint, because a trio of enormous men dressed in tight black T-shirts and wearing earpieces arrive. They cause a stir through the crowd as they approach our table. A nearby group of frat boys who had previously been egging each other on and getting close to consuming enough liquid courage to hit on Brix, suddenly find something better to do at the far end of the room.

While two of the bodyguards take up positions next to our table, Brixley gives the other one a handful of bills and tells him to buy fundraiser tickets, make sure to vote for the fudgy pretzel cookies, and for heaven's sake, try to blend in better.

"I requested discretion," she mutters after he walks away with the money. "This is not what I meant."

"The big boss wanted huge and intimidating," the one nearest me says, giving an accurate description of himself and his partners. "But we're not here for you, ma'am. We're from Alpha Lobo."

Aw, how sweet. That's Mike's company. And this proves Mike is keeping eyes on me, to make up for accidentally almost getting me killed in an explosion.

"This is kind of cool," Tanner whispers. "But now everyone is staring at me."

"You're celebrity adjacent now, get used to it."

"I'd like to," he says with a wink.

If I didn't know better, I would think he was flirting with me.

SIXTEEN

Cookie hangover might be worse than alcohol hangover. I wake up and my stomach hurts and my whole body wants to punish me. Too much sugar, especially since I've been (mostly) sticking to Powell's get-in-shape-to-perform diet. I owe myself an apology and an extra-long workout. And maybe Brixley and I should book spa appointments, too. For our health.

When I make my way to the kitchen, Brixley is already there. She's prepared herself a poached egg and a plate of greens. "There's tea ready," she says, pointing to the carafe. It's ginger—she must also be suffering from cookie-induced nausea. "And we're definitely hitting your gym today."

I pour myself a cup and toss one of Joel's egg-white omelets in the microwave. It was labeled with my brother's name, but he's not here to fight me for it. When I join Brix at the breakfast bar, she slides her tablet over to share the latest celebrity gossip.

> Supermodel Brixley made an appearance at a Scottsdale bar with bestie Cassidy Blaine-Corbitt, the late Jace Monroe's lover. Is she consoling Cass for her loss, or setting her up? They seemed to be awfully cozy with an unidentified man.

At least the picture was taken from a flattering angle, though the lighting is dim. It was shot after our guards arrived, but fortunately before we started devouring all those cookies.

"Tanner's going to love being called unidentified."

"I tagged him on Swifta, so they know exactly who he is. These gossip blogs just like creating drama." Brixley shrugs and finishes off her egg. "If you're going to date him, he'll have to get used to the attention."

"I don't know why you think dating is in my future." Sure, he's kind of cute. And funny. And he can bake. Oh, and there was that one kiss. But he's also a paparazzo, so nothing could ever work out between us. We're on opposing teams.

The security system sounds an alert, and a moment later I hear Powell opening the front door. He drops his bags in the foyer, like the lazy slob he is, and comes into the kitchen, followed closely by Mike. Neither of them look happy.

Powell hugs the both of us, and helps himself to my tea. "Yuck. Why didn't you put any sugar in this?"

"Stop taking other people's food. We've talked about this," Mike reminds him. "It's a security risk."

"Or a germ risk," Brixley says. "You don't want to be sick for the big show. Where's the rest of your team?" Devon, she's told me, is constantly surrounded by a platoon of five armed bodyguards right now.

"If you haven't seen them, I'm not going to tell you," Mike is smugly confident. "And if you have, let me know so I can fire them." The behemoths at the bar must not be part of his regular crew. If they were, I'd have spotted them before.

"See, Powell. This is why Devon keeps trying to steal him from you. When are your next contract negotiations, Mike? I may have a role for you."

"Not a chance," Mike rejects Brixley's offer, which is too bad for him. He'd get to travel to more interesting places with her. "Powell's my favorite client. He's the only one who lets me drive his cars."

"What? You said I had to! For security purposes!" Powell's outrage is somewhat manufactured. Mike is a skilled driver at high speeds. My brother gets a thrill out of the idea that they might be in an exciting chase someday.

"Yes. Security. That's why," Mike deadpans. He goes to the fridge and retrieves one of Joel's prepared meals. There are several in there marked with his name; he doesn't participate in Powell's restrictive diet plan, so his food is a little more appetizing. Maybe I should have chosen one of his breakfasts instead.

"Have you boys seen the hot news?" Brixley passes her tablet to Powell. Mike's interest is piqued, and he comes over eagerly. He claims it's part of his job to follow everything, but I think he also likes to gossip. I've seen who he follows on social media, and most of it is definitely not job related.

"Oh, that's just Tanner Smythe. His background check came up clean." He sounds disappointed, probably because last night's outing is not exciting news to him. His team likely sent him a minute by minute update.

"Except for the ex-wife thing. Did you know he used to be married?" Powell looks at me intently and Brixley gasps as though this is some soap opera level drama. I bet she's about to text Mason the next chapter in their ongoing gabfest.

"He got divorced shortly before moving here. Why'd you run a background check?"

Mike shrugs his powerful shoulders. "He showed up the day Jace died. Plus, since you put him on the list for permanent access, I had to, for security purposes." That phrase is starting to become meaningless, given how often Mike uses it.

"Omaha put him on that list! Not me! Why is everyone acting like there's something going on?" I'm getting frustrated with all the assumptions and insinuations.

"Speaking of something going on," Powell changes the subject. "The FBI is on their way over. Should be here any second." He turns in the direction of the front door and points. Nothing happens. He checks his phone. "Damn, I timed it wrong. Wait."

Because we are an overly indulgent group, we wait patiently until he receives the notification that someone was waved through the guard booth. And then we give them time to make the drive to the house.

"Should be here any second," Powell repeats, and points toward the door again. Now the doorbell rings on cue.

Mike lets them in. Our guests are the usual agents, accompanied by a third one, this time a man. He's younger than me and dressed in khakis and a wrinkled shirt rather than a sharp suit like his colleagues. They all freeze when they spot Brixley.

"Am I not supposed to be here?" Brixley asks when the stares start to feel awkward.

I've met Agent Benítez several times now, but this is the first time she's shown any sign of being anything other than firm, remote, and sort of scary. This time, she looks like she's desperately—but ineffectively—trying to not to melt into a puddle of joy.

"I'm sorry," the agent stammers at Brixley. "I was not expecting you. I'm a fan. A huge fan. I . . ." She's at a complete loss for words. It's kind of adorable. Her face is getting redder, and she can't seem to close her mouth. I suspect Benítez has a little crush. And from the smirk on her partner's face, I suspect Johnson is fully aware of it and finds this situation hilarious.

"We need to speak privately with the Corbitts." Agent Johnson finally takes over because Benítez is too starstruck to form coherent sentences.

"No problem, I have reading to catch up on anyway. I'll be by the pool." Brixley blows a kiss at all of us as she leaves, and I swear Benítez swoons. But as soon as Brixley is out of sight, Benítez morphs back to her all-business persona. Too bad. I liked her better when she was showing her softer side.

We migrate to the dining room, where the big table is, and we are finally introduced to the new guy. His name is Agent Walters, and he proudly describes himself as a hacker.

"You're an IT specialist," Johnson corrects. "Stop calling yourself that."

"Hacker is more exciting," he grumbles. "Fine. I'm an IT *genius* who specializes in hacking. Better?" This sounds like an argument they've had many times.

When they're through debating job descriptions, we get down to the reason they're here.

"We've discovered the origin of the money used to pay the mechanic to place the bomb." Benítez scrutinizes our faces, to analyze our reactions. Powell and I exchange a look.

"That's . . . good, right?" I ask, because the way she says it, it doesn't seem like good news.

"The money came from Blaine Holdings, LLC."

My heart drops. That's mine! That's the business name under which I own the gym and my other commercial investment properties.

"How is that possible?" I ask, suddenly paranoid that I have somehow been implicated.

"Somebody hacked into your system about six months ago and started funneling money away." As a self-proclaimed hacker, it's on Walters to provide the explanation. "I found traces when I was checking out your security cameras. They were conveniently down when the bomb was placed on Powell's car."

"They've been going down a lot lately. I've had someone out to fix them."

"We know." They are all watching me. They can't seriously believe I'm involved in this, can they? Does Powell?

I kindly turn to my brother to reassure him. "If I wanted you dead, I'd kill you myself. I have all the alarm codes and I know where you sleep."

"Same!" Powell exclaims, and we both laugh. It does not amuse anyone else in the room.

"Is Cassidy a suspect?" Mike asks. He puts a firm hand on my shoulder, and I'm unsure if he's signaling his support for my innocence or if he's preparing to incapacitate me.

"No." Benítez's answer gives me a sense of relief. I'd never harm my brother, and I'd certainly never murder Jace, and I would hope they knew that without me having to say anything. "But the bomber may be trying to frame her. Or this could be part of a bigger plan. For now, you need to go about your life as normal. Don't act weird and don't tell anybody about the investigation. It's possible that the mastermind is somehow connected to you."

"But I don't know anyone with the computer skills to pull that off," I tell them, immediately thinking over and dismissing every single person I've ever encountered. "Nor do I know anyone who wants Powell dead."

"Really?" My brother asks. "I do. Not thirty seconds ago, my own sister threatened to kill me in my sleep."

"Get a restraining order," Agent Walters suggests and is met with annoyed sighs from both his colleagues. He's definitely the odd man out on this team. "I was kidding. What, they can make jokes but I can't?"

"Walters, this is a murder investigation," Johnson reminds him. "Focus."

I am not surprised when Brixley decides she'd rather do poolside yoga with Mike and Powell than come to my gym, especially since I will be dealing with the annoying Agent Walters instead of getting in a good workout. I can't blame her. If given a choice, I'd prefer not spending my afternoon sitting in my office while a man who won't even tell me his first name digs through all my private files. But I am committed to finding out who is trying to kill us, and who stole from me. And hopefully getting them arrested.

When we arrive, Walters informs me he needs complete access to my work computer. Initially, I'm a little hesitant because I'm never comfortable with anyone looking through my things. Also, Mike pulled me aside after our meeting and gave me a strict lecture to not trust anybody.

But it's not like Walters is the hacker himself, unless the rest of the FBI team is in on it too. And I just can't believe that Benítez would consider even *bending* a law, much less breaking one. Alright, I've convinced myself. I sign on to my rarely used computer and let him have his way with my data.

Whitney pokes her head in the door while we're working. Or rather, while he's typing and sighing, and I'm watching impatiently. "Oh, sorry, I didn't know you had someone in here."

"This is just…" I wave my hand vaguely. Hmmm. I can't identify him as an FBI agent, and he refuses to reveal his first name, so I'll have to bestow one upon him. "Percival Von Sharkington. He's filling in for the regular IT guy and seeing if he can get the cameras back online."

The newly named Percival doesn't glance up from his work, but his annoyance is reflected in the monitor. Whitney appears skeptical. I guess she's not familiar with the famed West Coast Von Sharkingtons, and their prodigal son.

"Okay, Cass. Anyway, glad to have you back. I heard about your car accident."

Yes, *accident*. That's the rumor the FBI supplied. My staff signed a card for me and sent me a huge bouquet of flowers. Whitney texted a couple of times to check on me, but that's it. I'm not annoyed she didn't try to visit. Maybe we're developing a friendship—we've gone out to a few happy hours and saw a movie together once—but we're not close enough for her to witness my convalescence.

"Luckily, I survived with just scratches." I hold up one arm to show her my fancy new scars. It'd be a lot cooler if I could tell the real story. *These? Oh yes, one time I was in an explosion and narrowly escaped being blown to bits. No big deal.*

"Wow. Now you and your brother have both cheated death. That's amazing." Her tone is just sarcastic enough to make me wonder if she's minimizing the severity of my being in a car crash, but my lack of major injuries does make it seem like it wasn't so bad. She wouldn't have any idea how utterly the car was destroyed. Fortunately for Powell, he maintains full coverage insurance. And now he's rather excitedly shopping for a replacement. The guy still has eight other vehicles; there's no need to be greedy. But what can I say? He's a collector.

Percival—yes, I'm definitely calling him that from now on—tells us both to be quiet. He's studying my files and working his magic. Or perhaps he's helping himself to the rest of my money. Either way, he's doing something that requires his full attention.

"Fine, I'll be at the front desk," I tell him. I'd prefer to go get a workout in—my first since the "accident"—but it's probably better to not be sweaty and stinky if I have to return to my office and help with anything. It's just courtesy. "See you later, Percival."

"Where'd you find that guy?" Whitney asks as she walks through the gym with me.

"He came recommended by a friend." Not quite the truth, but not quite a lie. Agent Benítez isn't my friend, but I mostly trust her. And I kind of like her, especially after seeing her adorable reaction to meeting Brixley. It humanized her.

"My brother is an IT guy. I would have called him, if I'd known you were hiring out."

"Maybe next time." I'm only saying that to appease her. Once the FBI is done with their investigation, my computers will only be accessed by services vetted by Mike.

"Speaking of my brother," she says, even though we weren't. "He's in town visiting."

"Great. Did you talk to Owen about taking time off?" Owen is the manager, so he creates the schedules. I don't. And I don't like employees using their relationship with me to try and change their hours.

"I already made those arrangements. I only brought him up because I think you two might like each other."

"Oh?" I'm not interested in dating anyone, no matter what Brix keeps implying. But with Brixley leaving tomorrow evening, and Powell constantly singing—he says he's rehearsing, but I suspect he's doing it to annoy Mike—it would be nice to escape the house.

"I was thinking maybe we could go out to dinner the day after tomorrow."

"The three of us?"

"No, you should bring someone for me," she says with a wink, a wink that gives everything away—she's bringing her brother, so I should bring mine. She is doing exactly the same thing everybody else does, using me to access Powell. I saw this coming, and I'm not falling into this trap. This isn't the only time she's hinted about meeting Powell, despite the no-fangirling clause in her contract. She tried to invite herself over to my house before too, but I cut that off. I don't need someone taking advantage of me. I went through enough of that in high school. And during my one semester of college. And everywhere people find out that I have a celebrity sibling.

"Anyone?" I ask, silently daring her to outright state her goal. I had enjoyed spending time with her outside of work, so I'm sort of hoping she proves me wrong.

"Well, not that Percival guy. He seems kind of odd. And I think he lied to you about his name. Von Sharkington sounds more like a gamer tag."

While I'm glad I employ staff members smart enough to realize that was a fake name, I'm also mildly disappointed. I suppose I should have come up with a more plausible nom de plume. John Smith-with-an-I or something.

"I wasn't even considering him. You make the reservations and I'll find someone for you." Not Powell though. I have a better idea.

After an hour of standing around pretending to be working, but actually worrying, I am summoned back to my office. Agent Walters is leaning back in my desk chair, staring at the screen.

"Find anything out?" I ask hopefully.

"You donate more money to charity each month than I earn in a year," he says. I doubt it. I mean, I do give a lot away, but not in FBI-salary level quantities.

"If that's true, then you need a better job, Percival."

"Cassidy."

"What?"

"I was correcting you. My name is Cassidy. That's why I didn't want to tell you."

I'm trying not to laugh at how childish it was for him to conceal that from me before. Nothing is wrong with having a unisex name. "I wouldn't have made fun of you. We share an awesome name. But I'm older than you, so I get to keep it. You're stuck with Percival now."

He finally tears his eyes away from the computer monitor. "What makes you think you're older than me?"

Is it rude if I say his babyface? Or how he dresses like an intern who just rolled out of bed? Or the way his colleagues treat him, like he's a newbie fresh out of the academy? "I just assumed," I finally answer tactfully.

"Your birthdate is on your file. I'm older." He turns back to the screen, so distracted by my age assumptions he's ignoring that I've bestowed an unasked-for nickname upon him. "I completely misjudged you. I thought you were another one of those spoiled rich kids, but I'm going through your files. The food bank, domestic violence shelters, medical relief funds, you throw money at every cause."

"I grew up poor," I tell him, not that it's any of his business. He doesn't need to know about our homelessness after my dad's death, or the series of shelters and apartments with sketchy roommates. My mother's hard work and determination saved us from that lifestyle long before she married Hank. But now that I think about it, all of that information is probably in whatever dossier the FBI has created about me. "I like to give back."

"You do. But you haven't given money to any charities in the past six months."

"Yes, I have!" I know that for a fact, because I have auto donations scheduled.

"No, you haven't. Look here." He taps on my computer screen and I read the name.

"Maricopa County Coalition against Domestic Violence? I've donated to them for years."

"Carefully read the name again. Marico-Q-a."

I squint at it. He's right, there's a 'q' that isn't supposed to be there. I'm positive the county hasn't changed its name. "What's happening here?"

"Someone got into your finances and altered the recurring donations to accounts that mimic your typical charity names, but with slight misspellings. Those false entities are set up so that money flows into their off-shore account—one that changes monthly—but on your end, and, more importantly, on your accountant's end, it appears to be all going to the usual places."

"Do you think my accountant had something to do with it?" He's another friend of Hank's, and he's overseen Powell's finances for years too. I can't imagine he would be defrauding me.

"No, probably not. I bet he didn't notice the typos in the recipient names and that's how he missed catching where the money was going. This scam could have continued until next tax season, when the charities send out their annual donation letters and you found out you hadn't been making them."

"So what now?" My mind is wandering. Those charities depend on me. If I haven't been donating for months, are they cutting services? I donate a couple hundred a month to an organization that provides books to low-income children. Are all those kids being cut off? Why didn't they contact me? I'm going to have to make a few phone calls and get the money flowing again.

"Now we bring a forensic accountant in here to go through all your records."

"And they'll get my money back?"

"Maybe, but probably not. I'm more concerned with what it's being used for. You've had over a hundred thousand dollars stolen. The helicopter mechanic was only paid thirty thousand to place the bomb. We don't know who put the device on the car, but assuming they received the going rate, there's still plenty of money left over to pay for another attempt."

Coldness settles over me. Here I had been so focused on the charities' losses, I wasn't even considering the risks. I personally financed Jace's murder and mine and Tanner's injuries. And I could still be paying for someone to kill my brother.

When I finally leave my office—the other Cassidy still typing away—I rush out of the gym. I need to get home and talk to Powell. Also, Brix and I have massage appointments scheduled. But my priorities are in order, so first I'll inform my brother that there's still enough cash floating around out there to pay for his murder.

Before I can make it to my car, I hear someone call my name and turn to see Tanner. He's triumphantly wearing his Rusty Mug T-shirt.

"You're welcome," I tell him, pointing at his prize. His entry was delicious, but we all know Brixley's support is what earned him the win. There were some absolutely amazing gingersnaps that some brilliant person paired with a coffee stout, and they came in a distant second.

He thumps his chest proudly. "I got bragging rights, too."

"I remember. Alright, go ahead. Brag." I cross my arms and wait. His dimple appears.

"Hey, Cass, guess who makes the best cookies in an entire dive bar?"

"That's not the accolade you think it is, but congrats anyway. Oh, by the way, what are you up to the day after tomorrow?" I assume he's going to be hanging out in his van being obnoxious.

"Just hanging out," he says, leaving off the being obnoxious part. But I bet I'm right.

"You know Whitney, my assistant manager? She and I are planning a double date," I tell him. "Are you interested?"

A slow smile spreads across his face, and his damn dimple deepens. He can be cute sometimes.

"Really? Yeah, of course! That sounds fun. What time?"

I provide him with the details and tell him I'll pick him up, but he has to let me know where his van is parked or broken down, whichever it might be. My assumption is my back parking lot, but I'm still pretending to be unaware of his overnight trespassing.

That was easy. No Powell, no problem. Now to see how Whitney reacts. If she's mad or disappointed, I'll know who she was truly after.

SEVENTEEN

Whitney's back is to us when Tanner and I arrive at the restaurant she picked. It's one of those trendy places visited by young professionals after work, so the men in the crowd are wearing expensive ties with their shirt sleeves rolled up—the uniform of the casual businessman on the prowl. The women all have high class haircuts and designer dresses with heels. I fit in. Tanner is slightly out of place, in his 'nice' T-shirt and jeans. At least his shirt doesn't proclaim his favorite bar and his jeans are miraculously hole-free.

"Whitney!" I call out as we approach, and she turns. I'm watching her face carefully, and I see it: surprise and dismay. Just as I suspected, she thought I'd bring Powell. While I do enjoy being right, I wish I weren't. Just once, I'd like to find someone who doesn't want to use me.

She recovers well. "Tanner, right?" She extends a hand to greet him. "It's nice to see you outside of the gym."

Tanner shakes her hand and we sit down. Whitney and her brother—he introduces himself as Silas—have taken alternating chairs at the four-top, so I find myself facing Tanner. He does clean up well. He's unquestionably better looking than my date. Not to say Silas is unattractive though. His face is symmetric, at least, beneath his military-style buzz cut. But there's a coldness to his eyes that makes me wary. I've already decided any progression to intimate contact is off the table. Not that I was considering it anyway. This is just supposed to be a fun night out, not a potential hookup or anything.

Because this is a trendy bar, the drinks all have fancy long names that I'm not going to bother with, so I order a craft beer, as does Tanner. So does Silas, though he requests it by grunting "same" instead of actually ordering. Whitney ignores the ridiculously complex drink names and orders by pointing to a picture on the menu. When it arrives, it's a frothy pink beverage in a big glass with two straws.

"Interesting choice," Silas comments, and Whitney shrugs.

"I like froofy drinks. Bottoms up," she lifts her glass to toast Tanner, then drinks deeply. Her brother rolls his eyes at her. He gives off every indication of being annoyed and wishing he were elsewhere. If I had any interest in him, my feelings would be hurt. As it is, I'm going to be polite and try to have a good time and leave immediately after we eat.

Despite Silas' constant glowering, and Whitney's now-confirmed desire to date my brother, it is sort of pleasant to be here, out with ordinary people. We don't have to avoid camera flashes or maintain I'm-having-fun expressions on our faces even when we're not. This is quite different from when I'm out with Powell and other celebrities and we have to keep an eye out for . . . well, for people like Tanner. Funny how sometimes Tanner doesn't seem like the enemy. He's not nearly as bad as most of his brethren.

Right now, he's being downright enjoyable. He's chatty, friendly to everyone and seems to be in a good mood. And he can sense Silas' reticence, so he tries to help draw him out. But he uses an odd conversation starter: he asks Silas and Whitney how they met.

"My dad took me to the hospital and pointed her out," Silas says, laughing. So I guess it is possible for him to show some emotion other than irritation.

"I don't remember any of that, but then I was only a few hours old," Whitney adds. I can see the calculations going on in Tanner's brain.

"Oh!" he exclaims when he catches on. "You're brother and sister! Huh. I get it now."

"Don't worry," Silas reassures him. "I'm not one of those overprotective older brothers. You're safe. For the moment."

Tanner gives me the strangest look, a mixture of confusion and disappointment. What's his problem? I told him the date was with Whitney, and he enthusiastically agreed. So why does he care if the guy I've been set up with is related to his date?

The rest of the meal, Tanner focuses all his attention on Whitney. He barely looks in my direction, even though I'm seated right across the table from him and it probably hurts his neck to keep his head permanently twisted away. I don't know why he's acting like that all of the sudden. Yeah, she's his date and all, but we're out as a foursome and, selfishly I'm annoyed because his sudden exclusion of me means I have to continue trying to make small talk with Silas.

Silas doesn't want to discuss his work, he doesn't want to talk about his family or his friends, or the latest book he read. Why is he even here? Why on earth would Whitney want to hook me up with him when it's clear he has no interest? When she invited me out, she acted like she thought we'd hit it off.

"I heard you're related to a famous singer," he finally says.

"Yes, Powell Corbitt is my brother," I respond. I assume he knew that already, and my suspicion is confirmed when he nods. Is he going to ask for an autograph? Is this the point he pulls out his demo and asks me to pass it along? I've been through this before, more times than I can count. No wonder he hasn't wanted to learn anything about me. He had ulterior motives. But if he wanted a favor, he should have been a lot friendlier.

"I know who he is. I remember reading stories about the two of you. You certainly have a . . . close relationship." His cold eyes are locked on my face and his stare is making me uncomfortable.

"Powell is my best friend and my housemate," I say. "So yes, we're pretty close."

"It must be convenient to live together. Do you share a bed?"

I want to think Silas is socially inept and doesn't understand what he's asking, but the sneer on his face shows that he knows exactly what he's implying.

"Excuse me?" I can keep my voice calm, but my tone has turned frosty.

"Didn't he brag about taking your virginity?" Silas continues. "I swear I read something about that. Were you into it? Brotherly love? My sister and I would never do that sort of thing, but since you and Powell aren't technically related, you can do whatever you want."

The floor drops out from under me and my ears start ringing. I cannot believe he would bring up that ancient lie. What kind of guy brings up disgusting old rumors like that on a date?

"The tabloid story was a complete fabrication." My hands clench into fists and I hide them under the table. I can't let him see that he's getting to me. That's probably what he wants.

"Or so you claim. I heard there were witnesses, but you managed to bury them under legal threats. Kind of shady if you ask me. But money buys silence, doesn't it?"

"The only thing money bought was an apology, from the magazine to us. The supposed journalist who cracked the story was a fraud. He made the whole thing up. People only believe it because they like hearing sleazy underhanded things about celebrities, regardless of truth. It was ten years ago, it was a lie, and it was resolved in court." I wish I hadn't already finished my beer so I could throw it in his face.

Silas smirks. "Seems like you're protesting a little much. Whatever. You may have denied it back then too, but I've always had my suspicions."

What's his obsession with such ancient rumors? Has he been fixated on me for some reason?

Tanner and Whitney have finally stopped flirting long enough to notice the brewing animosity. Tanner has the slightest little frown and is looking at me with concern. Whitney is busy trying to shush her brother, and they are having an intense silent conversation, eyebrows furrowing, heads tilting, jaws jutting out. Whatever they're communicating to each other, it makes Silas bow his head for a moment. When he raises it back up, he's plastered on an ingratiating smile.

"I'm sorry. I shouldn't have brought up old gossip. The story was something I remembered from years back, and when Whitney told me about you, I was reminded of it."

His apology isn't enough for me. I will not pretend to forgive, and I will not tolerate being in his presence any longer. I stand up and toss my napkin on the table. "I think it's time for me to go. Tanner, do you need a ride?"

He looks to Whitney instead of me. She smiles flirtatiously, and he has the gall to smile back. "I'll catch one with Whitney, thanks anyway."

Fine, that's his choice. He can stay with them and seduce Whitney in front of her awful brother. I'm going to go home, hang out with my non-awful brother, and relax. And I'm not going to tell Powell that someone is bringing up those old rumors. He's under enough stress with concert prep and all the bombings. No need to pile on additional aggravations.

EIGHTEEN

It is finally June, and we are officially one week away from the Jace Monroe Tribute Concert. I will be so glad and relieved when it's all over. I've been getting interview requests, and I don't want to talk to anybody. Somehow word of the car bomb leaked, despite the FBI's attempts to keep things quiet. When it first happened, they were aided by the fact that it took place on the same night a serial bank robber led police on a dangerous chase through downtown Phoenix, culminating in crashing into a busy fast-food restaurant. Our dramatic explosion initially ended up as nothing more than a "car fire" line in the news. But now it's out and everyone knows that someone—possibly the same person who killed Jace—attempted to kill Powell. Plus, the aficionados over on the Rolls-Royce forums are in deep mourning for the car. Apparently, that particular one had some limited-edition features.

And I can't seem to escape the press even at home. I swear, I'm going to leave spike strips in the driveway to discourage uninvited visitors. How on earth did Tanner decide he has the right to just drop in whenever he feels like it? And why didn't the security guard patrolling the perimeter tackle him, preferably into a cactus?

When he rings the doorbell, I answer through the intercom. "What do you want?"

"You sound like you're in a bad mood," he responds.

"When you show up like this, it puts me in a bad mood."

"Good thing I'm here to see your brother and not you."

"Why? So you can harass him?"

"Cassidy, let the man in." Powell's voice cuts through mine on the speaker. "I invited him over."

"Where are you?" That's one thing I hate about this app—it doesn't reveal his location. Powell can just sit back and relax and make me deal with whatever random paparazzo shows up at our door.

"I'm in the basement. Bring him down, please."

Ugh. Here's the problem with living with my employer: I have to do what he says, even when I don't want to. But I put my book down and get up from my comfortable chair and go open the front door, where Tanner is buckling under the weight of his photography equipment.

"Finally," he says, as though *I* was inconveniencing *him*. "This stuff is heavy."

I take a bag from him and throw it over my shoulder. "Powell said I had to let you in. He's probably in his recording studio."

"I guess he didn't tell you I was coming. He needs publicity shots, so he offered me the job. The label was going to fly one of their usual contractors out for it." Tanner seems inordinately proud of being the chosen one. He follows me happily through the house and down the stairs to the lower level.

In addition to our Downstairs Drinkery—yes, I won the naming-rights battle—Powell has a recording studio and a small dance room for rehearsing, even though he prefers to use my gym. The one here is fancier though, with mirrors on two of the walls, so he can watch himself, and a camera to record videos so he can give himself scathing feedback. His ego is unmatched when it comes to his music, but he is hypercritical of his dance skills. One article fifteen years ago saying he had two left feet has made him permanently self-conscious.

Also our laundry room is downstairs. But I doubt Powell wants pictures there.

"So what's going on with you, Cass?" Tanner asks as I lead him down the hall. We haven't spoken much in the couple of weeks since our unpleasant double date. Well, it was unpleasant for me, at least. Everything seemed to work out just fine for Tanner. Whenever I encounter Whitney lately, she gushes about how much fun they're having together and how wonderful he is: *he's so sweet,* and *oh my goodness I can't wait to see him later* followed by a bunch of nonsense exaggerations about Tanner's attractiveness.

"Nothing's going on with me." I open the door to Powell's studio where my brother is playing with his soundboard. "Here's your victim."

"The word you're looking for is subject," Tanner corrects me with a grin, which makes that annoying dimple appear on his left cheek. It would make him attractive, if that were possible. But it's not, because no matter how cute he is, he's still kind of a jerk. If he were really my friend, he would have been supportive and stormed out of the restaurant with me when Silas morphed into a false-rumor obsessed jackass.

"Hey, come on in," Powell greets Tanner and leaves me standing outside. "Deedee, you want to hang out and watch?"

"Gosh, that sounds fun!" My exaggeratedly excited tone conveys the mockery I intended. Powell laughs and waves me away.

They are down there for over two hours, not that I'm paying attention to the time or anything. What could possibly take so long to shoot? Is Tanner so bad at his job that he can't make my objectively attractive brother look good in pictures? If so, he needs to find a new line of work.

Then my phone buzzes with a text. It's lazy Powell who can't be bothered to come and look for me.

Where are you?

Upstairs. Why?

Come down and have a drink with us.

Oh, no. They moved to the bar. That means poor Tanner is sipping expensive cognac and listening to Powell play old records and go on and on about the quality of vinyl over digital. And they want me to join them? I consider not going. Maybe I should head into the gym and get in my second workout of the day. Or maybe there's paperwork I need to do. Yeah, that's a believable excuse.

But I go downstairs anyway, where they are not drinking cognac and listening to blues. No, they've got gin and tonics instead, and Powell set up the sound system to play his self-made instrumental versions of his own music. Yes, he's showing off.

"You should try these, Deedee." Powell's cheeks are already pink from alcohol. Despite his well-stocked bar, he doesn't drink much. It exists primarily as a place to show off to guests, not as an alcoholic's fancy retreat. Moreover, he's not supposed to be drinking on his diet—his nutritionist would have a fit. "Tanner made them."

"Baking skills *and* mixing skills? Prove it." I perch on a stool and let Tanner mix me a drink.

"Challenge accepted," Tanner says as he starts measuring out the tonic water. "Why Deedee?"

"Don't call me that. And why what? Why should you prove it? You're the one standing on that side of the bar."

"No, I meant, why do they call you Deedee? How'd you acquire your nickname?" He acts genuinely interested.

"It's short for Cassidy-dee," I admit, though I hate sharing snippets of my life. But if I don't tell him, my brother probably will—he's chatty when he's drinking. "When I was little, my father used to tell me made-up stories of the adventures of Chickadee-dee and Cassidy-dee."

"Ah, that's why you have a stuffed chickadee wearing your dad's wedding ring." Tanner snaps his fingers and nods as if he's just figured something out. "That's kind of sweet. Tell me one of the stories."

"Absolutely not." But I am impressed he remembered my scruffy old chickadee. Tanner saw it for a minute almost four months ago. It's the only toy I've retained from my childhood, though I'm certain there's a box or two of memorabilia in my mother's storage shed.

"Please, Deedee?"

"No. And you aren't allowed to call me that. Family only."

"Fair enough, Ms. Blaine-Corbitt, ma'am. I presume this is your bar, so I'll be respectful of your wishes." He does an absurd little bow.

"Ummm . . . this is *my* bar," Powell corrects him. I raise an angry eyebrow and he backpedals. "I mean *our* bar. We share it."

"Oh. I just thought . . ." Tanner trails off, eyes fixed on the neon blue DD sign hanging on the wall.

Powell follows his gaze and his eyes widen. "Downstairs Drinkery? Damnit, Deedee!"

"We don't need to discuss how or why I came up with the name," I inform him loftily. "Sometimes I can be creative too."

"The initials are a coincidence? Maybe we should rename this. I'm thinking . . . Primary Cantina. I'll order a new sign."

"Forget it. Your accountant said we've already surpassed the neon sign budget this year."

"You have a neon sign budget?" Tanner interrupts. The next words out of his mouth are probably going to be part of his continuing anti-rich people diatribe.

"Apparently," Powell mutters, giving me a sullen glare.

"If he thinks we're going to replace my DD with his own initials, then yeah, we have a line item for that, and it's maxed out. Did you two get the pictures you needed?" My swift subject change elicits an equally swift mood change in my brother.

"Yeah, they're gonna look awesome. He got the shots the label wanted, and then he took a bunch I can use on my SwiftaPic later."

"He changed his shirt six times," Tanner offers his camera so I can look through the images, but I decline. I already know what Powell looks like with every possible shirt/hairstyle/facial expression combination. We've lived together since I was twelve; I've seen it all.

"Of course he did." I admire his foresight. He hates dealing with social media. Half the time I'm the one who reminds him to post and I'm usually the person who crafts the responses to his fans. It's all part of the job. And it certainly is easier when there's an array of pre-shot images to choose from.

"What's wrong with that? My hair looks fabulous today. I might as well memorialize it. And now I have things to post while I'm traveling."

Foolish Powell, announcing his schedule in front of a paparazzo. I guess it doesn't matter though, since we're both flying out to California tomorrow. Tanner can't afford to follow. Unless some sleazy blog covers his costs, but why would they when LA is literally teeming with photographers?

"You're leaving for the reunion concert already? It's not for another week." Tanner proves once again that he is a stalker who tracks our schedules, and that he has no understanding of how this industry works. What, we're supposed to fly out day of?

"We're going out early for rehearsals and media," I explain. "We need to make sure Xander can follow all of the steps." My brother snickers at that. Xander can dance just as well as the rest of them. Devon is the real concern: how can he perform without Jace at his side?

"It's going to be fun, right Cass? Getting the old crowd back together again?" Powell's happy smile fades as he realizes what he just said. "Except for Jace. It really hits hard sometimes, doesn't it? Like you think everything is fine and life is moving on and then bam! You're reminded again."

"It's never going to not hurt, but the pain will fade with time." I gently rub his forearm and try not to think about my dad. I've never forgotten that loss, but it's no longer a punch in the guts when I remember him. Same for Powell and his mom, I'm sure.

"It must be harder for you," Tanner says. He is watching my face with sympathy. Then he holds up his glass. "To Jace."

I don't think it's entirely appropriate that someone who never met Jace is doing a toast to him, but I won't reject the gesture. We clink our glasses and sip slowly.

"You're going to be on camera at the show," Powell reminds me. "Jace's long lost love and all that drivel."

"Shut up," I warn him. The alcohol is loosening his tongue too much. I don't need him exposing mine and Jace's relationship as one-sided in front of an inquisitive manipulative would-be reporter.

"It's not drivel," Tanner speaks up in misguided defense of me. "It's tragic. I can't imagine being in love with someone and never getting to tell them except in death. It's heartbreaking. If you care about someone, you should gather your courage and tell them while you're alive."

Powell's eyes glaze over and his face goes blank for a second, then he immediately stands up and leaves the room. Great. I know exactly what he's doing. Tanner doesn't, he's staring after him, concerned.

"Did I say something wrong?"

"No, worse. You said something *inspirational*. He just ran back to his studio." Usually he grabs for one of the ubiquitous legal pads and a pen, or his phone to sing into, but we were close enough he can use the real technology. Powell's going to disappear for either a few minutes or a few hours, depending on how it works out in his head.

"He's making a song out of what I said?"

"Yep. You'll have to tell Whitney when the song comes out."

"Why tell Whitney?"

"She's your girlfriend, isn't she? You can't talk about loving someone while you're in a relationship and not expect them to assume you're referencing them."

"She's . . . we've hung out a couple of times, but why would you . . . did she *say* she was my girlfriend?" Tanner stammers and seems confused, which is odd considering the way Whitney raves about him. He runs a hand through his hair and is starting to look distraught.

"My understanding is that the two of you are very happy together." I raise my eyebrows. Is it possible their relationship isn't as perfect as his "girlfriend" claims?

"Would that be a problem?" His attitude changes suddenly. His emerald eyes are fixed on my face like he's challenging me, and I flashback to the kiss he delivered outside the restaurant. The fake kiss that somehow infuriated him, even though he was the one who initiated it in the first place.

"Why would that be a problem? I set you up, didn't I?" Not quite intentionally, but he doesn't need to know that. I had suspected Whitney thought I was bringing Powell on our double date, and I didn't have many other options. I didn't know they'd end up actually dating though. He was meant to be my support person and a decoy to test Whitney's expectations, not an actual romantic option for my assistant manager. Maybe I should have explained that to him in advance.

"True, you did." Tanner looks away for a moment, his fingers drumming an agitated beat on the bar. Then he turns back to me. "And I should thank you. Whitney is awesome. We're having a ton of fun together."

"Great. Hey, you know what would be super fun? You should take a romantic getaway. Why don't you come to LA? I can get you tickets to the Last Barons concert."

"Are you serious?" He's clearly missing the sarcasm in my voice.

"Yeah, sure. I have some extras." They were intended for mom and Hank, but my parents were invited to host a charity viewing of the concert, where they'll be auctioning off a stack of signed merchandise. And that reminds me—I need to get Powell busy signing things this afternoon when he emerges from his studio.

"Fantastic. I'd love a romantic getaway. That would be amazing." He sounds rather aggressive and angry in his acceptance of my offering. Why are we sniping at each other like this? Oh, yeah, because he's a sleazy photographer who takes advantage of people . . . and now he's suckered me into giving him free tickets. Ugh, he won again.

NINETEEN

I have my usual list of complaints about Los Angeles, but I am kindly not airing them. Powell is already stressed enough with rehearsals and media events and the fact that someone is trying to kill him. He doesn't need to listen to me whine about smog and traffic and crowds. At least we have his condo to escape to. There's a rooftop pool and a decent fitness center. As an additional bonus, the building is quiet. The prior occupant of our unit was a heavy metal drummer, so we are completely soundproofed.

But I'm not spending much time there. Instead, in the interest of "security purposes," Mike has been forcing me to accompany them everywhere. I've resumed my traditional role of watching the boys practice and coming up with effusive compliments to greet my brother with when he comes offstage. And I have to do that while avoiding Xander, who wants to "set up a dinner" so we can discuss "album possibilities." Apparently, my repeated "you'll never sing Jace's songs" is not getting through to him.

Today, four days away from the memorial concert, I've finally managed to earn myself a bit of respite. Instead of listening to yet another interminable repeat of cheesy pop music, I am out with Brixley. We've just had a lovely lunch—I'm fairly certain Mike's undercover bodyguards occupied two of the tables nearest us—and now we are at the Butón studio.

In the old days, as a non-celeb hanging out backstage, what I wore to concerts didn't matter, as long as it was black. But this show is different because I'm making a public appearance as Jace Monroe's devastated lover. I'll be seated up close to the stage and cameras will regularly pan to me, which means designers were fighting to dress me. I fielded dozens of calls in the past two months, finally deciding on René Butón. He's very French, très chic, and also he's dressing Brixley, so I don't have to go alone.

Brixley is the one currently standing on a platform while René's assistants bustle around her with their pins and measuring tapes. Her gown is a gorgeous shimmery blue, which she would not have been wearing if this were the reunion concert rather than a memorial show. Had we gone through with the originally planned fun fan-centric event, we would both have shown up in vintage tour T-shirts and jeans. But now, since it's a tribute, we have to be glamourous. Not my favorite way to remember Jace, but despite my status as his great love, nobody asked my opinion.

"Is perfect, you are always perfect," René says to Brixley, making one final fussy adjustment to the hem. He had left it long, waiting to see what shoes she would be wearing. Brix is already a gargantuan six foot three and the heels she brought add an extra four inches. I'm going to look like a toddler next to her. I'm *only* five-eight, not tall enough to be a model, and just the right height to have short men be self-conscious around me. Even guys who are five-ten act like I'm too tall, because they don't tower over me as much as they'd like. Fortunately, I don't care about that kind of thing. I don't put up with insecure man babies. Maybe that's another reason I'm always single.

"You're up, Cass." Brixley steps lightly off the platform after she is divested of her gown. She sprawls on one of the couches, not caring that she's in nothing but her undergarments. Granted, she's appeared on billboards in much skimpier attire, so I suppose she feels quite covered up. Now it's my turn to cast off my studio-provided robe and subject myself to the stabs of a thousand pins. This must be how Tanner felt when he was lying in the cactus.

René helps me into my dress. I usually prefer to wear muted colors, and he respected that. This one is a light silvery silk, with an edging of lace on the bodice. The skirt of the gown is tastefully decorated in lace and beading that gradually gets darker toward the bottom, so it ends in black.

"You are both Jace's wife and widow in this," René explains the intention behind the design. I get it; the top is elegant bride, and it fades into funereal wear. Subtle, and beautiful. It'll definitely get people talking.

"Absolutely gorgeous," Brix gushes. "You look amazing, Cassidy."

I'll accept her compliment. I *feel* beautiful in his dress. I admit, I often try to pretend I'm too down to earth for this sort of thing, but I'd be a liar if I said I don't love to don luxury designer gowns occasionally. There's something about the sensation of the silk sliding across my skin, silk cut to my proportions and sewn just for me, that makes me feel special.

"Are you sure?" Maybe it seems like I'm just fishing for more compliments, but there will be a lot of eyes judging me and determining if I was worthy of Jace's affection.

"You'll make the best dressed list," Brix assures me. Or maybe she's assuring René. I would claim I don't have any interest in those lists, but I'd be lying. I'm hoping this will be better than the time I went to the Music Video Awards with Powell and got mocked for what I had thought was a trendy and fun dress. Turns out, feathers were out that year, and sequins were in. Pictures of me did not have flattering captions, traumatizing my twenty-year-old self.

"You had better," René says. "I turned down Zahna to make this for you."

That would be more complimentary if I didn't know Zahna's invitation was revoked. She had the nerve to go on a talk show and brag about how her actions indirectly saved Powell's life. She carried on as though she were some sort of hero for cheating on him. Her comments enraged Jace's fans and Powell himself. As soon as my brother heard his ex's claims, he started making angry phone calls, and hours later Zahna was on SwiftaPic expressing her sorrow that, due to circumstances beyond her control, she would be out of the country during the memorial tribute, but we'd be in her thoughts.

"If you want me on the best dressed list, does that mean my hair and makeup need to be professionally done?" I ask the question as innocently as possible, and the horror on René's face is my reward. From the way he's clutching his chest, I may have nearly given him a heart attack.

"Don't worry," Brixley promises him, after letting out one of her high-pitched cackles—her laugh is the one unattractive thing about her. "I took care of that. I lined J'Shanna up for the both of us."

René is suitably impressed and relieved. J'Shanna is a top-notch stylist, one so well-known she's only referred to by a single name. She worked with Powell once, but she's more often busy prepping big money movie stars for red carpet events. We've an appointment before the concert, when J'Shanna will show up with her crew, and she will supervise as they paint me and comb my hair and do horrible things with hot implements until it meets their standards. I'm going to suffer for a couple of hours but will come out of it looking phenomenal.

"Thanks, Brix."

"No problem. I can't wait until Tanner sees you. He'll know what he's missing."

"Tanner?" René asks, suddenly very excited by our conversation. "Tanner Woods, soap opera star? Or Tanner Vonn, action movie hero?"

"Neither. He's a pap with a crush on Cassidy."

"Oh." René loses all interest when he learns of Tanner's mediocrity, so it's not worth correcting Brix's description. She's wrong though, especially given how quickly Tanner jumped into a relationship with someone else.

René finishes his pinning and has me step out of the dress, promising to have it delivered to me backstage. While I haven't been looking forward to having to parade in front of the media play-acting about how sad I am about my lost love, I do kind of want to see the expression on Tanner's face when he sees how well I clean up. Not because of what Brixley said though.

TWENTY

Here we are, concert day. The day which, by Mike's calculations, is the day someone will most likely make another attempt on Powell's life. I'm nervous, but I'm doing my best to hide it. Powell is nervous as well, but he's pretending everything is fine. I'm better at doing that than he is.

One of Mike's security staff spent the night outside our condo door last night, so Mike would be well rested for the main event. The nighttime guard cheerfully shoulders Powell's duffel bag and escorts us to our waiting vehicle, which has yet another bodyguard in the passenger seat.

Excited energy radiates from my brother as the armored town car transports us to the rear entrance. "I've missed this," Powell says, looking up at the Castillo Center through the tinted glass. From the back, there isn't much to see. But on the other side of the building, crowds are already jostling for places close enough to spot the celebrity guests arriving.

"You've performed thousands of times," I remind him.

"Yes, but I've been doing it solo for so long. It's different with the guys. This is the biggest show of my career, and it feels good to be back with the old crowd."

"But it's not quite the same."

"No, not quite." We're both silent for a moment, mourning Jace. I think that's the real reason our parents didn't come. The charity watch-party/auction was just an excuse. This whole event is a reunion for everybody who spent nearly a decade working with the Last Barons on their albums and tours and media productions, and there's an enormous gaping hole in it. Every time we look around backstage, we'll be reminded of Jace's absence. It's going to hurt. And knowing that his death wasn't an accident makes the loss hurt worse.

"Don't sit around talking!" Mike opens the door and yanks Powell out. "How many times do I have to tell you to stop making yourself a target?" He's got a solid grip on my brother's collar as he drags Powell toward the backstage door and the rather imposing guards.

Mike acts like every step is a risk and killers could be lurking behind every corner. But I think he's overdoing it. We're going to be perfectly fine here. Security at the venue is tight. Everyone is going to have to pass through metal detectors after the red carpet. In fact, they'll be funneled through a press-free room where they may be subjected to an extra search. Nobody wants an embarrassing tabloid picture showing them all spread eagle while a security card waves a scanner around them and checks under their dresses. They're even going to make me go through the whole rigmarole when I make my grand entrance. And that's after the pat down at the back door.

We have several hours until showtime, but some entertainers are on stage and the lucky ticket holders are slowly trickling into the auditorium. Not the famous crowd, of course. They'll make their entrances through the gauntlet of reporters later. The early arrivals are super-fans who won contests (or had a lot of money), bloggers, and the second-tier acquaintances and distant relatives of the band.

I'm backstage right now, hanging out in the green room where I was ostensibly supervising the catering staff and the buffet. I've fallen back into old patterns—I wiped down all surfaces for any trace of peanut residue and harassed the caterers about the ingredients in all the little cakes. They received explicit instructions prior to my inspection, but it never hurts to be on the safe side. Someone is out to harm Powell; we can't be too careful.

Two people appear in the doorway and I glance up from the cookie I'm sampling—my mouth is an excellent peanut detector—to see my own guests. My unwillingly invited guests, I should say.

"Thanks for inviting us." Tanner is almost unrecognizable with combed hair and a suit. Based on how ill-fitting the sleeves and shoulders are, I assume he rented it. I should have sent him to Powell's tailor instead. Whitney is also in borrowed clothing, the tight red dress with a sweetheart neckline that I wore to the Grammys a couple of years ago. I might let her keep it, since she's my friend. Also, she had to have the waist taken in, so if her seamstress removed any material, I can't wear it again anyway. I'm not interested in dieting or losing my ab muscles to rewear an old dress, no matter how expensive.

"This is awesome! You're so lucky to lead such a glamorous lifestyle," Whitney says, surveying the room. Envy shines from her eyes. She's made enough comments about my undeserved riches lately, she's starting to sound like Tanner.

"Help yourself to the food," I gesture to the heavily laden table by the far wall. Tanner, being himself, immediately asks if he can take some pictures. Great, now he's become a still life photographer. He managed to convince Powell to upgrade his ticket with a press pass so he could bring in his ostentatious Hasselblad camera and a bag of spare lenses. Seriously, can't he take some time off and enjoy himself? Spend one evening without documenting every moment? When old folks talk about social media and cell phone cameras being the downfall of society, they forget that photography junkies like him have existed since the invention of film.

Tanner takes pictures of food, and of Whitney enjoying the food, and of me rolling my eyes at their excitement. It's not that impressive—the after-parties are where the real good stuff will be. Maybe I'll wrangle them invitations to one. Devon's is going to be epic. I stopped by yesterday and checked out the set-up.

I'm trying not to be annoyed about seeing them together. I had no claim to Tanner, after all. And he's clearly happy with her. He smiles when he looks down at her, and he doesn't shake her off when she clings to his arm. And she's whispered in his ear several times, bringing a blush to his cheeks. This trip is their first romantic getaway, so I'm sure they're having a wonderful sexy time of it. But I'm not jealous. I don't even care at all. Not one tiny bit.

After they sample some treats and take selfies with me, they head out to explore the venue. The main show, obviously, doesn't start for another couple hours, but there are numerous distractions available, including a large display of old tour merchandise and vintage T-shirts. No doubt Tanner can find something to photograph.

Once my slightly unwelcome visitors have gone, I take one last cookie—can't eat in my fancy clothes—and head down the hall to Powell's dressing room. My hair and makeup were done by J'Shanna and her flock of assistants earlier; all I have left is my gown and shoes. My brother has just finished up his pre-show massage, so he and the massage therapist courteously leave so that I can borrow the room.

My dress is hanging near Powell's post-show party suit and his outfit for the opening song, the only clothing left on the rack. All of his other costume changes have been taken to the wings, where the Last Barons will strip down between songs. I like to tease Powell because they wear literal stripper clothes so that they can rip them off quickly. Devon and Mason used to perform quite a provocative green room show sometimes, until Mason accidentally damaged the snaps in a very important shirt right before a performance and ended up having the wardrobe lady screaming at him. Good times.

Unlike them, I have to remove my clothes the usual way, unbuttoning and everything. I can't risk messing up my professionally done hairstyle by yanking things off. Then I step into my dress carefully, pull it up, and realize I have a problem. I can't zip this thing. I thought I'd be able to get the zipper at least part way up my back, but it seems to be stuck.

I poke my head out in the hallway, hoping a female PA is walking by. I don't want to go knock on someone else's door. And I certainly don't want Xander to see me holding the bodice up like this. But the hoped-for PA isn't available. The only person visible in the entire corridor is . . . *Tanner*. Seriously?

Oh, well. Beggars can't be choosers.

"Tanner, can you help me?" I ask, and he turns around, startled.

"Cass? What are you doing?"

"I'm getting dressed for the concert. What did you think I was doing?"

"I thought you were already ready."

"In a button-down shirt and jeans? You thought I was wearing that to a formal event?"

"I thought I was overdressed. I was going to ditch the jacket and tie." He tugs at his neck, clearly uncomfortable. That's fine, I'm sure Whitney will happily take it off him later.

"Can we not stand here in the hall talking about this? Get in here."

"Wow," he blurts out as he enters. "This is posh!" He's right, it's downright opulent. The guys were each assigned extravagant dressing rooms for this show because a documentary filmmaker has been coming through to interview them, and they want to convey success and grandeur. Not that they aren't successful. With the exception of Xander, they've all been doing extraordinarily well since the break-up. Mason's audience has shifted halfway around the world, and Devon is trying to figure out his next steps without his partner, but they're still better off than they were before.

"Just zip me, please," I tell him when he's done checking out the mirrors and peering behind the four-panel room divider, where I'm sure there's a pile of Powell's dirty clothes. My brother left here in a robe, unwilling to dress for the show yet.

"It's stuck," Tanner complains, after fumbling for a moment. "Hang on, a thread is caught." He kneels behind me to examine the teeth, and his fingers brush against the bare skin of my back, making me shiver. He apologizes.

"Why are you roaming around back here anyway?" I ask, to keep my mind off his fingertips.

"I'm not roaming, it's just the zipper is awfully low." His hair tickles my spine as he makes another attempt.

"I didn't mean your hands, Tanner. I meant why are you backstage?"

"Oh. Umm . . . Whitney thinks she left her purse in the green room, so she went back to get it." His hiss of frustration blows warm air down my dress, and I'm about to tell him to give up. I'm going to have to change clothes and find a seamstress. Someone probably has one available. And if they don't, Brixley can make an emergency call for me.

Tanner lets out a frustrated grunt, and then, finally a proud exclamation. "There! Defeated the string!"

I am relieved that his triumphant zipping did not result in a torn gown. "Well, thanks," I say as I turn to face him, and suddenly the space between us is charged with electricity. Why is the air so thick in here? It's hard to breathe.

"You . . . you look pretty. Your hair . . ." His voice has gone hoarse and his eyes have taken on an almost frightening intensity. Those are definitely not colored contacts. "Your . . . um . . . your neck is very elegant."

I try to take a deep breath, but my dress is tight and the air smells like cinnamon and I don't like this feeling I have, the way the blood is rushing through my body. We're too close together.

"Tanner . . ."

"I um . . . need to find Whitney. See you later?" He swallows and takes a step back, and I unconsciously lean forward before coming to my senses and stepping back as well.

"Yeah, good, you should go do that. I . . . I'll text you. I might be able to get you into one of the after-parties." The words come out accidentally and I regret them immediately. What's wrong with me? I don't want to spend the entire night watching them flaunt their happiness. I almost sound jealous. But I'm not. Seriously, I'm not. Tanner is welcome to date whomever he wants.

"Okay, um, that sounds fun." He edges past me to make it to the door. "I . . . okay. Bye!"

When the door closes behind him, I give myself a moment to regain my composure. I shouldn't let him get to me like that. I shouldn't let him make me feel anything.

Brixley is planning to meet me in the green room, and then we are going out the back door, hopping in a limo, and circling the block to the front of the building in order to walk the red carpet. It's flashy and frivolous but required for the press. I'm going to use her as a shield to avoid answering any reporters' questions about anything other than who I'm wearing. I promised René exactly how I'll answer: "This? Why, it's a René Butón, of course. Who else would I wear?"

So that's where I am, all dressed up and ready to go, when another security sweep comes through. Devon is filming a dressing room interview, and Xander is off doing whatever narcissists do, so it's just me, Powell, and Mason at the moment. Powell has an obnoxious tradition of not speaking out loud for an hour or so leading up to showtime in order to preserve his precious voice, so he's sipping honey tea and tapping a pen against the dry erase board he carries with him in case he feels the need to communicate. Mason is even more obnoxious: he is video-chatting with his baby. Yes, he's video-chatting a four-month-old, which basically consists of staring at the kid and saying things like "Hey, Cass, look at this, I think Sonit gurgled at me. Urvashi, move the camera closer! Urvashi, can you hear me, babe? Move the camera, he's trying to tell me something."

Since neither man is able to speak coherently to other adults, by default I'm forced to greet the security guard and his dog.

"I thought nobody was supposed to be in here yet," he says crossly. "We haven't cleared these rooms."

"They were cleared earlier." This will be the second sweep, or maybe the third. Mike has gone over it too, though unofficially since he's employed by Powell rather than the venue. Once this final one is done, the other non-band guests will be permitted to come in. At the moment they're schmoozing at some cocktail reception hosted by the production company off-site. Brixley texted me from there a few minutes ago, saying she'll be heading over soon.

"Alright, well let's let Mitzie check it out again." The guard tells me, entering the room. Mitzie is not a fitting name for the giant German Shepard he's got on a leash. She's pulling at it, like she's trying to lead him to something important. Concern flits across his face and he orders me to stay out of the way.

Mitzie heads toward the food, so my initial assumption is that she's not very professional. I'd head straight for the food too. But she doesn't mess with any of the spread, not even the meatballs. Instead she just sits, nose pointing at the table. The officer follows.

"Do you know how that got here?" he asks, indicating an item between two of the platters.

"The lens? A photographer was here earlier," I tell him. "He must have forgotten it. I can take it back to him." If I had noticed it before, I would have called Tanner. He's being careless. He's told me how much those things cost, but he was so distracted by the buffet—or by his girlfriend—that he forgot about it.

"Don't touch that!" He shouts something about a 996-T into his radio, then orders us to evacuate the building immediately. I don't recognize that code, but Mike obviously does because before we can even react, he runs in from his post outside the door, followed closely by Mason's bodyguard. I half expect him to throw Powell over his shoulder in a fireman's carry, but instead he grabs my brother's arm, yells for me to follow, and hauls Powell out the door and down the hallway. Mason's bodyguard is an ex-linebacker, and he puts his massive body to use, forcing a path for us as we run through the crowd of security personnel that are streaming toward the green room.

We make it to a safe area in the rear parking lot, where the venue staff are now milling about in confusion. Mike directs us to crouch down behind a vehicle while he focuses on the radio chatter. The positioning is easier for the boys than for me—they don't have yards of silk to keep off the dirty ground.

Vernon—we haven't been formally introduced, but that's the name stitched on Mason's bodyguard's shirt—draws his gun and is keeping watch over us. I catch a glimpse of Devon huddled with another group of burly guards, and Xander, wearing nothing but a silk robe, is arguing with some of the staff. Apparently, his clothes are extremely valuable, and someone needs to risk life and limb and *go get them right now! Don't they know who he is, damnit?*

"Urvashi, I'm fine. I'm sure it's a false alarm," Mason is reassuring his wife. He's holding his phone low so she can't see any of the chaos surrounding us. She's not stupid though. I hear her demanding to know why there's a tire in the background and why he keeps looking over to the side and cringing.

My calves are getting sore from squatting in heels while balancing my skirt on my lap and trying to keep from brushing against anything. I can imagine the fit René Butón would throw if there are any smudges on my dress when I walk the red carpet, assuming there still is a red carpet to walk.

Finally, after an interminable and indeterminate amount of time—in all honesty, probably less than ten minutes—Mike places a hand on Vernon's forearm and tells him to put the gun away.

"It's over. They're taking care of it now."

"Taking care of what?" I ask loudly, trying to be heard over the sounds of Mason making kissy noises at his baby.

Mike sighs and reattaches his radio to his belt. "That was a close call. There was a bomb in the green room. Not a sophisticated one; the bomb squad is disarming it as we speak."

"I didn't see it," Powell breaks his vow of silence. He doesn't have a choice, since he dropped his white board when we started running. I didn't notice either, but we aren't experts in bomb identification.

"It was disguised as a camera lens." Mike's words make my heart drop and I am momentarily lightheaded. I grab Powell for support. Tanner was the only photographer in the green room so far today. He left that lens on the table. Was it him, all along? Was Tanner the one who tried to kill us? That doesn't make any sense. He says he's my friend. And his background check was clear.

"How did it get there?" Powell asks. He was occupied with his massage, so he missed the pre-show visit from his favorite paparazzo.

"Tanner. It was Tanner's lens. He was taking pictures of the food, he had his camera bag . . ." I think I might throw up. He zipped me up and told me I was pretty, all the while picturing me dying in that dress. I hug Powell, burying my face in his chest and probably staining his shirt and smearing my makeup. This is my fault. I invited Tanner, I gave him the tickets and allowed him backstage. I provided a murderer another chance at my brother.

Mike summons the local FBI agents in charge of the case immediately. They aren't our usual field agents; these are two older men wearing bulletproof vests and FBI ball caps. I thought those were just a television gimmick, but evidently not. Powell is looking at them with envy. I suspect at some point he will pull out a wad of cash and acquire one of those hats.

They want to know everything, but what am I supposed to say? I made friends with a stalker who was lurking in my bushes and he happened to be a mad bomber? I briefly allowed myself to trust someone and he tried to kill my brother? And me? Crap, I trusted that man, and he tried to kill *me*.

"His name is Tanner Smythe—that's with a 'y'—and he's in the audience tonight," I tell them. "He's a photographer and he came by the green room earlier to say hello to me, before it was open to everyone. He and his girlfriend had some snacks from the buffet and then were going to find their seats."

"Do you think you can get him to come out and talk to you?" one of the agents asks. They want to take him down quietly. The bomb has been neutralized, but Tanner doesn't know he's been caught yet. The explosion was timed to go off in thirty minutes, when the remaining Last Barons would be gathered for a pre-show pep talk and vocal warm-up.

I agree to lure Tanner to a meeting, so I text him and tell him I need to see him. It's tricky. I need to get him someplace private for the arrest, yet he can't be made aware of all the FBI agents and police officers swarming around. Powell, whose eyes are glowing with excitement—perhaps because he has not fully processed Tanner's epic betrayal—offers his dressing room for the sting operation.

Unfortunately for Powell, Mike forces him off to a secure location, so he won't be in the vicinity if Tanner has additional explosives. I can sense his disappointment that I'm the only one risking my life as he gives me a quick hug and wishes me luck. Three officers escort me there and hide inside ready to jump out and seize Tanner. The rest of the backstage hallways are kept clear so that he isn't spooked by security.

I pace the room, waiting. My stomach is in knots. Tanner was the mastermind behind everything. A little voice in my head insists it couldn't be him—he was in the car explosion with me. But that could easily be explained. He'd placed the device expecting Powell to drive, and when he saw which car I was driving, it was too late to argue. That's why he suggested the scenic route, and why he claimed he saw someone messing with the car. He knew the timing on the bomb. He cut our escape a little narrowly, warning me when he did, but I guess that benefited his diabolical plan. It helped him trick me into trusting him.

When he knocks, I swallow my fear and answer the door. He enters and stands a little too close to me.

"What did you want to talk about?" he asks in a husky voice. Oh my god, he's turned on by this. He thinks in a few minutes his bomb will explode and kill everyone in the green room, and meanwhile, he's going to put the moves on me. Sick bastard.

I try not to let my eyes betray the hiding spots of the concealed agents. I need to be bold and call him out. Maybe if I tell him I know his evil plan, then, like a Bond villain, he'll reveal everything. I'm safe, the other men in this room all have guns.

"I know what you did," I say, forcing myself to remain calm.

"You do?"

"Of course. It was obvious." Is that vague enough? It must be too vague because he frowns.

"Did Whitney text you?"

Hmmm. Should I pretend she did? Is that possible? Did he reveal his bomb-dropping to her and she tried to warn me?

She should have called 911 instead. Or alerted one of the many guards.

"No. I just knew anyway."

"Because you feel it too?" He steps closer and I back away.

"Feel what?" I'm confused now.

"Are you talking about my ending things with Whitney?"

He did? When? After he told her he was a psychopath that was out murdering people for fun? Or did he do it because he's a gentleman and wanted to save her from being known as the girlfriend of a killer?

"Cass," he continues, and his voice drops to a more intimate register. "There was never anything happening there anyway. I let Whitney mislead you, but . . ." He brings up a hand as though to touch my face. I edge away.

"No, I'm talking about how you . . . you forgot one of your zoom lenses."

"I did?" He pulls a convincing confused face. But he's wasting his acting skills. He's not going to fool me again.

"You left it on the table in the green room."

"I don't think so. I wasn't using one in there." He reaches toward his camera bag as if he's going to check. The movement is too much—he might have another bomb—and that's what triggers the hidden agents jumping out to seize him.

It's over rather quickly. They take his gear and cuff him, and the whole time he has a bewildered expression on his face, like he can't believe he got caught.

"Cassidy," he tries to call to me, but I watch dispassionately.

"You tried to murder me and my brother. I have nothing more to say to you until I see you in court."

"I swear, I didn't do it," he says, quoting every bad guy ever, but he is dragged out, and my part in this is over. All I want to do is cry. I want to sit down in a comfy chair, wrap myself in a blanket and weep. I've never been so betrayed in my life.

But the big show is starting soon, and Brix is waiting for me, and I have to go pretend nothing happened. I check my makeup and am pleased to find it has remained undamaged, possibly because of the thick coating of setting spray J'Shanna covered my face in. Good. I'm presentable. I can do this. I square my shoulders and stride out as confidently as I can. The show must go on.

Brixley holds my arm as we walk the red carpet. I'm blinded by the flashes. This is a new experience for me. I've walked the red carpet many times before, but as someone's date. When you're there with a celebrity, you trail a few paces behind them and do your best to stay out of the way of the cameras. Lesser informed press will accidentally take your picture and try to nab a short interview, but they'll move on when they realize you're a nobody.

But this time, I'm not a nobody. I'm the love of Jace Monroe's life, arriving at an event to memorialize his death. They request quotes from me, wanting soundbites beyond my planned "This? Why, it's a René Butón, of course."

"This is difficult for all of us," I tell one. To another I say, "Jace would have loved this. I still feel his presence with me, every day." I tell a third, "I am so honored to be here on behalf of Jace." Then I repeat the cycle for the next set of interviewers. Brixley is answering her own questions, but hers are more focused on the design of her dress—why, it's a René Butón, of course—and the fabulous jewelry she's wearing.

We finally make it through the first gauntlet, and arrive at the second, the security checkpoint.

"I've already done this, multiple times," I complain to the guards. "Besides . . . never mind." I was about to say that an arrest has been made, but we're keeping that confidential for now. Brix knows, and she was almost as horrified as me that it was Tanner.

"No wonder he was so obsessed with you," she said when I shared the top-secret news. I found that rather insulting, since she'd previously insisted he liked me. I guess I'm not likable, except when someone needs my help to commit murder.

"Have they figured out Tanner's motive?" Brixley asks me when we find our seats. She covers her mouth when she talks, overly cautious in case any lip readers are watching the live video feed. I doubt this is being broadcast yet, since the enormous clock in the back of the auditorium is still counting down. Despite Tanner's terroristic intentions, he didn't even delay anything.

"Not as of the last time you asked me, five minutes ago," I say, after checking my phone. Mike said he'd update when he heard any news. I assume it's going to turn out Tanner was a deranged fan, maybe someone still upset over the breakup of the Last Barons. Or maybe he was a hired hitman, sent to wreak havoc. He was cold-blooded, I'll give him that. All those times we hung out and I never once suspected a thing. I even let him kiss me once. And I asked him to take those pictures for the magazine. He must have been secretly gloating the entire time. "I feel like a terrible judge of character," I confide.

"It wasn't just you. He fooled everybody. I had him on my SwiftaPic. Once they let us release the information about his arrest, I'm going to excoriate him."

"I won't stop you." At the moment it's being kept secret because for all they know, he wasn't working alone. He may have had an accomplice, somebody skilled at making bombs. Though perhaps Tanner made them himself. He drives around in a beat-up old van. Isn't that an indicator of maladaptive behavior? He's one of those off-the-grid hoodie wearing manifesto writing lunatics. I bet when they search his van, they find stacks of notebooks detailing his nefarious schemes.

The lights over the audience dim and the voice of a ghost comes out through the speakers. "Hello, America! Are you ready for the Last Barons of Sound?" It's Jace, in a recording from years ago that sends chills down my spine.

Five spotlights illuminate chairs on the stage, with four men standing behind them. Mason is on the far left, with the same devilish grin that won him so many hearts and got him into so much trouble. Next is my brother, the golden boy, with his easy smile and boyish charm. On the far right is Xander, perfectly coiffed and exuding the charisma he can switch on so easily for an audience. Devon is posed casually behind the chair next to him, but I can see the tension in his body, and Brixley hisses out a sympathetic breath. And there in the middle, is an empty chair. Jace's death has never felt more real than it does right now, as the opening notes sound, the remaining Barons strike a pose, and the show begins.

This first song, with the infamous chair dance, is painful to watch. My eyes are drawn to the heartbreaking void in the center. I can picture Jace, with his effortless sexiness and smooth movements, in his customary position as the anchor of the group.

I am overwhelmed by grief now. All I can think is that Jace was murdered, and I befriended his killer that same night. Tanner must have been so proud when I called him to take Powell's photo, worming his way in with hardly any effort. I wonder how long he was stalking us. It had to have been for months before he made his move, since my computer systems were hacked long before the first bombing. I knew he was good with digital manipulation software—though he claims he rarely uses it—but I had no idea he was talented in other forms of manipulation. He tricked me and I despise him for it.

Brixley's hand finds mine, and we cling tightly to each other throughout the performance. She tears up multiple times, especially when Devon steps up and begins singing their new single, *Fallen Brother*. It's the last song of the night, and cynically, I know the producers timed it so that the downloadable version goes live the instant the Last Barons hit the final note. The profits are intended to go to Jace's foundation, but I've seen how record companies define profits. Little of the money will ever arrive in the charity's coffers.

When it's finally all over and Brixley and I make our way backstage to begin our circuit of post-show events, I am too drained to continue.

Devon and Mason are doing shots, Powell is sprawled in a chair where he's being fawned over by one of Brixley's supermodel friends, and Xander is apparently waiting for me. I find myself wrapped in his smelly embrace. The cologne he swam in earlier doesn't fully mask his dance-sweat odors. None of them have bothered to shower yet.

"Stop touching me," I slip out of his arms, hoping he didn't leave stinky wet marks on my dress.

"Jace . . ." he says, and his eyes well up with what I can only assume are false manipulative tears. Please, just stop. I need the whole messed up world to stop and give me a chance to breathe.

"The tribute was beautiful," I tell him, because even in my weakest moments I can still be diplomatic, and then I go join my brother. He's relieved to see me. Even the boobs spilling out of the supermodel's dress weren't enough to distract him. He's tired and miserable, despite all the applause and the glory of having put on a stellar performance. He trusted Tanner too. He let him into our home on numerous occasions. He is almost—but not quite—as betrayed as me. At least Tanner never kissed *him*. That I know of.

"Deedee, you want to get out of here?" he asks hopefully. "You look like you aren't feeling well. Can I take you home?"

"Yes!" I say immediately. I want to go back to my brother's condo and chisel the centimeter-thick layer of cosmetics off my face and soak in a hot bath and mourn. Mourn for Jace, for my friendship with Tanner, for experiencing the ultimate betrayal. Alas, it is not to be. Or not to be for one of us.

"Sorry, Powell, it's in your contract. You're required to go to the after-party." That comes from Liam, my brother's manager. He used to be an assistant on the group's tours, and he was the one roped into handling this concert. He's a great manager, he always does a fantastic job. But he's also a stickler for rules, and he won't bend them, not even just this one time.

Powell makes a face. "I'm tired." But he knows better than to breach a contract. "Fine, I'll have one of Mike's men escort you instead. I'll see you in the morning."

Poor guy. If he were to ask, I would attend the party with him. I don't want to, but I'd do anything for my brother. But since he made the offer, I go in search of Mike and request a car before Powell can change his mind.

TWENTY-ONE

My poor exhausted brother arrived home at four in the morning, just in time to shower and change and head back out to appear on a morning show. I was waiting for him with a big cup of coffee with cream, the first dairy he's been allowed to have in months.

After the show, where he carefully made no comments about Tanner's arrest, despite the hosts asking over and over about Jace and the car explosion and Powell's contact with the FBI, we finally get to go back to the condo.

No surprise, he falls asleep on the ride home, so I nudge him awake when we arrive.

"Come on, sleepyhead. Let's go upstairs."

"Five more minutes," he mumbles, attempting to burrow his head into the tinted window he's been slumped against. With the assistance of the driver and Mike's lobby-stationed guard, I drag him out, slip my arm around his waist and let him lean on me as I guide him to the elevator.

Once I tuck him in, I sit at the kitchen table and stare into space. I'm thinking about how angry I am, how betrayed. And how hungry. This whole situation has made me so nauseated I haven't been able to eat since my green room snacking early yesterday afternoon. I should probably get some food in me so I can keep my strength up in order to plot ways to hurt Tanner back. Not that there's much I need to do. I'm sure federal prison isn't a pleasant place, especially for someone as lean and pretty as him. He'd better find himself a protector, fast.

While I'm heating myself up a frozen meal—Powell's nutritionist keeps this kitchen stocked—the intercom buzzes. I want to ignore it, in case it's someone from the media. The only people we should be talking to are the FBI agents and it can't be them since we have an appointment to go down to their offices this afternoon. They wanted a statement last night, but Mike argued them out of it. It would have been bad publicity to delay the big show by questioning Powell.

The buzzer goes off again, so I may as well answer, if only to tell the vultures to go away. And I'm surprised. It's Whitney.

"Cassidy, can I talk to you?" she asks. I didn't know she knew where we stayed out here. Maybe Tanner found out as he stalked us and accidentally let it slip. Poor Whitney, I should have called her last night and told her what happened when Tanner disappeared on her. In all the chaos, it didn't even occur to me. Some friend I am.

"Sure, come on up." I tap the button to unlock the building door.

As it turns out, Whitney isn't alone. Her brother Silas is accompanying her. I wish she had warned me—there's something about Silas that unsettles me. I would have met her downstairs in the lobby instead, under the safe eyes of Powell's current babysitter. Or bodyguard. Whatever.

Silas' bulk takes up the majority of the doorframe, so I step aside and reluctantly let them in. I haven't seen him since our aborted double date, when he brought up the terrible old tabloid story. Speaking of that date, I should apologize to Whitney for hooking her up with a deranged killer in the first place. Though to be fair to me, I was fooled by him too.

They survey the room. "Where's your brother?" Whitney asks.

"Sleeping, so we need to be quiet. Would you like some coffee or tea?" I'm nothing if not a good hostess.

"No thanks," they both say, but they willingly sit down at the table with me. I don't want to eat in front of them, so I leave my food in the microwave.

Then Whitney continues. "The reason I'm here is because I got the strangest phone call, supposedly from the FBI wanting to question me. Do you know anything about that?"

"Did you hear about Tanner?" I respond. I'm not surprised that the killer's "girlfriend" would be questioned in this case.

"About Tanner? No. Why, what happened? I mean, what happened after he broke up with me and abandoned me at the concert by myself? He totally disappeared. I tried to reach you afterward, to get those after-party tickets you promised, but you weren't answering your phone. I sort of suspected the two of you ran off together." That's a sordid assumption. She almost sounds like Brixley, or at least Brixley a few days ago insisting that Tanner liked me. Yeah, it wasn't me he liked. He liked the idea of killing me.

"Oh, right, sorry about that. I was busy." I take a deep breath because I know my next words will shock her. "Tanner was arrested last night. We found out he's the one who bombed Jace Monroe's helicopter and Powell's car. He placed another one in the green room, but the security dog found it before it went off. The bomb squad managed to disarm it without anybody knowing." Yes, I realize this is all supposed to be kept confidential, but she's going to learn all those details anyway, when she meets with the agents. If creepy Silas weren't with her, I'd invite her to tag along with me and my brother. We could get all the questioning out of the way together and then go out for drinks and a long session of bad-mouthing Tanner.

The siblings exchange a meaningful look.

"So they think it was all Tanner?" Silas clarifies.

"Yes, they do. He hid the last bomb in a camera lens. That's how he smuggled it in, and how they figured out it was him."

They exchange another look. They're as good at wordless communication as Powell and me. Or rather, probably better. Powell tends to understand when I'm conveying "let's get out of here," or "stop talking now" but he misses out on higher concepts.

"He's been to this condo before, hasn't he?" Silas asks.

"No." Powell didn't have any photo shoots over here, so he had no reason to come around. Though really, what do I know about the guy?

"Actually, I think he has," Whitney says. "In fact, I'm sure of it. He snuck in here yesterday, after you two left to prepare for the show."

"What makes you think that?" I haven't seen any evidence of a break-in, and surely the security guard would have noticed Tanner sneaking around. Although, given that Whitney was with him, she would know. He told me they'd toured some photography museum, but he's a dirty liar.

"Because of the killer peanut flour scattered all over the place." Silas grins at me, showing all his teeth. The hair on the back of my neck stands up. I suddenly feel like he's a predator, and he's about to gnaw the flesh from my bones.

"What peanut flour?" I ask, but Whitney has already reached into her purse and she flings a handful of nutty smelling powder at me. I try to duck away, but the dust cloud hits my face and gets in my mouth and eyes. The rest settles on my clothing. I am so bewildered by this sudden turn of events that I can't do anything but wipe at my face and gape at her.

"Die!" she screams as she throws a second handful. Now I unfreeze enough for a minor reaction. I put up my hands to block it and jump to my feet, trying to brush off the flour. This might be the weirdest thing that has ever happened to me, and considering I toured with a '90s boyband, that's saying something.

"What are you doing?" Everything has been so bizarre in the past twenty-four hours that my mind is having a hard time processing this. Did she really just attack me? With flour? Really? Am I dreaming?

"You killed our father, so we're going to watch you die." Silas' voice is cold, and now he's studying me like a scientist. He's waiting for an anaphylactic reaction, but they picked the wrong Corbitt for that.

"Who's your father?" I pinch myself, and it's not a dream. But I'm frozen in place. My limbs are heavy with shock. I should run, but I can't control my body. Fight, flight, fawn or freeze? Apparently, my trauma reaction is to choose freeze. I wish I'd known that before.

"Don't pretend you don't remember," Whitney taunts. "Frank Markoff? The reporter?"

"I've met lots of reporters, and I haven't killed any of them." I have no idea who she's talking about, and I want to think this is a strange joke. The condo has numerous interior security cameras, maybe they know about them? Maybe they have an online prank show and they're doing this for laughs? They'll expect me to hand over the footage later so they can post the video to their channel. But the powder does taste like real peanuts, and their expressions are deadly serious.

"This isn't a game, Cassidy," Silas tells me. "Our father was a respected journalist, until you and your brother sued him. You know exactly who he was!"

The name still doesn't ring a bell, but the mention of the lawsuit bangs a huge gong.

"Are you talking about the tabloid reporter who falsified the story of Powell and me sleeping together? I didn't even know he was dead!" I assumed that guy was living in a trailer park in the desert with all the other washed-up journalists who screwed up an article. I always imagined him drinking cheap beer and shaking his fist at the sky.

"He didn't falsify anything. He had a source, a valid source. But a true journalist can't share that information, even when held in contempt of court. So he didn't. And he ended up hanging himself in disgrace when he lost his job. That was you, Cassidy. You and Powell killed him, so we're going to kill you." Silas delivers the whole speech in a calm monotone. He's a psychopath, I realize. No wonder I was instinctively creeped out by him before. And no wonder he mentioned that story on our date—he kept it stewing in his mind for a decade.

"It was you all along? You're the bombers!" I've solved the mystery, but far too late. Were they working with Tanner this whole time? Or no, wait. Did they frame him? I can't worry about that right now. All I know is I have to keep them talking so I can formulate an escape plan. There's a table between us, but they're blocking both my exit and the nearest panic button. And I'm covered in a substance that will kill my brother, so I can't make a dash to warn him. I can only hope he hears the commotion and calls the police, without leaving his room.

Of course my luck isn't that good. The next sound I hear is Powell's bedroom door opening and his sleepy voice asking, "What's going on, Deedee?"

"Get back in your room and barricade the door!" I scream. Powell has worked with dozens of directors and choreographers through the years, and I must have matched their authoritative tone because he obeys immediately and without question. His door slams shut and the lock clicks. My eyes slide to the charger in the kitchen, where I count four phones. Crap. He doesn't have one in his room.

"Actually, Powell," Silas calls in a sing-song voice. "You're going to want to come out. You should at least try to save your sister."

"It's a trap! There's peanut dust . . ." and that's all I'm able to say before Silas punches me in the face.

I've never, ever been hit in the face before. Not ever. Not accidentally in a gym class, not in a mosh pit, not even when I was in an explosion. It hurts. *It hurts!* The pain is so agonizing it chases every thought from my head and I reel back, pressing a palm to my eye in shock. I think I heard my cheekbone crack.

"Why isn't she reacting yet?" Whitney asks Silas.

"Because I'm not allergic to peanuts," I say, which is a tactical error. I should have faked anaphylaxis, collapsed on the ground, then waited while they tried to unlock Powell's door. Then I could have crept up behind them with a weapon. Not that we store weapons in the condo, but I'm sure I could improvise something. It would also have given me a chance to press the nearest panic button. I'm going to assume Powell activated the one in his room and help is on the way. That means I just need to survive a few minutes. I'm tough, I can survive anything for a few minutes.

Here's the problem, though. I am stronger than the average woman. I'm in great shape and I'm fast. But Silas is a big man. He's bigger and stronger. Maybe not faster though, but Whitney might be. And it's two on one.

"I guess we have to do this the old-fashioned way," Silas says and lunges at me. I dodge and manage to get in a good kick before he tackles me to the floor. "Hey, Powell, I'm killing your sister now. You should come watch; it's going to be fun!"

I struggle under his weight. "Whitney, please, I thought we were friends, please help me."

She flinches. I hope she regrets her decisions here. But she doesn't change them. "My father died because of you. I told you, I've been plotting revenge for ten years. I'm not going to let a few happy hours and movie nights take that away from me."

I had always thought that if I were ever attacked, I would fight. I would be ferocious, and tenacious, and I could defeat any bad guy who came my way. Silas disabuses me of that notion rather quickly and decisively. He incapacitates me with another excruciatingly painful face punch, and then his monstrous hands come around my throat. I can't breathe, which sends me into blind panic. I writhe and squirm and try to pry his fingers off, but he is far too strong. My vision starts to darken, and I feel . . . regret. Surprising, that my last emotion would be regret, but it is. I regret not spending more time with my mom. Not being able to save my brother. Not being able to apologize to Tanner for mistaking him for being a terrorist. So many things . . .

I close my eyes, surrendering to the darkness. But before I succumb, Silas' grip loosens. He's not going to finish killing me? I stay still, unmoving, waiting. My mind is slowly forming tendrils of actual thought again, and I can feel emotions beyond panic and regret. Now I have time to formulate a plan. My left eye is swollen shut, but I crack my right eyelid the smallest bit I can, hoping to see what's going on. Silas is still on top of me, but he's undoing his pants. I keep my breathing as even and shallow as possible. Let him think that he choked me into unconsciousness. I'm only going to get one chance.

"Hey, Whit," he warns. "You might not want to watch this next part."

"Do whatever you want, I'm still working on this lock. I bet she has the keys somewhere." Whitney is getting frustrated with Powell's door, which if my brother is smart, he barricaded. I hope he didn't think he was dreaming when I told him to get back in his room, that he didn't fall down on his bed and go back to sleep. I hope I'm not struggling in vain. I want us both to escape alive, and the only way we will is if he triggered the panic button. Or if he develops a time-travel machine and goes back to last night when he told Mike he didn't need him to stay over. I'll pin my hopes on the button.

Silas grabs the neckline of my shirt and rips, tearing it right down the middle and exposing me to his evil hands. I concentrate on not moving at all, not even twitching, no matter how much he hurts me. I'm still peering out from a tiny slit in my eyelid, waiting for him to get in the right place. He leans over me and . . . now!

Using the strength I've gained from thousands of abdominal crunches, I slam my body upward as swiftly as I can, smashing my forehead into his nose. My angle is slightly wrong, so I don't drive bone shards into his brain to kill him instantly as I had hoped. Instead, he yelps in pain as hot blood sprays my body. I use the distraction to roll over and try to crawl out from under him, but Silas catches me by grabbing a fistful of my hair and yanking me backwards, sending a new shockwave of agony through me.

"You're going to pay for that," Silas hisses directly in my ear. He's holding me so tightly I can't get away. That's when Powell's door flies open and he runs out, wearing a T-shirt tied over his face so that only his eyes are exposed. It must've taken him so long to come to my aid because he was constructing an anti-peanut mask. He's brandishing one of the heavy wooden curtain rods that used to be over his bedroom window, which is probably the closest thing to a weapon he had in his room. I hope it's effective.

"Deedee, are you okay?" he calls out, at the same time winding up and hitting Whitney hard in the head, sending her to the ground. She tries to get up, but he whomps her again, this time in the spine, and she collapses.

"That's my sister!" Silas yells, ironically upset that someone would dare harm his sibling. He finally releases me, tossing me aside as easily as if I were a piece of garbage.

"The police are on their way," Powell shouts to me. "Cass, answer me, are you okay?" I don't look okay, since half my face is unrecognizable from being battered, and I'm kneeling on the floor, shirtless and covered in blood. Thankfully, it's not my blood, but Powell wouldn't know that.

"I'm fine. Watch out!"

Silas dives at Powell, who swings the curtain rod. His blow glances off Silas' shoulder, and they both crash to the ground. Now I can act. Nobody hurts my brother. I lurch to my feet, twist the remains of my shirt into a rope, and leap on Silas' back. I loop my makeshift garrote across his throat, the ends wrapped around my wrists for extra traction.

He was trying to punch Powell, but now he's rising to his feet, fighting to throw me off. I jam my left knee into his back for leverage and hang on with all of my might. He lets out a choking sound, and stumbles backwards, clawing at the fabric that is slowly cutting off his air supply. When he can't get his fingers under it, he pulls a knife from his belt, one I'm lucky he didn't use before. I'm terrified of the blade, but I can't let go. I have to strangle him, because if I don't, he's going to kill us both. Silas tries to slash at me behind his back, but the angle is awkward for him and I can dodge. He must not be thinking clearly, or he'd simply slice the loop around his neck. His slashing motions grow weaker and more erratic, and I keep twisting away without lessening the pressure I'm exerting on his windpipe.

"Hang on Cass," Powell yells. He tries to hit Silas with the curtain rod, but with the way Silas is thrashing, he accidentally hits me instead. Luckily, he pulled back at the last second, so, while I'll probably have a bruise on my shoulder, it wasn't hard enough to make me release my grip.

"Get the knife!" I shout at him, and Powell drops the rod and grabs for Silas' wrist. Silas is weakening, I can feel it. His movements are becoming jerky and slow, and he stumbles to his knees. Powell is trying to pry his fingers off the knife when Silas collapses on top of him, with me still clinging to his back.

Silas isn't moving, so I finally let go of the garrote as I slide off him, and land in a spreading puddle of blood. Oh no.

"Powell! Powell, are you okay?" I yell, frantically trying to shift Silas' body. He is huge and heavy. There is a muffled groaning coming from beneath him, and then Powell pushes upward, helping me shift Silas. "Whose blood is that?"

My brother emerges, with blood all over his forearms and shirt. "His, I think? I'm not sure."

"Are you in pain? Did he stab you? You should know if it's yours!"

He pulls the mask off his face and examines his arms, then lifts his shirt to look for wounds. Nothing. Good.

I want to collapse. I'm tired, my face hurts, my muscles ache, my shoulder is numb, and . . . in all the excitement we've forgotten about Whitney.

"First my dad, now my brother?" Her eyes are wild as she staggers toward us. She picks up her purse and reaches into what must be a magical never-ending bag of peanut flour. Before I can call out a warning, she throws a handful in Powell's face. His eyes widen. He probably doesn't recognize the smell since we've kept him so sheltered from his allergen. But he definitely recognizes the sensation.

"Kitchen drawer," I shout, reminding him of the location of the nearest EpiPen. As he sprints to the kitchen, I take the opportunity to grab the curtain rod. I hold it, poised to defend my brother from Whitney, but she's no longer interested in us. She rushes to her own brother and drops to her knees next to him, weeping and promising that everything will be alright.

While she's distracted, I run to check on Powell, laying on the kitchen floor next to the contents of the drawer he'd ripped out of the cabinet. He's already jabbed himself in the thigh with the first EpiPen. "Get me an ambulance," he gasps. His breathing is labored and his face is already swelling and turning red. He's having a bad reaction. I grab the other Epi from the set. If I'm remembering my training correctly, we need to wait five minutes.

I'm about to call 911 when Mike bursts through the front door, gun at the ready. I've never been so happy to see someone in my life. I wish he'd been here ten minutes ago. Or twenty? I don't have any idea how much time has passed since Silas punched me. It could have been thirty seconds for all I know; my senses are skewed by pain and fear.

"What's going on?" Mike asks, his gaze doing a sweeping assessment of the room. He cautiously approaches us.

"Peanuts," Powell struggles to force the word out, so I jam the second shot into his thigh.

"Call an ambulance, now," I order Mike. "Two, probably. And have those people arrested." I point to the other set of siblings. Whitney is draped over her brother's body, sobbing hysterically.

Mike takes off his cardigan and places it over my shoulders to cover my bare skin and my blood-spattered bra. Yes, Mike, security guard extraordinaire, was wearing a powder blue cashmere cardigan on his day off. I'll try to remember to tease him later.

"It'll be okay. We'll handle this," he reassures me in a soothing voice. I want to believe him, but I don't. Powell is gasping for breath and his face is more swollen than mine.

More footsteps are running down the hall and the police thunder in, guns drawn. Mike holsters his weapon and puts his hands in the air while he identifies himself and us. The cops are initially hesitant to arrest Whitney, as she's a weeping woman clinging to a presumably dead body, but I'm able to convince the officers that Whitney was one of the attackers, and they cuff her. She's going to need to get checked out as well—Powell cracked her pretty hard in the head—but she's going to the hospital in handcuffs.

An officer touches my shoulder softly, trying to pull me away from Powell. The paramedics have arrived, and they are trying to get me out of the way. I want to obey them, but I can't bring myself to let go of my brother's hand. I don't understand why these EpiPens didn't make him better. Aren't they supposed to fix everything?

"Cassidy, come on, we need to get you taken care of too," Mike unhooks my fingers and gently pulls me to my feet. "Let the paramedics do their job." He leads me to a chair and makes me sit while they check my vitals and examine my broken face. The adrenaline is wearing off now, and I'm starting to shake.

Powell is carried down to the waiting ambulance on a stretcher. It takes a little bit of arguing and me clinging tightly to the ambulance door, but they finally agree to allow me to ride with them on the bench seat. They'd prefer to strap me to my own stretcher in a different vehicle, but Mike warns them of the uproar I will create if they try to separate me from my brother. As the doors close, I see Silas being wheeled out to another ambulance, with an oxygen mask over his face. I guess we didn't kill him. I don't know how to feel about that yet. I suppose it depends on whether my brother survives.

TWENTY-TWO

Little known fact: Many hospitals have fancy luxury suites for the wealthy. Some of them, including a certain well-known Los Angeles facility, have clandestine tunnels by which celebrities can enter. That's where the ambulance takes us, to the hidden private entrance, where a team of medical professionals is gathered in wait.

Powell is whisked away quickly. As they're wheeling him off, a police car pulls into the secret garage and Mike leaps out before it comes to a complete stop. He chases after Powell's stretcher.

I'm left behind with the paramedics and one nurse. Way to treat me like a second-class citizen.

"Are you . . ." the nurse asks hesitantly.

I don't want to sound like a spoiled brat, but I've just been beaten rather badly, I can't see out of one eye, my entire body aches, my brother might be dying, and I want to be cared for and coddled and injected with a lot of pain killers.

"I'm Powell Corbitt's sister, and I expect the same degree of treatment he receives. I'll be paying with my black card."

Those are the magic words. I'm in an exam room immediately, surrounded by experts. I also get bumped to the front of the line for the CT machine. I'd feel bad about cutting, but I know that if one of the patients ahead of me was dying, the hospital wouldn't squeeze me in. Money buys convenience, but not at the cost of lives.

Even with my priority rush treatment, it still takes a couple of hours before I am brought from the radiology department to my luxury suite. The suite is already occupied by Agents Benítez and Johnson. I knew they were supposed to fly out here this morning to help wrap up the case, but I didn't expect to encounter them in the hospital. Can't they give me a break?

"Cassidy?" Agent Johnson eyes me cautiously. "Is that really you?" I know I look bad, but I didn't realize I was unrecognizable.

"It's me." My voice is quiet because the swelling prevents me from opening my mouth very far. The entire left half of my face is swollen. It's not painful though, thanks to the morphine.

Benítez pulls a chair next to my bedside. She's positioned herself on my right, by my functioning eye, so I can see her. "We watched the security footage."

"From the condo?" Our cameras are state of the art. They have sound, a fact that Powell sometimes exploits by songwriting loudly in the living room.

"Yes. Cassidy, you were brave. You saved your brother's life."

"He saved mine." It's hard to talk. All I want to do is to check on Powell, and go to sleep. In that order. And preferably in the next thirty seconds.

"Whitney confessed to everything. She gave her brother access to your computer system and he got into all your accounts and moved the money around. He built the bombs and paid the mechanic to place the one on the helicopter. Silas personally attached the bomb to the car."

"The mechanic?" I ask. I vaguely remember something about him being killed. "Did Silas murder him?"

"We haven't proven it yet, but there was DNA taken at the scene. I'm confident it's going to come back a match."

Agent Johnson peers over her partner's shoulder, with an expression that suggests she's trying to be reassuring but is actually horrified to look at me. "Don't worry, Cassidy. We heard everything they said. You aren't going to be charged with anything. Neither is Powell. It was all clearly self-defense."

"Okay." It hadn't occurred to me that I might be in trouble, or that this could be anything other than a straightforward case of self-defense. They entered the condo under false pretenses, attacked me, and tried to kill both me and my brother. Even in California, we're allowed to defend ourselves.

"Enough." My personal nurse cuts Johnson off when she starts to speak again. "Everybody out. My patient needs to rest now." That's another perk of the luxury suite: private medical staff dedicated exclusively to my well-being.

"Wait," I try to grab at Benítez's sleeve, but miss. There's one more urgent concern that needs to be addressed. "Tanner?"

"The photographer? He's still being questioned, but it looks like he might not have been an accomplice. He'll be out soon. We think..."

"I said that's enough," my nurse has a sharp voice that commands obedience. "Get out, now." This is her domain. She outranks the FBI within these walls, and they obey without question. Honestly, the nurse is so intimidating I'm surprised the agents don't salute or bow to her as they hurry out of the room.

"Thank you," I whisper when she closes the door firmly behind them.

"No more talking, sweetheart. Your body needs rest." She uses a kinder, more sympathetic tone with me. "Your brother is going to be fine. He's right next door, and he's asleep. We've dosed him heavily with antihistamines, and he's breathing on his own again. You can visit him tomorrow."

That was all I needed to know. Concern about Powell was the last thing keeping me awake. Now I can relax and let the morphine carry me away.

When I wake up the next morning, a very skilled—and expensive—plastic surgeon is brought in for a consultation. He examined the x-rays and scans of my shattered cheekbone in advance and he optimistically promises to make me look "just as beautiful as before." It's just going to require some tiny incisions and a titanium plate. My surgery is already scheduled, and they want to start prepping me.

But I'm a cranky and demanding patient. Before I'm willing to go under the knife, I insist on visiting my brother. My nurse has assured me he's alive, but I'd like to see that with my own two eyes. Well, one eye, right now.

"You look terrible, Deedee," Powell says when they wheel me into his room. So does he. He's reclining in his bed, hooked up to several IVs. There's a monitor for his heart and breathing. His face is discolored, probably from the swelling yesterday.

"Right back 'atcha."

"No, I look wan and sexy. There are legions of fans who would love to nurse me back to health." He's right. They'd fight for the chance to give him a sponge bath and check his vitals and make sure he's comfortable.

"Does the media know you're here?" I haven't heard singing crowds, so I imagine they don't. Devon was hospitalized once for appendicitis, and there were hundreds of loud fans clustered outside the building having a candlelight vigil, crying and belting out Last Baron songs, and generally being a nuisance to all the other patients.

"Mike says one of my neighbors has been blabbing that he spotted paramedics leaving my place, so I posted one of those shots Tanner took the other day and claimed to be back home. We should be good."

I'd sigh with relief if it were physically possible. I don't want anyone trying to sneak in while I'm sedated to take gruesome pictures of me for some online gossip mag. Though it's not like they can get up here. This floor requires a special elevator key, then they'd have to evade the security guards. Tanner is the only one who has developed a magical ability to circumvent all of our safeguards, but he doesn't know we're here either.

"Have you heard about Silas?" I ask. The FBI has likely spent more time in here than in my room, so Powell's information might be more up to date than mine.

"Yeah, he has . . . he has . . ." Powell looks to his personal nurse for assistance. The guy looks like he should be in a street-fighting match, not scrubs. I bet Mike hand selected this one.

"Hypoxic-anoxic brain injury," Nurse Brute supplies. "He's not expected to recover."

"You strangled him good, sis." Powell gives me an approving nod.

"You stabbed him though. I think that contributed to his condition."

"Yay, teamwork? The Corbitt siblings solved the mystery and captured the criminals." He tries to laugh, but it turns into a cough, and his nurse leaps across the room to make sure he's not choking and chastises him for talking so much. Powell's throat is still scratchy from the tube. I hope there are no permanent effects. We sort of rely on his voice to make a living.

"And nobody will ever know."

"That's right. My publicist already crafted a statement about Jace's killers being caught and attributing it to Mike. I told him he can't raise his rates on me now that he's going to be in higher demand. And maybe he should hire you on a freelance basis."

"So then I get double pay as your assistant and bodyguard? This is why you have a business manager, to keep you from making silly financial mistakes."

"True." Powell snorts out another attempt at a laugh, triggering another coughing fit. His nurse glares at me, as if it's my fault.

My own nurse clears her throat. "We need to go. It's surgery time."

I hug my brother as best I can, without tangling our tubes.

"Hey, Cass," Powell reaches out and takes my hand before I can be wheeled away. "He's going to be okay."

"Silas? I hope not."

"I was talking about Tanner."

"Oh." I have been forcefully keeping him out of my mind. The way he looked at me during his arrest, the pain and surprise and betrayal in his eyes, that was all real. He wasn't putting on an award worthy performance, he really was innocent. And no matter how I try to justify blaming him—the bomb was in a camera lens!—I can't.

"Mike said he was released this morning. I'll buy him a plane ticket or whatever he needs. Don't worry."

"I'm not worried," I inform him, but Powell can see right through me. And yes, maybe I am a little worried. Okay, a lot worried. Tanner has been sitting in jail, probably terrified. Or perhaps furious. That would be my reaction to false accusations of murder. And all that fury will be directed at me, which is fair enough, given the circumstances. We're probably not friends anymore. If I were him, I certainly wouldn't forgive me.

TWENTY-THREE

I accidentally step on Powell when I get out of bed. He reacts by grunting and rolling over. We've been back home for a week, and he's spent every night camped on an air mattress on my floor, with a baseball bat at his side. I've told him it isn't necessary, that I can cope with my nightmares on my own and I don't need his protection, but he won't listen to me. I think he's doing it more for his own peace of mind than mine. I also sort of wish he could get himself a girlfriend so he could have someone to sleep with in his own damn room.

I leave him lying there, while I go to the kitchen to make myself breakfast—and by make myself breakfast, I mean get a frozen smoothie packet out of the freezer and toss it in the blender with some yogurt. I'm still on a liquid diet, though I should be able to move on to soft solids soon. It no longer hurts as much to open my mouth and the stitches inside my cheek are dissolving. My face isn't as swollen, but the skin on the entire left side has become a rather lovely shade of yellowish green. Well, Powell not-so-kindly described it as "vomit colored" but I think it's pretty. Maybe I'm becoming an optimist.

The doorbell rings, and I can't help it, I jump. I'm not used to visitors popping by lately. We've still got a security lockdown in place, although the threat has ostensibly passed. We're not even being harassed by the media, since we've kept most of the real story private. As far as anyone who wasn't involved in the case is concerned, Mike is the hero. I don't know what they threatened Whitney with, but her attorney hasn't made any statements to contradict that. Maybe she's decided cooperating is in her best interest, now that she's facing the death penalty. Federal prosecutors don't look kindly on people who bomb helicopters. Eventually the full truth will come out, but by then we should be prepared to handle it.

The bell rings again, and the app on my phone shows a familiar face. Tanner. My heart sinks. I'm not ready for a conversation with him yet, not like this, when I'm still bruised and battered. I want to wait and see him when I'm healed, when he won't look at me with pity. We could maybe sit down together at a bar—next to each other because it's easier to apologize if I don't have to look directly at his face while I do it. I could have a drink first, to prepare myself, and ply him with enough alcohol that he becomes bright-eyed and forgiving.

I watch through the camera as he aggressively paces back and forth on the porch, talking to himself and moving his hands as though rehearsing whatever he plans to say. Okay, he's chosen the time, not me. I have to go through with this. I gather my courage, but when my fingers touch the deadbolt, I change my mind.

"What do you want?" I ask through the intercom instead. He jumps, just like I did a minute ago.

"I want to talk to you." He's using a demanding tone, which decreases the likelihood of me opening the door. I've had enough of welcoming visitors only to be assaulted.

"Fine. Talk."

"Open the door."

"Why? So you can attack me?" That's certainly the vibe he's giving off, with his vigorous gesticulations and stomping around.

He tilts his head to look directly at the security camera. "I'm not here to attack you. Yell at you maybe, but not attack you."

"I'm not letting you in to yell at me."

"Cassidy, open the door, please. Can we talk? No yelling, I promise."

"Do you have any peanuts?" Powell's voice cuts in on the intercom. I need to delete this app from his phone. I don't need my brother forcing me into repairing a friendship before I'm emotionally strong enough.

"I know those aren't allowed in your house," Tanner replies. He holds up his empty hands. "I didn't bring anything, not even a camera."

"Doesn't matter, you can't come in," I say, but then Powell comes wandering up behind me. He's still in sweatpants and an old T-shirt. For all his money, you'd think he could invest in some decent sleepwear, but he likes his faded holey old Last Barons shirts. It takes a special kind of vanity to wear your own picture on your pajamas.

"Just let the man in. He didn't do anything wrong, remember?"

I block him with my body. "Whatever he wants to say, he can say over the intercom."

"Don't you think you owe this to him? You can't avoid him forever." He stretches past me to undo the lock.

"Seriously, Powell? You deal with him then." I walk away as Powell lets our unwelcome guest in. I don't need him to see me like this. Apologies have never been my strong suit. I haven't had enough time to prepare myself for an awful heart-to-heart conversation, where I say I'm sorry for accusing him of murder. That's supposed to come later, on my terms.

The two of them are talking in the hall, but I can't make out all the words. They must be discussing Whitney though, because Powell says, "She sure had an explosive interest in us." No surprise, Tanner—like everyone else he's made that joke to in the past week—does not laugh. My brother needs to find better sycophants. He should ask Xander where to hire an appropriately fawning entourage.

Now Powell is warning Tanner that I'm not very talkative right now, though he doesn't explain it's because I can barely open my mouth. Tanner's reply is unintelligible, but the rise in inflection at the end suggests it was a question. "She's not coping well," Powell replies, probably intentionally loud enough for me to hear. That's a lie. I'm doing just fine. I'm always fine. I'm resilient, whether my brother believes me or not.

Tanner enters the kitchen, and I keep my back to him.

"What do you want?" I ask quietly.

"Why are *you* mad at *me*?" he responds. "I'm the one who's supposed to be mad at you. You accused me of trying to blow up a concert. It's your fault I got arrested. Do you have any idea what that's like? The FBI confiscated my camera, and they trashed my van. I spent two days in lockup, wondering if I was going to prison for life, for a crime I didn't commit, and it was your word that put me there." He sounds livid, and I would be too in his situation, but the evidence against him was pretty damning.

"The last bomb was in one of your lenses," I remind him, without turning around. I've got my head in my hands and I'm willing him to go away or for Powell to kick him out. But no, Powell's gone off elsewhere in the house, leaving me alone with Tanner. So much for being the protective big brother.

"That wasn't even the same brand. I shoot with a Hasselblad! A Hasselblad, Cassidy! Do you think I'd use a knock off lens with a Hasselblad?" So his big issue is that I failed to identify the logo on the bomb case? I want to laugh but laughing is bad for my recently sewn cheek.

"Sorry I didn't read the fine print on a bomb." Sarcasm also hurts my cheek, but it's worth it.

"It's not just about the lens. I thought we were friends! And you thought I blew up a helicopter? And the car that I was in? And that I tried to kill you backstage? That hurts."

"I don't know if you saw the news, Tanner, but your girl-friend was behind it all. She used your press pass to smuggle the bomb into the venue." What is wrong with me? He's giving me the opportunity to apologize for everything and repair our relationship, but I can't stop being defensive.

"You set me up with her! And you gave us the tickets!"

"So now this is my fault?" Admittedly, I've been thinking that myself.

"That's enough, Cassidy, I'm not going to keep arguing with the back of your head. Turn around!"

So much for his promise not to yell. He grabs me by the shoulder and swivels my stool to face him. His eyes immediately widen and his jaw drops. Yeah, I know, I look awful.

I try to rotate back to the counter but he blocks me. I'm getting awfully tired of men trying to control me, but at least his actions come from a place of concern, unlike Silas.

"It's nothing," I say, but obviously he's not a moron and doesn't believe me.

"Cassidy," he whispers, and his fingers come close to grazing my injured cheek. His eyes flicker from my face to the marks on my neck, the discolored bruises left by Silas' massive hands. When I bring up my own hand to self-consciously cover them, he spies the bruising on my wrist. "Are those ligature marks? What happened? I thought Mike . . ."

"Mike's arrival was not as timely as I would have liked," I reply, making the understatement of the year. "Silas was . . . violent." Another massive understatement.

Tanner stares at me, his expression a mix of horror and sadness. Then he steps forward and carefully wraps me in an embrace, holding me comfortingly against his chest. Until this moment, I didn't realize how much I craved physical contact. Everybody else has been so careful to avoid brushing up against me. Even my mom, who worries that I'm developing PTSD, doesn't want to touch me. She's been treating me like I'm made of glass and might shatter in her hands. I'm glad Tanner has no such qualms.

I find myself relaxing for perhaps the first time since this nightmare started. I sag against him and allow the steady rhythm of his heartbeat to soothe me. His familiar cinnamon scent—maybe it's cologne?—gives me a sense of safety, of stability. This is exactly what I need right now.

When we eventually separate, Tanner rests his forehead against mine. Tears rim his lashes.

"Cassidy, I spent the past week waiting for you to apologize to me. Every day that passed without a phone call made me so angry, and this morning I finally got up the nerve to come over here to confront you. I know you don't like to admit when you're wrong, and I thought maybe you were embarrassed about accusing me. I was all set to yell at you, and demand an apology, and make you grovel. And this whole time you've . . . you've been suffering and in pain. I can't imagine what you went through."

"It was no big deal," I say, because I like to compartmentalize. I've already set the attack aside, locking the trauma deep down in a box, next to Jace and my father.

"Can you tell me . . . do you want to talk about it?" He takes a half step back, still looking intently into my eyes.

"I'd rather not."

"I'm a good listener. But if this is about your trust issues . . ."

That stings. I don't have trust issues; I simply maintain strict criteria for people I trust. There's a difference. But that's not my reason anyway.

"No, it's not about trust. I just can't . . . I can't keep repeating it. I need a break." I must have described my ordeal a hundred times, to FBI agents, police officers, Mike, Brix, my parents. Eventually I'll have to rehash the nightmare all over again, at a deposition, maybe at a trial.

"I understand," he says gravely, and I believe he does. He's probably the only one who would. He's not in his exploitative photographer mode, he's showing me the friend he's always tried to be. He gently tucks a strand of hair behind my ear. "Maybe I should go."

"Wait!" I grab his arm. "You were right. I owe you an apology. I'm sorry, Tanner. You were my friend and I didn't even pause to consider whether you were guilty or not, I just jumped to conclusions. I've lived so much of my life not trusting anybody, so I always have this expectation that people will let me down. I'm really, truly sorry."

"Did that hurt?" The corner of his mouth twitches, and that adorable-yet-sometimes-infuriating dimple makes its first appearance of the morning.

I touch my cheek softly, probing the small patches where the nerves aren't healed and sensation hasn't returned yet. "Not too badly."

"I didn't mean your face, I meant your pride."

"Maybe a little. But I'm not finished. It's not only setting up your arrest that I'm sorry for. I should have called you when I got out of the hospital or when I got home. I should have checked on you and made sure you were okay. You went through an ordeal too, one I knew about. I owed you a call, at the very least."

"True." He pulls out the stool next to mine and sits. "You know, your apology would go over much better with coffee."

"Didn't you claim to be the perfect modern man? Make it yourself." I tease as I gesture toward the espresso machine.

His lips quirk in amusement. "I don't think you understand how apology coffee works, Cass."

I do, I do understand. I understand that in this moment, I am forgiven, and he is making an attempt at lightening the mood and working toward rebuilding our friendship. Because yes, that's what it was, friendship. A real one. I didn't realize how much I enjoyed his company, how much I've come to trust him, until he hugged me today and reminded me.

So yeah, I'm going to make him coffee.

"Caffè latte, right?" I ask as I pour beans into the hopper. I hear his affirmative response over the sound of the grinder.

He is quiet while I operate the somewhat noisy machinery, but I can feel him watching me. I try to keep my hand from shaking as I focus on pouring the steamed milk and trying to make a picture on the top of his drink. I'm good at swirls and hearts, but those wouldn't be appropriate, so I'm attempting something else. It looks nothing like what I intended.

When I finish and slide his mug over to him, he looks down and snorts. "What did you do to this?"

"I'm not a foam artist. It's a camera. Don't critique my apology coffee."

"Do I need to bake you some apology cookies now?"

"I wish. I can't eat them yet. I'm on soft foods only." I point to my sad smoothie, now warm and even less appealing than it was before.

"Oh. How about some apology . . . hmmm. Pudding? I can look up a recipe."

"Just drink your latte. Don't worry about me." I sit back down and toy with the straw in my cup. I don't want the smoothie. I don't want anything. I want to crawl back into bed and have everything go away. I want to wake up and be magically transported to four months ago, and I tell Jace not to go on that helicopter. I want to notice the money laundering and put a stop to it before anyone gets hurt. I want to put my head on Tanner's shoulder and close my eyes and sleep without dreaming of Silas' hands around my throat.

Tanner clearly understands my desire not to talk right now, so we sit in companionable silence. I know that if I need someone, he's here. After a few moments, he nudges me with his elbow.

"I watched the concert."

"Federal prisons do pay-per-view concerts? Lots of Last Barons fans in there with you?"

"I wasn't in prison during the show, I was in a holding cell where Agent Roth—did you meet him? He's big and scary—took great pleasure in telling me my evil plans had failed and the concert was going off without a hitch. But no, I didn't watch it live, I downloaded a bootleg copy yesterday."

"Why?"

"Because buying it costs twenty dollars, and I didn't think Powell would mind."

"Not why'd you pirate it. Why'd you watch?" I've watched it myself several times with Powell, while listening to his running critique on everything from a misstep Devon made in a dance to the way the lighting was a lumen short of what he desired. The camera panned to me often, and each time it caught me looking sad, holding on to Brix. And each time my name combined with the false description of my relationship with Jace flashed across the screen.

"I figured they'd show the audience, and I wanted to see your face. Honestly, I was still mad at you, so I kind of wanted to see you cry, but you didn't. You were your usual self, stoic and self-contained. You are the strongest person I know."

"It does take a lot of strength to keep a straight face through some of those songs. Grown men singing about meeting a girl at her locker? That one didn't age well."

Tanner laughs. "True. Did I ever tell you, one of my sisters was a Last Barons fan? I recognized some of the music. She used to blast them loudly from her room."

"I toured with them four times. I memorized all the songs and the dances too."

"Yeah, I saw you in the gym rehearsing with Powell. You've got the moves." He nudges me again, teasingly. Next time my brother is prepping for a show, I'm going to paper over the windows to the gym studio and save myself some embarrassment.

"I'll teach them to you," I offer, but for some reason he doesn't want to take me up on it. He finishes his latte and goes over to the sink to rinse his mug out.

"So what happens now?"

Great, he's bringing the conversation back to serious subjects. I shrug, feigning unconcern.

"A trial, I guess. So far Whitney's cooperating, though, so it's possible we never have to go to court. Maybe we sue for damages, so she can't write a tell-all and profit from what she did. And Silas, well, he's probably not going to recover, so we won't have to worry about him." Someday the real story will be leaked, and everyone will know that Powell and I were attacked and how we fought back. But for now, Mike is a hero, Powell and I are safe, and nobody needs to find out what went on in Powell's condo that day.

"That's not what I meant. What happens for you? The entire time I've known you, you've been dealing with the aftermath of Jace's death. I don't expect you to get over the love of your life this quickly, but the memorial is done with. Where does that leave you?"

There's an error I need to correct in that statement. I won't argue with a dead man, but I can share my own truth. "Jace's will was what he wanted to say. It didn't dictate my feelings. All it did was push me into a more public role than I wanted, because I can't be the one to . . . you know. Correct him. He's dead, I'll let him rest in peace and privacy."

"So you're not mourning the loss of your one true love. Good to know." There's that dimple again. "But seriously, the concert has passed. What do you do now?"

"Besides preparing for Whitney's trial? Powell has a new album coming out, and we're going on tour at the end of the summer."

"I don't care about them. I'm asking about you. What's next for *you*?"

And I don't have an answer for that. My life revolves around others; there isn't anything for me.

I shrug helplessly. "I don't know. Going back to work at the gym, once my bruises fade."

He steps closer. "Cassidy, there has to be something you want. Think about yourself, for a change. What do *you* want?" Is he challenging me? He is slowly getting closer, eyes fixed on mine. The air is getting too thick and I can't catch my breath.

"I . . ." I search for an escape, a way to get away from the fluttering in my stomach and the electricity in the air. I'm not ready for this, not yet. "I want . . . to swim. Today's the first day since my surgery that I'm allowed to swim, and that pool is calling my name."

"Oh." He finally breaks eye contact, glancing over his shoulder out the doors to where the pool water is beckoning. And now he's chewing on his lower lip and avoiding looking at me. I just can't seem to get things right between us.

"Tanner, is your swimsuit in your van?"

That brings a tentative smile back to his face. "Are you inviting me to swim?"

"I'm inviting you to spend a day lounging around in the vicinity of my pool. If you want to swim, you can. And then later, you can wander back into my kitchen and figure out how to make apology pudding. I recommend chocolate."

His smile widens, and the dimple is in full force. "It's going to be okay, isn't it? You and me, Cass . . . friends again?"

Yes, that's what I'm ready for. That's what I need right now. Friends again. Because it turns out, we were all along, I just wasn't able to admit it.

"We're better than okay, Tanner. Go get your swimsuit."

**The Corbitt Calamities #2
Matchmaker Mayhem**

Her brother's plans to settle down have her on red alert. Can she keep him alive when dubious hotties threaten possible homicide?

Cassidy Blaine-Corbitt never has a dull moment. With her superstar brother on a hopeful search for love through an extremely expensive matchmaking service, she reluctantly also joins to make sure his heart emerges unscathed. But she's shocked to hear a rumor that the hapless men are being set up with murderous femme fatales.

As her sibling ignores her warnings while he falls hard for one of the beauties, Cassidy vows to expose the truth at any cost. But when her investigation leads to a suspicious discovery, she fears she'll be too late to rescue the lovestruck man from a heartbreak that might prove deadly.

Can she save him from a lethal passion plot posing as happily ever after?

Also By Sara LaFontain

The Corbitt Calamities Series

Unexpected Encore
Concerted Chaos
Matchmaker Mayhem
Tour Saboteur (coming in 2023)

The Whispering Pines Island Series

That Last Summer
Say the Words
No Longer Yours
Cherry Christmas, Baby!
If This Were a Love Story

Acknowledgements

This book was derailed by the pandemic, but I'm proud to finally put it out there. As always, I did not create this without support.

Many thanks to Kimberly Zach, Book Coach. Her advice helped me get this novel on the right track and made it stronger.

My beta readers were fantastic; thank you Y.M. Nelson, Alison Butler, and Red L. Jameson.

Thank you Ryan Williams, for everything, all the time. But most especially for supplying me with chocolates throughout the writing process. You know the way to my heart.

About the Author

Sara LaFontain writes books featuring unreliable narrators, flawed characters, and things working out in the end. Prior to embarking on a writing career, Sara held a variety of jobs including wildlife tour guide, purveyor of fine chocolates, cafeteria worker, ESL teacher, domestic violence victim advocate, and family law attorney. She currently lives in Tucson, Arizona with her husband and two children. When she isn't writing, she's experimenting with new crafting projects, knitting, gardening, and bragging about desert winters.

The Whispering Pines Island series of standalone novels is about love, healing, and finding happiness.

The Corbitt Calamities series is a fun chick lit series featuring explosions, attempted murders, invasive photographers, and, at the heart of it all, an unbreakable sibling bond.

www.ingramcontent.com/pod-product-compliance
Lightning Source LLC
Chambersburg PA
CBHW010842190726
48286CB00012BA/2956